# WANNABE

# WANNABE

## M. WALLACE HERRON
### With Tim O'Mara

Down & Out Books
3959 Van Dyke Road, Suite 265
Lutz, FL 33558
DownAndOutBooks.com

The characters and events in this book are fictitious. Any similarity to real persons, living or dead, is coincidental and not intended by the author.

Cover design by Eloise B. O'Mara

ISBN: 1-64396-203-5
ISBN-13: 978-1-64396-203-0

*For Carole Monferdini,*
*The Essential Element*

# PROLOGUE

If you look at the front of the residence, a small Arts and Crafts structure at the end of the road, you'd never know anyone was home. But he's in there, hunting and pecking over his keyboard. The only way you'd you'll ever see him is to amble through the backwoods of his property. His writing window faces that way. At this hour, he's more a silhouette than anything else, the top of his head halfway above the opened laptop. Or he might be pacing back and forth across the short room, searching for inspiration, for just the right words. He's taller than you'd imagine, judging from the picture on his older dust jackets. He hasn't allowed a new author photo in years.

He's a diligent worker. Rarely ventures out during the day. And his day commences early. Sometimes three, four a.m. The soft yellow light in the bedroom announcing he's awake. Then the blue-gray glow of the computer in the next room. The only sustenance he avails himself of at this hour is a liter bottle of liquidity he removes from the refrigerator and carries with him to his workspace.

He doesn't consume on a regular basis. Not

in the ritualistic sense of breakfast, lunch and dinner. He snacks. Departs the room for a few minutes and returns with a sandwich in his hands. By the time he gets to the table the nourishment has been dispatched with. He brushes his hands across his torso to remove the crumbs and sits back down. He seems to have had enough from the bottle; it just sits there. Expectant. Growing warm. He goes through at least one of them a day. On recycling days there are a couple of transparent bags at the end of the driveway, full of plastic empties.

Occasionally he stretches. Leans back and puts his arms straight out to the side. Raises them up and interlocks his fingers. Then he'll bring his clasped hands down and rest them on the back of his head. He'll sit like that for a while, staring at the screen. Reading what he has written, his lips moving almost imperceptibly. Then he drops his hands, leans forward and begins typing again. This will happen three, four, five times a session. It's when his hands are locked over his head and he cracks his knuckles that you know he's finished for the day. He holds his hands up there. Rotates his head, working the stiffness out of his neck. Then he returns to the keyboard, makes a couple moves, and the ghostly light goes out. He closes the laptop and walks out of the room.

It's a sad, lonely life, but it fascinates me.

I could watch it forever.

# CHAPTER ONE

My name is Ezra Lockert, and, as far as I can tell, I'm Glen Dower's biggest fan. Have been since I was a teenager and picked up *Swallow My Soul*, his first novel. Clearly not his best, but crammed in there between the battle of man and vampire, he wrote of a loneliness in a way that told me he knew where I lived. What it was like to be alone. Outside the normal social whirl of the nine-to-five world. He saw it for what it was: a never-ending dance of institutionalized rhythm. Punching a clock. Repetitive motion. The endless shuffle around this mortal coil.

But there was another world. A step outside the boundary of what my parents taught me was real. He would go there. And take me with him. Show me things no one had ever seen before. *Swallow My Soul* pulsed with more life than I had known could possibly exist.

Shakespeare said it best. "There are more things in Heaven and Earth, Horatio, than are dreamt of in your philosophy." And it still holds true today. Only nobody cares. Nobody wants to know. Their reality begins and ends with a scarcely remunerative paycheck and what it can and cannot acquire. People refuse to acknowledge the existence of what to them is the unreal. And that gives

The Others unique power. Their own society outside the norm.

An underground, if you will, but not another dimension; their world coexists with ours. And, because our sense of reality denies their existence, we are easy pickings. Like stabbing wieners on a grill. The Others swoop down, feed, and retreat.

It's up to the few of us who know, who accept the unreal as truth, to protect the rest of the world.

It's a dirty job, but somebody's got to do it.

That's where I come in. I'm a fourth-generation Eliminator. If this were a baseball game, I'd be the cleanup hitter. But it's not a game. It's all too real.

And there's only one rule: Anything that threatens my world must be eliminated.

That was written years ago. Fifteen strange and quirky novels—as book reviewers have called them—ago. He's never had that runaway bestseller, but he's consistent. Sort of a utility player. Goes where he's needed. Sci-fi. Horror. Mystery. He's touched all the bases, and his fans have followed. One of us even started a web page for him. *The Unofficial Siting* it's called. Weeks will go by before anything new is added.

I left early during a reading event on his most recent book tour. (Recluse that he is, he still ventured out on the road to promote his latest work.) A brief recurrence of my anxiety flared up. I had to sneak out the back, because Glen has it in his contract that attendees at his signings have to remain in the store for five minutes after he leaves—to relinquish their cell phones lest anyone take unauthorized photos. In addition, this affords him the security of not being followed by any of his more...ardent fans. He has had issues with some of them in the past. Getting too close, running into him at hotels, stuff like that. This also explains the basic disguises Glen wears during his tours:

dark sunglasses, baseball hat, various forms of artificial facial hair.

I stayed in my car and then followed as he took some folks to the local bar next door for a meal. I couldn't believe it. Out in public. I was so nervous I sat in the parking lot for half an hour just trying to get myself calm enough to go into the place. After going back into the bookstore to retrieve my cell phone, I got a table right behind him and his friends. I didn't look over too much. But they noticed me. I smiled and nodded. Returned to my meal and the book I was reading. It wasn't one of his. That might creep him out. Make his friends take him some other place.

He never turned around. I could see his—was it his?—greying hair under his baseball cap. He never took it off the whole time they were eating. The sunglasses, either. He could have. No one was paying him any attention. Except for the people he was eating with, I was probably the only one in the room who knew who he was. He had to wave to get the waitress' attention for the check.

"Could you put a rush on it, please? We've got to go."

*Blues By The Case.* The book he was touring behind. I took my vacation days and caught the Midwest swing. Five cities in six days. I'd gotten my book signed the first night. His first two novels, also. He was pleasantly surprised.

"Wow," he'd said. "Where'd you get these? The remainder table?"

I couldn't speak for a moment. Not quite the anxiety, but... Then I mumbled something about liking vampires. He thanked me for coming. He shook my hand.

I had to leave the store, pretending to have an asthma attack. Against Glen's policy, they had to let me outside for air and also return my phone. It seemed like forever before my heart returned to its normal pace. Before my skin fit again.

I waited down the block. Watched the front of the bookstore. He never came out that time. I only saw the folks who had been helping us open our books to the right page for the signing. They must have snuck Glen out the back exit. I went to my car. It was a five-hour drive to the next city, and I had to check out the store. See where the reading would take place.

And I needed time to think.

# CHAPTER TWO

Why do we make the connections we make? What makes one person want to camp and fish, while another prefers to sit and read? One drives a sports car while the other owns a station wagon. These are the things that make us different from one another. Individuals.

We may share the same workplace. Do the same job. But when we get home, one person collects coins. Another stamps. Another may collect guns. And not just any coin, stamp, or gun. It could be silver dollars, French airmail, or derringers. Like doctors. They start out learning about the entire body, but, somewhere along the way, something clicks. Attracts their interest. And they delve deeper into the myriad mysteries of the heart. Lungs. Feet.

We all specialize.

Why does one fish in the tank settle into a motionless suspension just over the sand while another darts back and forth as far and as fast as it can? What makes one person watch these behaviors for hours while another may look and then tap on the glass, just to agitate the fish?

When I was young, I went from one thing to another, looking for my connection. I was good at sports, but not great. I liked music, but after being told repeatedly to stop singing, I figured out I was tone deaf. I couldn't draw a straight line to save my ass.

Maybe I should have gone into modern art.

I've always been kinda funny. At least my friends say so.

I was a teenager before I finally found my connection to the world. I was torn because it turned out I actually had two. One was cooking. I happened upon it quite by chance while trying to impress a girl. I was good at it. It came naturally. And if it had been my only connection I might be a chef with my own restaurant.

But I had another connection.

Writing.

I would sit in my room for hours. Lost in my imagination. The clack of the typewriter— and later, a laptop—talking to a blank page or screen. I used my allowance for typewriter ribbons and then ink cartridges. I wrote dozens of stories. Sent them off to magazines. They all came back—first in envelopes and later, electronically—with form rejections.

But that didn't stop me.

What stopped me was reading. In every author interview I read, in every writing book I devoured, there was one sentence that was sacrosanct.

*If you are going to write, you must read.*

So I read. Some writers, I wondered how they got published. They were just bad. Some writers were wonderful, and I know my next efforts were puny imitations of their prose.

Then, one day, I picked up a paperback by Glen Dower.

And I stopped writing.

He was that good. So far above anything I might ever do.

I have a friend. A guitarist. He's a terrific player. Been offered jobs with touring bands backing big stars. One night he heard a guitarist who made one guitar sound like three. He put his guitar away. Only plays at home now.

I have no doubt he could have learned to play like the guitarist he admired. But he didn't try. Maybe the other man's ability scared him instead of inspiring him to be greater than he was.

That's how Glen Dower affected me.

It wasn't until his third novel that I got it. I started to become attuned to his rhythm. His sentence structure. Word choice. What some critics saw as weaknesses, I saw as strengths. I started searching out articles. Interviews. Anything I could find about him. His writing. His life. I kept copious notes. I saw how he cannibalized his own life. Reworked truth into fiction. Creating a greater truth.

And once I saw what he was doing, I was no longer afraid to try.

I began writing again.

And the rejections returned. I became frustrated. I admit it. Glen was writing books. Getting published. Making a living at his art.

I was now working at the post office to support mine. And my words were every bit as wonderful as his. Just not in the same order. There had to be something more to it than just the writing.

And I needed to find out what that something was.

# CHAPTER THREE

At Glen's next event during the tour, I recognized some of the people from the reading the night before. They had been in the audience. Asking questions. I think he noticed, too. It kind of set him back. (The word "fan" *is* short for the word "fanatic.") Then he smiled.

"For those of you who've seen me before, there's not much new. I'm reading the same section again tonight. But thanks for coming."

I didn't ask questions. The story was enough. I just took a seat in the back of the room, listened to the familiar questions, and then hung around when the signing started. Glen left through the back door and after the requisite five minutes we were allowed to pick up our phones and leave.

I hit the road for the next city and found a hotel parking lot along the way where I could settle in pretty much out of sight of anyone who'd care. I'd be able to sleep in the car for a few hours and then wait for that night's reading.

A sharp rapping on my window roused me before daylight. Even with the car windows cracked an inch, I was sweating from the humid night. Some man in sunglasses and an old winter cap was staring in at me. His head moving between my face and his open, outstretched hand. I shook my head violently and rolled the window up the rest of the way. He got the hint and stepped back. His clothing was soiled. I watched his shoe soles flap silently. I looked up just in time to see him expel a large amount of mucus. If it had been a bullet, I'd have been dead. It hit the window right between my eyes. Hung on solidly and then oozed down like an invisible slug's trail toward the door handle. I looked back to see the man as he returned to his own world.

I pulled the visor down and flipped open the little cosmetic mirror. It had two small lights, one on each side, but they didn't do crap. I turned on the interior lights. *Wow.* I could have been the bum's—*okay, street person's*—brother. I looked like a maniac. My hair was all over the place. I had a big crease along my left cheek where I had been lying against the door. The top of my T-shirt was rimed with sweat.

I could smell something stale. Since there was no food or drink in the car, it had to be me. And my breath was just as bad. I was on a pretty tight budget and sleeping in the car was one way to save. But maybe it was time I put in a night in at a motel. Break out the credit card. Use the shower. Brush my teeth.

I looked back at the vanity—ha!—mirror and ran my hand over my neck. I could use a shave, too. Didn't want to give the evening's bookstore the wrong opinion of Glen's readership. I closed the mirror. Raised the visor. Looked up at the hotel across the street. One light on. I counted. The seventh floor.

Could that be where Glen was staying?

I looked at my watch. It was 4 a.m. I turned the key and put the car in gear.


The night clerk looked a little nervous when I first walked into the lobby.

"Help you, sir?"

"I need a room."

After I showed him my wallet, he visibly relaxed. A fake smile. "Well, you came to the right place. Single or double?"

"Single's fine. Anything on seven?"

"Sir?"

"Seventh floor. It's my lucky number. Seven. I always try to stay on that floor."

He touched a couple keys on a computer. "You're in luck. Lucky seven, huh?" He looked up and smiled a little more real. "I can give you 707. How's that?"

"Perfect." I put my credit card on the counter. "Two sevens."

"That'll be a hundred and twenty-nine dollars. Checkout's at ten a.m." He swiped the card through the machine. As soon as it started spitting out paper, he smiled. Looked up. "But I think I can give you a late checkout, no problem. Let's say...noon?"

I nodded as I signed the receipt. All that money for eight hours.

If this by some chance was where Glen was staying, those two sevens could prove to be incredibly lucky. I could be right across from him. I could look out the peephole and watch him. I could leave after him. Maybe even follow him to the elevator. Share the ride down.

"Good morning," The Author said.

"Morning," I returned, rationing my syllables in case I needed more later.

"Thanks for coming to the readings." He closed his eyes. "And for not bugging me the way those other freaks do."

"You're welcome." He had recognized me.

"Hey, you wanna grab some breakfast?" The Author asked as the elevator doors slid open. He let me in first.

Oh, God. Could I do that? Would I be able to lift a juice glass or a coffee cup without shaking? Maybe I should decline.

```
"No, thanks.  I don't want to intrude."
"No intrusion at all. The road gets a little
lonely, and, frankly, I'd welcome the company.
It's always good to see a friendly face."
```

*Friendly.* Me? We could become friends. Exchange phone numbers. I ran my hand over my face. Damn. I had better shave. Clean up a bit.

My hair was still wet and I was whistling, standing over my small suitcase, picking out a clean T-shirt when I heard a door opening. I dropped the shirt and stepped quickly to the peephole. It was his door. He stuck his head into the hallway. Looked in both directions. Then he closed the door.

It was not Glen Dower. Of course it wasn't. Way too tall. But what was this guy's issue?

Had he heard something that spooked him? My whistling? If I could hear his door opening, he could probably hear me. Did he think there was someone in the hallway? Someone walking past his door?

Was he someone deserving of being stalked? Maybe he was cheating on his wife and expecting to see her outside his door. Or—better yet—the husband of the woman he was cheating with. And the guy's got a gun. That would make for more conflict.

*Holiday Inn-Fidelity.*

After getting my stuff together, I stretched out on the bed and must have been more tired than I thought. Because...

# CHAPTER FOUR

I don't believe I ever got the wakeup call. I had left it for ten. There was someone new at the checkout who swore I was called, basically accusing me of sleeping through it. If the maid hadn't knocked and entered at eleven, I probably would've slept on. Ended up being charged for another day.

Now I was stressed. A couple hours off my schedule. I needed to get from Dayton, Ohio, to St. Louis, Missouri in about six hours. If I didn't stop for anything but gas, I should just make the start of the next reading.


It was all highway driving. I kept a watch for cop cars. Kept my foot pushing the gas, edging up around seventy-five, pushing eighty, the whole way. Trimmed some time. Managed to grab a microwave burrito when I got gas. Later on I got gas again. From the burrito.

It was a flat ride. Not much to see. That was good because I couldn't see too well. Had the sun in my eyes for most of the ride. I should have sprung for some cheap sunglasses when I bought the burrito. One thing I remember, though, outside of Brazil, Indiana, I passed an old barn, weathered and forlorn.

Painted on its worn side in blood red: *God, Guts, and Guns Made America Great.*

Everybody out here credited God for both the good or the

bad. That was true about the guts. Coming to a place you didn't know. Taking it away from the current residents. Making it yours. And guns were what made that possible. Don't know if I agree with how it came about. But I wasn't there then. I was here now. Involved in a literary endeavor. Something those early Americans were probably too busy to do. I smiled for progress.

But that sign back there got me thinking. That guy rapping on my window. If I was going to be spending time sleeping in the car, maybe I should think about some protection.

I got lost in St. Louis. The sun had all but called it a day by the time I found my way to the small bookstore off Highway 40. I put the car in some bar's parking lot. The Barney Fife rent-a-cop on duty outside the bar looked me over. I walked through the parking lot into the bookstore. Some guy in a linen shirt was stacking up folding chairs.

"I missed it?" I asked. "I thought it started..." I looked at my watch. "...about now."

The guy—his nametag identified him as Sam—stopped, a half-closed chair in his hands. "Supposed to. Dower got a phone call. Some family emergency. Reading's been canceled."

Canceled! I came all this way. "He say what it was?"

He gave me a look like what business was it of mine. "Just a family thing."

He didn't have a family. Not really. I knew that. Both parents, gone. No siblings. What was going on here? Was he sick? I didn't know if he was flying or driving the book tour. I assumed flying, but I should have checked closer.

"How do you know that?"

Sam kept on collecting chairs. "Know what?"

"That it was a family thing?"

He stopped and thought about what I'd asked. "Look, you know what I know. He got called away. Reading's canceled." He picked up another chair and folded it.

He was lying about something. *What?* "But he's okay?"

He didn't even look at me. "Whatever."

I wanted to shake the guy. Instead, I used my words. "*Whatever?* He's a great writer. It would be a terrible loss if he…" I let the words hang, not wanting to complete the thought.

"He's good," the clerk said, "but he's a midlist guy. About six people were here when the publisher called. Half of 'em already had books. We'd be lucky to sell the other three."

I didn't pause. "Give them to me."

"What?"

I was already digging into my pocket for my credit card. It kept me from stuffing my fist down this jerk's blowhole. "Give me the three books."

Sam looked at me. There must have been something in my eyes. I felt hot. Jammed up inside. If he didn't move soon, I'd start screaming.

He moved. Carrying a chair in front of him. He walked back to the display, such as it was. Set the chair against the table. Picked up the remaining three copies.

He hurried over to the counter and started ringing up the sale. I turned away. I couldn't afford this, but this guy was a hack. He sold books like products. I had to show him. Let him know some people were concerned about artistic expression.

The card was hot in my hand. Digging into my skin. I should have thrown it at the vendor. That's what he was. A salesman. *An errand boy.* It could be widgets or candles or books. It didn't matter. If he could separate a mark from his money, it was all to the good.

I took the card over to the counter. He backed up a step. I set it next to the cash register. It took him a moment, but he picked it up. We completed the transaction in silence. I signed as he bagged the books and handed them to me.

I was opening the door when I stopped and turned around. He had his cell phone up to his ear. I went back to the counter and set the bag down. Opened it. Took out a pristine copy of

*Blues By The Case.*

"Here." I handed it to him.

"What?"

"Take it, Sam. Read it. Learn what good writing's all about. What life is all about."

He stood there with the phone at his ear. "Just...just a moment."

His other hand came up. Closed around the book.

I pulled the bag off the counter. Walked out the door.

I was pissed. At myself. At Sam the Bookstore Guy. I went back to the bar where I had parked. Went inside. The scene was so familiar. I wasn't sure why but...then I knew. Glen's mystery novel, featuring his loner anti-hero hit man for whom the book was titled: *Houston O'Halloran.* I could sense the character as I sat down. Recalled his condescending snide attitude.

It was a bar like so many others. Long and wooden with metal-legged stools. Naugahyde seats, pleated to look expensive. The button in the middle just another target for another asshole.

And there were three of them sitting there. Assholes. They looked up as I walked in. They didn't recognize me and returned to their beers and shots. I could smell their better-than-the-rest bonhomie.

But I knew three things they didn't know.

One: the person who had hired me.

Two: who each of them was.

Three: they would all be dead before midnight.

I walked into the bar and was greeted by, "Tough luck, huh?"

It was two of the regulars from the book tour. One chubby,

the other blonde. Ardent fans.

"Yeah." The bartender put a napkin on the open space in front of me. "Absolut cranberry," I said.

"He was there, you know."

"Who?" I asked.

"The Man Himself. Mr. Dower. He was at the bookstore."

"I know. The publisher called him and canceled the thing."

"No. The publisher called the store. The clerk gave the phone to Glen and Glen said he had to leave. Signed all the books, though."

Blondie leaned over and looked at me. I looked back and said, "Really?" I was even more upset now. I downed the vodka. Motioned to the bartender for another. "Run it by me. What exactly happened?"

Chubby shook his head; the fat on his face moved. "We don't know. He was there when we walked in. There were like only two people in the audience, but he was smiling and talking."

Blondie leaned in again. "He looked up. Saw us. Nodded. Then went on talking to the people up front. They handed him their copies and he signed them. He talked for a couple more minutes. Then he excused himself and took out his phone."

"Then what happened?" I asked.

"He came back and then the guy at the store said there was a phone call for him."

"On the store's phone?"

Blondie shrugged. "I guess. Guy pulled a cell phone off the counter and said it was a call for Glen. Musta been the store phone."

"And Glen just walked out?"

"Not right away. He shook hands with the two people up front, signed the rest of the books, apologized to the store guy and then he left."

I already had my second vodka in my hand. I wanted to throw it in this guy's face. "You bastards," I said instead. Using my words.

"What?"

"He left because of you guys," I said. "You lean on him too hard. You ask the same dumb questions in every town. He can't stand you. You drove him away."

"You're full of shit."

"Besides," Blondie said. "You follow him around, too."

"Yeah. But I don't get in his way. I let him say what he has to say. You guys crowd him. I can see it in his eyes. He hates it when you enter the room. You monopolize the event." I took a medicinal sip before I did something rash. "And I wasn't there tonight. He left because of you."

Chubby slapped his palms on the bar. "He left because of the phone call."

"Believe it if you want." I signaled the bartender for another. "You guys make me sick."

Blondie was standing now. "You talk like you're better than us. You're not. You're just too much in love with the guy to even approach him."

"What?"

"Face it. You're queer for the guy."

It was almost funny. I probably should have blown up, but he was so far off the mark I had to smile. "Can't I just appreciate someone's talents without people thinking there's some sexual thing involved?" I took a sip. "Besides, I could say the same thing about you two."

The bartender had been watching us like she was at Wimbledon. Her eyes following our volley back and forth. Now she was grinning like an ace had been served.

"We are."

"What?"

"We're gay. And so are you."

I shook my head. "Doesn't bother me, but no. I'm not."

Blondie was climbing back into his seat. "Then what are you doing here?"

"Having a drink. Probably gonna get a burger."

Chubby was mock-shocked. "In a gay bar?"
I looked at the bartender. She nodded.
I laughed. "How are the burgers?"
"Real good," she said.
"Medium. Cheddar. Slice of raw onion."
"Anything else?"
I looked at the guys down the bar. "I don't want mayo."

The burger was good. And the guys turned out to be not all that bad. We discussed Glen's writings. I didn't agree with their take on everything. They tended to, understandably, notice a homoerotic subtext I just didn't see. But, by the end of my meal, we had struck, if not a friendship, a peaceful coexistence. For some reason I lied and told them my name was Ira. I apologized for blaming them for making our favorite author bolt the bookstore. I still thought they were guilty, but without some sort of proof, my accusations were delusions fostered by an overactive imagination.

I bought a round of drinks to show there were no hard feelings, paid my check, and got up, my credit card feeling a bit lighter in my pocket. I left one of the books behind as a tip for the bartender. My newfound acquaintances called me a class act and applauded me out the door.

Before I claimed my car from the lot, I walked by the bookstore one more time. It was locked up tight, an iron gate pulled down in front.

I'd have to come back in the morning. I wanted to speak to the bookman.

I drove around. Checked a couple motels, but they were too expensive. When I complained to one desk clerk, he suggested I check into one across the river in Illinois, only twenty minutes away.

And it was cheaper. Nineteen ninety-five a night. I got a

room across the highway from a metal structure with a big neon sign. *Honey's A-Go-Go.*

I got up to my room, but couldn't sleep. It wasn't quite midnight and my mind kept playing over the conversation with the gay guys. I got up. Stood at the window. Looked out.

Honey's.

May as well go over for a drink. Assert my masculinity with a lap dance. Or two.

All I remember is a few more drinks and a topless woman walking me to the ATM machine. Helping me get a two-hundred-dollar cash advance on my credit card.

I don't even remember how I got back to the room. When I woke up, I still had my shoes on. My pants were around my ankles. My shirt was on but unbuttoned. And there was a message on the dresser mirror written in bright red lipstick.

*Thanks for the book baby I had a real good time*
*xoxoxoxo*
*Tiffany*

I forced down breakfast at a truck stop on the Illinois side. Lots of coffee. By the time I was back in St. Louis, I was feeling better. I found the bookstore easier this time. Parked on the street and went in.

Sam was behind the counter. He remembered me.

"I'm calling 9-1-1," he said, showing me his phone.

I raised my hands. "Wait. I came to apologize. I was tired. Cranky. Please. I just want to ask you a couple questions. About last night."

He was wary. "What about last night?"

"About the reading. The emergency."

He kept the phone in his hand the whole time. But he answered my questions.

"So is there any way you can find out who called him?"

He looked at the phone. At me. Waited a beat. "He got called on the store's phone, but I wouldn't give out that kinda information. It's private."

"Right," I agreed, nodding. Then I left the store.

He was lying again. I knew it. I just had to figure out a way to get a look at the store phone. So I sat in my car a block away and watched. Delivery trucks stopped and off-loaded boxes. He stood at the door. Held it open and smoked a cigarette.

This could take a while. What was it Glen had written about stakeouts? The trick was to become numb? No, trancelike, that was the word.

A lot of people get bored on stakeouts. They drink too much coffee or eat crap food and spend hours in agony. Or they relieve themselves only to find their mark has split by the time they get back. That's about the only reason why partners are good. Bathroom breaks. Most of the time they're too obvious. Two guys sitting in a car call more attention to themselves than one man does. Who are they? Are they casing a place? Looking to rob somebody? But one man, if he's noticed, can check his watch like he's waiting for someone. Or get out and grab a window seat at the coffee shop across the street.

With me it's a Zen thing. No coffee. No food. No partner. I take care of Mother Nature before she calls. I blend in, become one with my surroundings, my head barely showing above the window line. Disguises help, too. A change of appearance lets you get out and walk around, yet still keep your quarry in check.

But the true secret to good stakeout technique is to ignore everything else. Focus on your mark. And, if you enter the proper trancelike state, everything else will ignore you. You'll be like a ghost in the car.

A citizen of another dimension.

And when your mark drops his guard, he's as good as yours.

I tried to be trancelike, but after a while my butt hurt. And I couldn't get out and walk around. Sam might see me. But I must have been doing something right because I saw him first. He stepped outside about five o'clock. Closed the door. Taped a piece of paper to the glass. Walked up the block. Around the corner.

I moved quickly. The note on the door said Back in 15. I tried the doorknob. Locked. The old door rattled in its frame. I took out my lock pick and inserted it in the aging doorframe.

Okay. Time for some inside info on your friendly neighborhood mail carrier. A lot of us carry lock picks. Sometimes we need to get inside an apartment building and drop off a package. It's either use the lock pick or carry the package around and try again the next day. Sometimes the regular lock jams in those multi-address boxes. A lock pick comes in handy. Trust me; we get the packages to you and the less you know how, the better. Like making sausages.

The old bolt gave easily and the door lurched open.

"Can I help you?"

I palmed the pick and turned around. The store guy was there. *What the hell happened to fifteen minutes?*

"I thought you might have forgotten to take down the sign."

He shouldered by me. Used the hand holding the keys to tear down the sign. "Well, I didn't. I came back to make sure I'd locked up. Forgot last time."

All I could come up with was, "Looks like you goofed again."

He glared at me. I stepped back.

After he pushed past me and locked the door, he turned and looked at me. "I'd appreciate it if you would never come to this store again. I thought I made that clear."

"If that's the way you want it." I turned and walked away, muttered just loud enough for him to hear, "Thought I had a big sale for ya."

"What's that?" he said.

"Never mind," I said. "I was just going to offer to buy up any unsold Glen Dower books you might have left."

"You already did that," he said.

Right. *Think fast, Ezra.* "What about remainders?" I asked. "You have any unsold Dowers in stock?"

He thought about that. "Not on the floor," he said. "Maybe the basement."

"Would you mind checking? I'll pay full price for any you have left." I could practically feel my credit card squirming in my pocket.

"Really," he said. "Full price?"

"And another twenty for your time." *Ouch!*

More thought. I upped the offer. "Even if you don't find any, there's a Jackson in it for ya. Just for checking." *That's a few extra lattes for ya, Sam.*

"Come on in," he said. I followed him. "Wait here. I'll check the basement."

"Thanks."

He walked toward the door in the back, unlocked it and disappeared. I went behind the counter and immediately found what I was looking for: a cell phone. Had to be the store phone because Millennial Sam may forget to lock up every once in a while but I was pretty sure he went everywhere with his own phone.

I pressed the home button and, to my delight, I didn't need a code to open the phone. I went to the telephone icon, pressed Recents, and a bunch of numbers came up. I wasn't sure how much time I had, so I took pictures of all calls going in and out of the phone over the past two days. I heard Sam coming back, so I put the stores' phone down and slid mine into my pocket as I got out from behind the counter.

"Whatta ya know," the guy said as he locked the door behind him. "You're in luck. I found three old paperbacks in storage. Alphabetizing is a wonderful thing."

"Great," I said. "How much?"

He looked at the books, did some quick mental math, and said, "Let's make it forty bucks. Plus the extra twenty. I'll need the twenty in cash, of course."

"Of course," I said.


I took the same route home to Cincinnati, but decided to cut down I-74 South in Indiana. It was still almost six hours, but I drove leisurely, not caring about the time.

I figured I'd try the numbers—a few dozen—when I got home. If I could just get a region of the country. Something to narrow my search. And once I found that area, I'd put my newest developing plan into effect.

I'd tell the post office I needed to relocate.

Tonight I'd be sleeping in my own bed. I drove the rest of the way home with a smile on my face.

# CHAPTER FIVE

I was working my way through a medium pizza. The box took up most of my small kitchen table, but there was still some room for my laptop and my phone, which contained the pictures of the phone numbers that had come into the St. Louis bookstore.

I used a fingernail to pick some pepperoni from between my back teeth. Dragged it across the front of my mouth, sucked it back in, chewed. My concentration moved back to my phone.

There had only been enough time for me to take two pictures of the store's phone log, but that was enough. I just needed to know who had called Glen, causing him to cancel the event. My plan was simple: Call every number—the ones with only names didn't help me—on the Recents list and see what happened. I was using a pre-paid cell—what cops and crime writers call a "burner"—I'd picked up earlier from a convenience store two towns away from my apartment. I didn't want anyone I called to be able to identify my own number. Call me paranoid. John Lennon would have called me someone with a sense of heightened awareness. I called it playing it safe.

I wasn't able to tell the times of the calls; they all said Yesterday. I started with the most recent Recent—ha!—and got a recording.

*"You have reached Four Star Publishing. Our office hours are eight a.m. to five p.m., Eastern Standard Time. If you know your party's extension, enter it at any time. For a directory of…"*

I hung up. So either Glen's publisher called the bookstore or the bookstore called the publisher. Or someone using the bookstore's phone. I entered Four Star Publishing into the search engine and was not surprised by the info I found. It was located in New York City and the main number was the one I had just dialed. Not much help there.

I punished myself with another slice of pizza. Dialed the next number.

A woman's voice. Sleepy. "Hello?"

I hung up. Pictured her lying atop wrinkled bed sheets. Her hair a jumble of silk she pushes out of her eyes. The bed creaks as...

...her husband rolls towards her.

"Who was it?"

"A hangup. I don't know."

"That's the third night in a row with a hangup."

"So?"

"So who's calling and hanging up?"

"How the hell should I know? He hangs up."

"*He?*"

"He. She. They. I don't know; they hung up."

"But you said 'He.' Why'd you assume it was a he?"

I licked the grease off my fingertips. Pressed the third number. Listened to it ring for as long as it took me to eat another slice. I'm not used to constantly ringing phones anymore. Usually you get a voicemail or an out-of-service message.

The fourth number was a Chinese restaurant. I hung up. I dismissed the immature thought at first, but it just sat there like immature thoughts do. So I acted on it. Called the restaurant back. They picked up after two rings, and I said, "Hey, it's Sam from the bookstore."

"Hey, Sam. The usual?" the guy asked.

I said yeah and to double the order.

"Okay, Sam," the guy said. "Thirty minutes. Busy tonight."

I hung up and hoped Sam the bookstore guy was hungry.

The fifth number? That one blew me away when I realized the voice on the outgoing message was Glen's. Monotone. No personality, no name. Just the number and "Leave a message and I'll get back to you."

I was listening so closely I forgot to break the connection. Like I expected him to pick up. I didn't say anything. I hung up, glad I couldn't say anything and that I was not using my regular phone. Maybe my breathing was on the recording. Could I be ID'ed by my breathing? It was only a couple of seconds.

I sat there. Shaking. I had done the unexpected.

I had discovered Glen Dower's cell phone number.

Now what?


But who had called whom? I didn't have the time to check when I took the photos of the recent calls. All I knew was that the call was made the day before. Was it before or after Glen had canceled the event? Did Sam the bookstore guy call Glen to wish him well? That was a dumb idea; they'd been at the store at the same time. Did Glen call Sam to apologize for having to cancel? See above.

But one thing was true: a call had been placed by someone between Glen's phone and the store's.

And I was still concerned about Glen's family. They were never mentioned anywhere. How close were they? Did they live in the St. Louis area? Is that why Glen was called away? He mentioned once living in the southwest before pulling up stakes and moving God knows where.

Jesus. I could worry about that later. I had his number! With an area code I typed into the search engine: 207.

Zero-point-eighty-six hundredths of a second later it produced about twenty-six million results. But the lead was Maine.

Two-oh-seven was the area code for Maine. All of Maine.

That was great news. The bad news was that Maine is a huge state. More than thirty-six-thousand square miles. I looked it up. There were more than one-point-three million residents of Maine. I looked that up, too. How many had cell phones? How many had cell phones with the state's area code? Had Glen done what many people had: removed his landline in lieu of a cell and kept his original number?

Why would the store have Glen's personal number? They would deal directly with the publisher or his agent. Especially with someone as reclusive as Glen Dower.

They wouldn't have his personal number, I concluded. And that led to my next conclusion: Glen had called the bookstore. But why? To clarify the details of the event? To ask about local eateries? To...

*To cancel his event while he was still in the store?* Maybe I wasn't the only one with anxiety flare-ups. Maybe there was no family emergency. If that were the case...

I felt much better. More alive. I had convinced myself I had made another connection. Glen and I were on the same wavelength. He made intuitive leaps look easy. I was struggling. Taking time. Learning.

Learning how his mind worked? This knowledge would shape my thoughts. My approach to writing. And the more I learned, the better my writing would get.

It was almost midnight and I had to be at work in the morning. Start paying off my credit-card debt. I was too wired to sleep. I needed to celebrate. Blow off some of this energy so I could sleep.

And five a.m. never took its time arriving.

The jukebox was loud. The crowd was loud. I hunched over my

beer at the end of the bar. I thought a beer would relax me. Put me in a better place for sleep. I was wrong. It was all I could do to hear my own thoughts.

Why couldn't I walk out my door, down the street, and into a nice, quiet local bar? Someplace where, if there was music, it played at a respectable level. Maybe even live. Seems the noisier the background music, the noisier the crowd. Is that a business decision? Does it sell more drinks?

Everyone did have a drink in his or her hands, leaning into their drunken conversations. Spittle and screams. Raucous laughter. The place was like cable TV: five hundred channels but nothing on.

My beer had lost all of its flavor. I dropped a five on the bar and left.

I spent five minutes going over Glen's number. Committing it to memory. Pressing the numbers into my phone without pressing the phone icon. Its musical tones became a song I couldn't shake. A golden oldie that pops up and stays with you too long. It kept my mind racing and my body from sleeping.

I couldn't sleep. The mice scurrying across the linoleum— skaters on ice. My bed sagged and moaned like an old man with every toss and turn. The springs complaining with a nails-on-chalkboard wince.

I couldn't turn the neon lights off in my mind, their flickering, sizzling glow pointing to...where? It was there for me to find, but I couldn't make the connection. And that was bad because I made my living making connections. Maybe I was in the wrong line of work—again. Maybe I needed to try something new. Go someplace where no goons were constantly wanting to rearrange my nose or fit me for cement shoes.

Maybe someplace on my own. Why did I continue down this path if I could get away from people?


*Maybe, Baby, Why and If.*

It took me less than a minute to realize what was keeping me awake.

After finding Glen Dower's cell phone number, I was now going to use that info to find The Man Himself. Maybe we'd end up being friends after all.

# CHAPTER SIX

I was at work. And I was tired. Physically. Mentally. Tired of opening mailboxes, inserting mail, removing rubber bands from mail groupings. Same old, same old. Everyday.

At least walking is good for you.

One thing my little drive-away vacation had showed me was how much I wouldn't miss my job. I knew I could walk away from it anytime. That gave me power. Power to plan. To get to where I wanted to be.

A writer. With my own novels. Published.

Let somebody else deliver *my* mail.

I had spent an hour after work browsing the travel section of the bookstore at the mall. I took my purchases and retreated to a quiet spot by a small lake overlooking the downtown area of Cincinnati, a box of cheese Coneys beside me, a UDF extra-thick chocolate shake sweating alongside. The rest of the afternoon was spent reading about the oddities and interesting things Maine had to offer.

It had an enormous maritime history and quite a few famous authors. Past and present. Evidently, the winter months were so disagreeable that there wasn't much for a writer to do except put pen to paper or fingers to keyboard. No procrastination.

I liked that. It would help me. I would have to write or go out of my mind from boredom.

You ever notice there's never a bad picture in a guidebook? There are hokey ones. There are gorgeous ones. But nobody ever publishes a slightly out-of-focus shot. Or a shot of a family with their heads cropped out. A finger protruding over the upper left corner of the print. I guess they realize no one wants to see that stuff.

But I do. It's real. Honest. And it says, Yes, you could have a good time here. Even better than these people are having. With all the perfect pictures, you know going in you'll never see a sunset that captivating. Or catch a fish that big. You go on your expensive vacation, and it's just never as good as you'd hoped because you're expecting perfection. So you get to be the jerk with the finger over the lens. The picture of Aunt Molly's neck growing atop a sweatshirt with some cute slogan about moose.

But that's okay. I'm not going to vacation there.

I'm going to live there. And write.

Just like Glen Dower.

But how do I get there? The transfer idea is solid. To wherever Glen lives in Maine. I become his mail carrier. I learn from him.

But where does he live?

"I need a transfer."

"'Fraid not, Ezra. I need you here."

Larry and I had come up through the ranks together. Started the same day. Both carriers. But Larry always had his eye on the prize. The desk job. Big bucks. Larry also always had his eye on the ladies. Still does. Even though he's married.

"Look, Lar, it's important."

"Sorry, Ez. Can't let you go."

*Play your card, Ezra. Don't let him shut you down.*

"How's Tammy?" I asked. "That new clerk? You...showing her the ropes?"

"She's fine. She's gonna be a good addition around here."

"To the postal staff? Or to your staff?"

That got a rise—ha!—out of him. He stood.

"I think this meeting is about over, Ezra."

"I don't. I can't stand it here anymore, and I'll do what I have to do to get a transfer. If that means ratting out your little love harem on the pages of the local paper or placing a call to your wife, I'll do it."

Larry was turning a shade of crimson I had never seen before. He couldn't speak.

"So sit down and let's see how this is gonna happen," I said.

Larry exhaled a blast of hatred. But he sat down. Took a moment to compose himself.

"Where would you like to go, Ezra?"

"Maine."

"Where in Maine?"

*Good question. Where in Maine?*

"I'll have to get back to you on that."

Larry grinned and shook his head.

"You never think ahead, Ezra. That's why you're still a carrier and I'm sitting here."

*Keep him under your thumb, Ezra.*

"And why I'll *still* be a carrier. And you'll be gone once word is out. No paycheck. No benefits. No pension. You wanna start over again, Larry? At your age?"

I stood up. Walked to the door. *Parting shot, Ezra. Give him a parting shot.* Got to the door. Turned back to Larry. "Think on it. I'll be in touch."

\* \* \*

I was brushing my teeth. Staring into the mirror.

Larry was right. I didn't think ahead. I should have had all my ducks lined up before I went in and unloaded on him.

Think. It can't be that hard.

How do I find out where Glen lives?

All it took was a little reductive reasoning. Thinking backward about the whole mail delivery apparatus.

Before we get the mail to deliver at our local branch, the stuff gets sorted and distributed. And that's where I needed to be. A distribution center where I could watch the mail for anything going to Glen's address.

"A distribution center, Larry. Where the mail gets sorted. Routed."

"Crap. You know you can't do that."

"Why not?"

"You're a carrier, for chrissakes. Distribution's a clerk category."

He was right. Maybe I should take the clerk exam, too. I'd be like a guy with two degrees. In demand. *Now stepping up to the plate...the ambidextrous mailman. Look at him, ladies and gentlemen. He sorts left. He delivers right. He does it all.*

This is gonna take way too long.

"I gotta think on it some more. If I have to, I'll take the test again. For a clerk."

"You're a waste of time. Get out of here."

The phone rang late Friday night. I answered to a whisper.

"Ezra?"

"Yeah?"

"It's Larry."

"You got a cold?"

"No. I can't talk long. Listen. You know the Good Morning Diner? Fourth and Walnut?"

"Yeah."

"Noon. Tomorrow. Your treat."

"I know a good burger place."

"I bet you do. But I like the Good Morning. It's about your transfer."

He hung up.


I was in the booth, waiting on Larry. A nice-looking waitress handed me a menu.

"Welcome to the Good Morning. I'm Ellen. Anything to drink, dear?"

"Coffee. Black."

"Be right back."

And she was. Thick porcelain coffee cup. Steaming hot. Before I had gone over even half the menu, which was only two pages.

"Wow. Quick."

The pencil was raised over the pad.

"Know whatcha want?"

"Not yet. Sorry. I'm waiting for someone."

"Take your time."

And she was gone to refill another coffee cup at the next table.

The bell over the door tinkled merrily. Ellen looked up. A grimace crossed her countenance. But there was a lilt in her voice.

"Larry. Good morning. The regular?"

"Sure thing, sweetness." He slid into the booth across from me. "You met my friend Ezra?"


Larry liked his eggs runny. I was going to suggest he use a spoon, the way they kept wavering and threatening to slip off the tines of his fork. He should have used a bowl instead of a plate, but it wasn't my concern. I knew I wouldn't be eating a lot of meals with this man, and I liked that fine. Hell, he probably relished the idea more than I did. Get rid of me fast and keep on keepin' on. So if I had to watch him slip those quivering forkfuls into his mouth, it was a small price to pay. At least he used a napkin after every bite.

"I think I got an idea as to how you can move inside."

"Yeah?"

He set his fork down and lifted his coffee cup with both hands. Held it as he studied me.

"You may not like it, but it's been done before."

"What has?"

Larry leaned over the table as far as he was able. His voice a whisper. I swear there was a smile wrapped around his words.

"On-the-job injury," he said. "I'm thinking broken leg."

"Jesus, Larry." I shivered like men do when they see another man get jammed in the nuts. He took a sip of coffee, his eyes watching me. There was a vivacity in them I'd never seen before. He was enjoying this. "I was hoping it wouldn't be painful."

"You wanna get inside, and the next test ain't for a while yet."

"I know, I know. It's just..." *Just what, Ezra? A sacrifice?* What about the ends justifying the means? Am I willing to endure physical pain to get to where I need to be? And what would be the limit of that pain? Doesn't a broken bone take a long time to mend? And I'd be out of commission. No money coming in. Unless it happened on the job. I could claim workers' comp. Hell, by the time I was healed, the next test might be within reach. I was seeing some room for negotiation. "Couldn't it be a bad sprain or something?"

Larry gave it a moment's thought. Then he shook his head and drank his coffee.

"How about just the ankle?"

He considered that as he sopped up the last of his eggs with a piece of toast.

"Ankle'd work," he said. "But it better be convincing.

\* \* \*

I'm not a big fan of when writers sum up a few days in one long sentence, but I spent most of the weekend at home, psyching myself up; deciding which ankle I would sacrifice; practicing how I'd walk with a limp. I also slept and ate.

Monday, I walked my route, looking for the perfect spot. I found it in front of a building construction site. The sidewalk had been cracked and uprooted into a jagged hunk of concrete with a gap just about wide enough to step into.

The noon sun bore down as I looked around for witnesses. The construction area was deserted. I let a car pass then slipped my right foot into the gap. An almost perfect fit. I was getting nervous and felt the need to pee. Maybe the work crew wouldn't mind if I used their portable outhouse.

Afterwards, I went back to the crack and took a few deep breaths. I had thought about drinking some alcohol or taking some anti-anxiety meds but didn't want to screw up my plans by having something show up in my system during the post-injury blood test. Something the post office—or an insurance company—could claim was responsible for the accident.

The more I thought about what I was about to do, the more reasons I came up with for not doing it. That was bad. This was for me. For Glen. For our future relationship.

It was time to stop thinking and start doing.

With my cart in front of me, I stepped toward the crack. My ankle slipped into the crevice and I keeled over, letting gravity do the rest of the work.

They probably heard my screams back at the post office.

# CHAPTER SEVEN

Turned out, it wasn't so bad. After two weeks at home—how's that for a quick summary?—I was inside, sorting mail at Larry's branch, my ankle properly secured in plaster as I slotted envelopes into their proper places. My lawyer advised me that if I wanted to settle the case quickly, I shouldn't ask for too much. Enough to make it worth my while, but not enough to keep it in the legal system for months, even years. I figured out what I needed to make the move to Maine and doubled it. I kept thinking I should have held out for more, but I didn't want to have to wait and then possibly have to return home after getting settled in Maine. I wanted to move forward at my preferred pace.

When it happened, it happened quick. Less than two weeks.

"Ezra!"

"Yeah?"

"Larry wants to see you in the office."

He was still working at this hour? Everyone on the first shift was gone. Was this about my transfer? Or was it about the job I was doing here? Maybe I wasn't as fast as some of the other people in my department, but I was injured. He had to realize that. Hell, he's the guy who...conspired with me and my ankle.

*Calm down, Ezra.* At most he'll complain about your work. He can't fire you. You could create all kinds of problems for him. Just you getting this job was out of normal procedures.

This can't be about performance. It has to be about Maine.


"Pack your things, Ezra. You're outta here."

I didn't know how to respond. It sounded like I was being let go. Fired. It must've shown on my face. Larry exploded in laughter.

"Oh, that look. It was worth all the phone calls and string-pulling for that look." He used his index fingers to dry his eyes. "You're outta here and on your way to Maine, shithead."

"I am?"

"You are. Mail distribution center outside of Portland. You're a clerk until the leg heals. Then you're a carrier again."

I thrust my arm over the desk. Hand extended.

"Thank you, Larry. Thank you so much."

He let my hand hang there in the air. Empty.

"Sit down. We gotta go over a couple things."


It was slightly more complicated than I had thought. I had to sign a paper saying I was leaving to care for an elderly aunt in the state of Maine and that I had no intention of returning to the Cincinnati area for postal work.

"Once you leave here, Ezra, it's like you never existed. I don't want you running to me demanding your old job back."

"Gee, Larry, it sounds like you don't like me."

"Because I don't."

He slid an envelope across the desk. I picked it up.

"Read it."

It was a letter of introduction—written on official USPS stationery—to the Postmaster at the central distribution center in Portland, Maine. One paragraph.

*This is to introduce Ezra Lockert. Ezra is*

*qualified as a mail carrier and as a clerk. Due to a recent job-related injury, he has been performing the duties of a clerk. Once his injury heals, he will be fully able to return to delivery work. He is moving to Maine to care for an elderly aunt. Any consideration you can give him would be appreciated.*

I looked at the letter again, this time reading it slowly.

"There's no promise of employment here," I pointed out. "What if I get to Maine and they tell me there's no work?"

"There will be. Your timing is magic, Ezra. You're catching a generational wave. Lots of old-timers getting ready to retire. You have an appointment with the Postmaster a week from tomorrow. Show him that letter. We've talked. He'll have something for you."

"A week? Don't I need to give you two weeks' notice?"

"You did that. I've just been so busy I forgot to report it. Tonight's your last night. Stop by Payroll before you leave town. You gotta sign something so they can cut your last check."

I stood, folded the envelope, and put it in my pocket.

"Thanks, again."

Larry didn't get up.

"Don't let the door hit you on your way out."

I rented a U-Haul truck with a tow bar for my car. Stopped some kid I had seen mowing lawns on the street.

"You wanna make twenty bucks?"

He eyed me suspiciously. "For what?"

"Get a friend or two. Help me load the truck."

"Twenty bucks each?"

"Yeah."

"How much stuff you got?"

"Not a lot. Take maybe four hours tops."

He contemplated.

"That's only five an hour."

"You want it or not?"

"For twenty bucks, not. Make it forty for me. Thirty each for my crew. Two buddies."

*Now he had a crew?* A hundred bucks. Still cheaper than professionals.

"Deal."

We shook and arranged a time for the next day. I spent the rest of my day boxing books and clothes at my apartment. Kitchen and bathroom stuff. Furniture was minimal. A couple tables. Some chairs. A sofa, TV, bed, two dressers, and the bookshelves. I'd be traveling light.


The little bastards made out like bandits. It only took two hours to load the truck. I put my old sleeping bag and a pillow in the thrunk of my car. I gave them each an envelope.

The kid I had contracted with opened his and looked inside.

"What, no tip?"

"Consider the two hours I didn't use you and your crew a tip."

I had one more thing to do before leaving the great state of Ohio.

# CHAPTER EIGHT

It could have been the twin of that sign about *God, Guts, and Guns* I'd seen in Indiana on my return trip home. Next to this one was a big piece of cardboard on a stake. Just to the side. I almost didn't see it. But there it was, like a personal missive to me.

**Gun Show**
**Saturdays and Sundays**
**10 a.m.-10 p.m.**

Did I really need this? I thought about that street guy and his saliva bullet. I thanked my ankle for the insurance settlement. I couldn't afford this a few months ago. But Fate sometimes just shows up. No announcements. And here I was being given an engraved invitation.

*Yes,* I convinced myself. *I needed this.*

I signaled a turn. Slid over to the inside lane.

"Any priors?"

"Priors?"

"Convictions? Arrests?"

"No."

"Doesn't really matter," he said, and handed me a piece of paper. "Fill this out."

"Why doesn't it matter?"

"I'm not a licensed gun dealer. I'm a guy selling guns at a gun show."

*There's a difference?* "But you *are* selling guns."

"Yes, sir. But I'm not a dealer. So you find something you like, you're walking out of here a proud, newly armed supporter of the Second Amendment."

I wasn't going to push my luck. "You got a pen I can borrow?"

I took the form over to the snack area. Got a hot dog and a pop. Read over the form. The guy was right. There was no waiting period while they checked your background at a gun show. I filled out the form. Went back to the booth.

I handed him the form as he considered me. "What you need a gun for anyway?"

"Protection."

"From what?"

"What do you think," I said. "People. I've got nothing now. What if someone tries to enter my apartment? Rip me off. That's why I need a gun. Protection. It's my right."

"Damn straight. It's every man's right. Kinda job you do?"

"I'm a mail carrier from Cincinnati."

"You know you can't carry on that job, right?"

"I'm not planning to. This is for my off-hours protection."

"Probably should let you guys carry while working. More good guys out there with guns, the better. And you're already in uniform, right?" He paused. "Do need to see some ID, though."

I removed my license from my wallet. He checked the ID and handed it back. He looked down at his display. Rearranged a silver pistol.

"This is a lovely weapon, isn't it?"

I didn't know what it was, but it looked like it could do some damage.

"Looks good to me. How much?"

He picked it up. Handed it to me. "Three hundred."

*Dollars?* I kept my cool. "That's a bit high for what I need."

I could probably afford it, but I really just needed something to make me feel more comfortable on the road and in Maine.

He showed me a few more. Again, all a bit high for what I needed. He picked up on that after showing me five other pieces. "Mister," he said, "I don't think I can help you. I gotta make a living here, y'know?"

I tried a new approach. "You have any...merchandise not on display here?"

He leaned in. "I'm not sure what you mean."

"I think you do. Do you have any guns that you might not be able to sell at this show, but might be available for sale elsewhere at a lower price?"

He grinned and tugged at his lower lip. "You really need a piece that bad?"

"You should see the neighborhood I live in," I said. I ran two fingers up and down my left arm in the universal sign of darker-skinned people. "And my neighbors."

Another grin. "There's a burger joint down the street. Be there quarter after ten tonight. Bring one-fifty. Cash."

"Okay."

He took my form and ripped it up, the pieces ending up in his wastebasket.


With my new financial situation, it turned out to be relatively easy to get my hands on a hundred and fifty dollars. I hit my bank's ATM. I was going to use my credit card but the interest rate was sky-high. Twenty-something percent. How can the government go after shylocks and gangsters for charging that much, but leave the banks alone? They must all be in bed together. Good thing I had made more deposits than usual as of late. I took out the cash I needed, happy in the thought that I was also avoiding a paper trail.

\* \* \*

I was occupying a booth in the back when the gun guy entered. I waved. He nodded and went to the counter. Bought some burgers and a drink. Had them bag it. Then he walked over and sat down across from me.

"You got the money?"

"Yeah."

He smiled. Took the burgers out of the bag. Took a slurp from his drink.

"Be right back."

He stood. Picked up the empty bag. Went into the men's room. He was only gone maybe half a minute. When he returned, he sat down and pushed the bag across the table to me.

"Pick up the bag. Follow me to my car."

He got up. I stood. Picked up the bag. It was heavier than I had thought. I followed him outside the restaurant.


He had parked in the back of the lot. We were on the far side of his van. No one from the restaurant or road could see us. And the brick wall behind us was blind.

"Gimme the money."

I took the gun out of the burger bag. It wasn't any of the ones he had shown me at the show. It was a small black thing. It looked like a cap gun.

"This isn't what you showed me."

"You mean the ones you said you couldn't afford? Like that sweet .38?"

I don't know if it was a .38 or not, but I nodded. "Yeah."

"That'd run you a few hundred past your budget. One-fifty looked to be your limit. Maybe even a little over it."

He glanced around the parking area.

"That's a .22. It's a good gun. It'll stop someone up close. Surprise them." He put his hand out. "You don't want it, no harm done."

I pulled the gun back. "No. No. It's fine. Just not what I was expecting."

An idea was forming in my mind. Triggered—ha!—by something Glen had written in *Swallow My Soul*, before his hero realized a bullet wouldn't really stop a vampire.

The guy had the shakes. He was constantly moving, scratching his arms. A junkie and I was gonna give him money for his habit. But he had something I needed.

"Let me see the gun."

It took him awhile to pull it loose from the back of his pants. He held it by the grip and pointed it at me. I could see the shells in the revolver looking my way.

"Hey. Take it easy there, sport. It's loaded."

"Yeah. It is."

I gripped the barrel and he let go, his hand turning up for the money.

But now I was in control. I had the gun.

Maybe I could keep this gun and retain my one-fifty. I pulled the hammer back.

"Why don't you just get in your van and drive away?"

He shook his head. "I should've known soon's you said you were postal. You just seemed too desperate." He turned back to the van's door.

For a big man, he was awful quick. When he spun around again, the silver .38 was in his hand and pressed against my forehead. His other hand slapped the .22 down to my side. It was no longer much of a threat, what with his gun touching my head. Not unless I thought I could outdraw this guy. And I knew that wasn't going to happen.

"You are one dumb shit. Never threaten someone with an empty gun."

This was cool. Like something in the movies. Then my nervous system took over. I could feel sweat break out all over. And with it came the decaying stench of fear. I felt alive.

"Sorry. I'm sorry."

He lowered the .38. "You sure are." He dipped his chin downward. "You want that gun or not?"

"Yeah. I do."

"Then give me my fucking money."

I dug into my pocket and extricated seven twenties and a ten spot. He wrenched them from my grip. He put the .38 back against my forehead. He pulled the trigger.

I had just started to feel the adrenaline erupt when I heard the hammer click on an empty chamber. Relief feels weird when you know everything's okay mentally, but your body still hasn't registered the fact. Like forgetting you're belted in on a huge downward roller coaster hill.

He laughed. A loud snort. Then he pulled a small glassine envelope from his shirt pocket. Six skinny pellets. He tossed them at my feet.

"Don't pick them up until I clear the lot. And for God's sake, put that gun away."


I was aware of the gun and bag of bullets the whole ride home. I started out with it in the glove box. That lasted to the first rest stop. No matter where I tried to hide them, under the seat, in the trunk, they seemed to give off a glow that made only that part of the car shine. As if they were saying, *Here we are. Look at us.*

I kept glancing in the rearview mirror. Did I look different? Nastier? More dangerous? Just having the weapon around changed my entire perspective. Could someone tell I had a gun just by looking at me? Were the police trained in that sort of thing? I eased up on the gas. Kept the car just under the speed limit. I did not want to call attention to myself. Just in case.

By the time I turned into my apartment's parking lot, the gun was resting peacefully under my seat. But it throbbed in my head like a toothache. Dull and insistent.

Glen's tour was over. There would be no more sleeping in the car. Why did I even buy the damn thing? Oh, yeah. *Protection.*

I parked in front of my apartment. And sat there. The old woman next door was walking the dust mop she called a dog. She waved at me. I nodded back. Didn't say anything. Would my voice sound different to her? Make her suspicious?

I watched her progress in the side mirror. I toggled the switch. Swiveled the glass. Followed her reflection until she turned the corner. Checked the street.

Empty.

If I was going to do this, now was the time. My eyes scanned up and down the block. Using the mirrors as backup. I leaned forward, my head still erect so I could keep watch. My right hand groped under the seat until it closed on the brown paper bag with the metal meal inside. I brought it up. Stuck it in my waistband. Bag and all. Draped my shirt over it.

I opened the door and stepped out. Checked myself. Not bad. If I leaned forward just a bit, my shirt hung straight down. And the forward tilt said progress. *This guy is going places.* I closed the door. Lean-walked back to the trunk. Opened it. Took out the sleeping bag and pillow. As I dropped the lid, the car heaved a sigh of relief to be rid of the revolver.

I might be sleeping rough tonight, but at least I'd be armed and ready.

# CHAPTER NINE

My new gun and I traversed the expressways. We were on our way to Maine to find a place to live and unload the truck. Make my appointment with the Postmaster.

I figured three eight-hour days would get me there without too much stress on my butt or my busted non-driving ankle. Leave me a couple days to find an apartment. I hit the road every morning at five a.m. to get a jump on the commuter traffic. Stopped for breakfast at seven. Lunch a few hours later. With bathroom breaks and gas fill-ups, it was usually around four or five when I started looking for a motel. I could have pushed, but there was no reason to rush things now.

I should have brought pen and paper or a tape recorder. As I left the populous city areas and ventured out into wooded country and farmland, huge rock slabs of mountain, and fog-shrouded morning vistas, I felt renewed. Born again. Not in some pseudo-religious way, but creatively. There was something about the rhythm of the road, the miles passing by, that freed my mind. Meditations flowed. Snatches of songs. Poems. Story ideas. Beginnings, middles, and ends. I'd repeat them to myself, trying to hold their ephemeral beauty, but by the time I got to the next stop they'd be gone. A small throb in my memory. I was like a drunk without the hangover, trying to remember what I had done the night before.

And Glen rode along with me. Bits of his dialogue, his descriptions.

It was what the travelers called "a lookin' plum" town. You look once and you're plum past it.

I took my meals in fast-food joints just off the highway. I used the drive-throughs, laughing as I steered my life back toward the highway because I knew the pimply faced kids who sacked my burgers had to stay there. Most likely for the rest of their days, and I was free to move. To find where my perfect fit would be.

I welcomed Glen back as an old friend. I talked. He listened. We traveled together. One spirit. One mind.

And the road beckoned me onward, leading me to some unknown destination. My fate unwrapping down a concrete ribbon. What surprises would await me at the end of my journey?

I'd hit a rest area and watch families sharing sandwiches and sodas. I felt a bit lonely sometimes, watching their easy banter. Their closeness. But I told myself it came with the territory. Other writers had made a similar choice. Kerouac, Thompson, and Glen came to mind. They sacrificed themselves on the altar of experience. Led solitary lives, but shared their thoughts with a multitude, touching so many.

But did they make a difference? I thought so, but at the end of the day, what was more important, the touch of someone close or listening to a completed page making its way through the printer?

# CHAPTER TEN

After the concrete and burbs of Cincinnati, with their tended yards and measured squares of public greenery, the wilderness of Maine was a new frontier. An outlaw area of reclaimed majesty. Horace Greeley had said, "Go west, young man," and, apparently, most folks had listened. Those who had stayed behind had settled into a new naturalism. A Garden of Eden.

I had spent most of my existence up to now in a hilly city in a flat state. Whatever wilderness had once greeted those Greeley-inspired travelers had been clipped back, poured over, and relegated to fenced-in areas where couples could stroll without turning an ankle, or bash a baseball a hundred yards or more before it would endanger any passing pedestrian or automobile. After seeing the ancient, roaming forests of Maine, I could understand why, in Ohio, we greatly valued our preserved state parks.

I had come here in search of a teacher, but I couldn't ignore the other feelings I was experiencing. There was something here that spoke to the soul. Oh, there were small towns scattered about, but they weren't delineated like Ohio towns seemed to be.

Here it was a coexistence with the land, and maybe not always a peaceful one. As I drove over two-lane roads, it seemed each municipality sprouted from the earth itself, and could just as easily, at any time, slip back into the maw of Mother Nature.

Maybe it had something to do with the springtime and its

profusion of new buds and fresh greenery, even while an unfamiliar chill still loitered in the air. Maybe the first harsh winter would make me look in the rearview mirror.

*Ezra, you made a big mistake,* something whispered in my ear.

But I didn't think so. I let the colors and scope wash over me and stored up their impressions in my subconscious. The writer in me would call them forth at the appropriate time.

I found a cinderblock motel on the outskirts of Portland that would serve as my base of operations until my first couple of paychecks gave me some cash for an apartment's expenses: first month's rent, security deposit, gas and electric. The motel wasn't too expensive and was within ten miles of where I'd be working. I could have afforded something better with the insurance payout, but I decided to play the spendthrift until I found a real home. I put a week's worth of clothes in the cheap dresser, its veneer chipped and curling at the edges. I stored the rest of my things at a self-service storage facility nearby. They required a three-month minimum, and I needed the largest room they had available. I cringed at the cost—see what I said about needing more money?—but three months would give me plenty of time to leisurely move stuff into whatever place I eventually found.

I had paid my credit card down before I left Cincinnati. Now it was starting to sprout again like the buds on the trees. I just hoped it didn't grow wild like some of the greenery I'd seen. With the motel and the storage fees, my self-imposed budget would be pretty tight, but my other expenses shouldn't be too bad. Basically food and gas. I'd get to know the area. See where I wanted to live. I'm sure people at work would be happy to suggest an area or two. Then I'd get a real apartment. Maybe with an extra room. *A writing room.* It could be a walk-in closet for all I cared, but it had to be a separate space, so I'd know going in there was only one thing to do.

And I had to keep it clean. No dirty clothes hanging on the chair or lying on the floor. No bills, newspapers, or periodicals piling up into a mountain of clutter on the desk, slipping over the edge and turning into a recyclable sea.

No distractions. When I was in that room I would write. Nothing else.

# CHAPTER ELEVEN

He had kept me waiting a half hour. When his door finally opened, he stood there. Studied me. Shrugged. His eyes were still on my letter of introduction.

"How's the leg?"

How much had Larry told him? Was it even Larry who had talked to him? Or was it someone above him who was turning the screws?

"The ankle. It's healing well. Doctors are impressed."

"C'mon in back."

I caught the door as it was closing. He had turned in front of his desk, waiting. I handed him the envelope I had been carrying in my hand since I arrived.

"Take a chair. Sorry for the wait." *No he wasn't.*

He walked around his desk as I sat. Squeaked into an ancient leather-padded oak chair that rocked back from his weight. His desk was matching oak, just as old if not older. It looked like it might have been a library table at one time. Now it held paper instead of books, his nameplate, black plastic mail trays from some office superstore, the usual desk accessories, and a perfectly pruned little bonsai tree.

He had yet to introduce himself. He leaned forward, accompanied by another squeak, and set his forearms on the green blotter.

He looked up over the piece of paper. Over the little glasses he read through. Granny glasses. I remembered some rock-and-rollers wearing glasses like that years ago. Full beard and matching gray hair pulled back and tied off into a ponytail that trailed down his back. The light from a large aquarium behind him reflected off the back of his head, his shoulders.

I checked the nameplate on the desk. *Simon Hillacre, Postmaster*. Ran it through my memory bank. Nothing jumped out and waved at me.

"It's not that I don't need people. I do. But I gotta tell you up front I'm not happy about this. We got some part-time flexies here deserve a staff position. Then you show up."

He sat back and turned to his left. Opened my letter to its full length, then eased it down behind his desk. A moment later the gnashing of a shredder gobbled it up.

"You either got some heavyweight connections, you know where some bodies are buried, or you know who's doing something or some*one* they shouldn't be doing. You don't play that game here. You do your work. Only your work. As soon as that leg gets good enough to last a route—we have docs who'll check that—you're on the street. I want to get you outta here as fast as I can. Morale's good around here. I don't need some...tourist screwing it up. You're bottom of the ladder. Understood?"

"Yes, sir."

He stared at me. Fixing me in his mind. His voice lacked all enthusiasm.

"Welcome aboard." He nodded toward the outer office. "Lizbeth will walk you through the paperwork and such. You start next Monday. Any questions?"

"What shift?"

He smiled for the first time since I had seen him.

"Overnights.

I had a week. Finding a real apartment topped the list of things to do, and, thanks to Elizabeth, I had a couple of areas to check out. But that would be tomorrow. Tonight would be a celebration.

Lobster. And wine.

I slept well. Too well, actually. It was almost lunchtime when my feet found the floor and padded their way to the bathroom. I thought I'd have a headache, but I felt great. I had killed two bottles of wine. One with dinner. Another at home. God no, I couldn't start considering this motel home. I'd never leave. That thought alone got me showered, dressed, and out the door.

I found a place with a big neon sign that said *Diner*. I tore through a huge stack of pancakes and a pot of coffee while I looked over the local paper. I was circling some apartment rentals when the waitress came for the plates.

"You lookin' for an apartment?"

"Yeah."

"You got a job?"

May as well try it out. Get used to saying it. I glanced at her nametag.

"Well, Donna, I'm a writer."

"Oh." She smiled. "Written anything I might know?"

"Some short stories. I'm working on a novel." She just stood there. Was she waiting for me to tell her the titles? "No. Not really."

"Uh-huh."

She took the plates away and I went back to circling apartment rentals.

"You want a warm-up on that?"

She was back, holding a fresh coffee pot over my cup.

"Please."

She poured.

"Reason I asked, our cook's uncle died a couple weeks ago. He had this cute little cabin back off the highway. I'd rent it myself, but they're thinking of selling it once the estate's all cleared up. I know I couldn't afford to buy it, so why move all my stuff in just to move it out in a month or two?"

A house. It'd be perfect. No neighbors through thin walls. I could write all day.

"Sounds good. Could I see it?"

Donna turned and made her way toward the kitchen. I looked over and saw an older man in a T-shirt and hairnet staring our way. Donna came right back.

"Well, I told the cook, you're a writer, and he wants to know...you ever been published?"

Ah, the regular Joe's measuring stick. You're not a writer until you've been published. Like all the pages I've pumped out are just so much masturbation.

"Nope," I shook my head and smiled up at Donna, "but I start a real job with the post office on Monday."

"Honey," she grinned, "you may have just found a place to live. I'll be right back."

She hustled across the restaurant, conferred with Amos for a few seconds. She must have mentioned the post office because he got a big smile, looked over and gave me a thumbs up.


I made arrangements with Donna to come back around three when things were slower and Amos could come out and talk with me. I returned to the motel and called a few of the listings in the paper. I squeezed in a few look-sees, talked with the landlords, the rental agents. It was the same story. First month's rent. One month's security deposit. Everyone was glad to hear I'd be working at the post office, but they all wanted their money up front. It looked like I'd be at the motel as long as I'd originally planned. It wasn't that bad, just industrial. Concrete walls, concrete floor. Not what I'd call cozy. I didn't realize how badly I wanted to move into a place of my own. Just looking at apartments got my relocation glands salivating.


It was a little after three when I walked into the diner and sat down at the counter. Other than a couple and their two kids finishing up in a booth, the place was empty.

Donna came over quickly. "Coffee?"

"Please."

She set the cup in front of me and poured. Disappeared into the kitchen. A moment later she reappeared with Amos. He stuck out his hand.

"Amos Gallatin."

"Ezra Lockert."

"You mind we go out back? I own the place and can't even smoke in here." He glanced at my cup. "Bring your coffee."

I followed him through a spotless kitchen, out into the green, landscaped backyard. He sat down at a wooden picnic table. Pulled a pack of smokes from his pocket.

"This is a nice surprise," I said.

He smiled as he stuck a cigarette between his lips. Lit it. "You like?"

"Very much."

The yard was completely enclosed by a six-foot-tall stockade fence lined with flower beds. A chaotic yet carefully controlled choice of colors.

I told him so. In those exact alliterative words.

"You talk like a writer."

I watched him flick his ash into a beanbag ashtray. The brass bowl polished to a high gloss. "Thank you."

I thought he'd talk about the plants, but he plowed straight ahead.

"It's a small cabin. Comes furnished."

I pulled out a map of the area one of the rental agents had given me.

"Where is it?"

He studied the map. A well-trimmed nail struck paper.

"Here."

It was just outside an area Elizabeth had recommended.

"How much?"

He drew in some smoke. Let it wrap around his words.

"Not really sure. I just mentioned it to Donna yesterday. Thought she'd jump at it."

I took the rolled-up newspaper from my back pocket. Opened it up on the table.

"Here's your area." I ran my finger down three apartment listings. "You can see what they're asking."

Amos studied the apartment rents. His lips pursed into a silent whistle. I agreed but didn't say anything. The apartments had turned out to be more than I wanted to pay. There was little reason to believe I was going to get an entire cabin.

"Donna tell you what we wanted to do with the place?"

"Yeah."

"So you know we're gonna put it up for sale?"

I nodded.

"We, my sister and me, just wanted to rent it out to help cover any expenses we might have with it. Mainly taxes, utilities. My uncle owned it free and clear."

"Uh huh." *Non-committal.*

He studied those rents, the hairnet keeping his silver hair from falling forward. The ash on his cigarette got longer.

"Got twenty acres out behind the place. You walk to the end and there's a lake. Fishing's pretty good. You fish?"

"Used to. Haven't in a while." Shit. Lakefront property. No way I can afford this. It goes up for sale, some rich guy buys it. Levels the cabin and puts in a long drive. Builds some huge McMansion closer to the lake.

Amos was sure taking his time with the bad news, and I was beginning to wonder about his hair. The more I looked, the more I thought it might be a wig. I put it together with the neatness of the kitchen and the backyard. The trim fingernails. It made perfect sense in what I could see of Amos' world. A hairnet over a wig. I wanted to see if it moved when he spoke directly to me.

"Maybe we can make us a deal." He stood and took a piece

of paper from his pants pocket. "Here's the directions. You go take a look at the place. You like it, we'll talk serious."

I took the paper. "I'll go check it out right now."

I walked to the kitchen.

"Young man?" When I turned around, Amos was dangling a key from his right hand. "You might need this."


What can I say? It could have been a hovel and I would have loved it. But it wasn't. It was a small, one-bedroom cabin with a living room, kitchen, and bath. Comfortable furniture. Neat and clean. No basement. No upstairs or attic. It was built on a slab of concrete and nestled under some ancient pine trees about a quarter mile back from the road. A prefab aluminum structure served as a one-car garage.

But it was the view from the kitchen that made it perfect.

There was a good-sized outbuilding. Amos had told me his uncle had used it as a workshop. It had electricity and appeared to be fairly well insulated. His saws and lathes and other things I couldn't even begin to name were organized neatly around the single room. That neatness must have been a family trait. And it worked to my advantage. I wouldn't have to bother with the machines. I could just concentrate on my writing on the large worktable smack dab in the center of the room.

All I needed to do was find the proper chair.


I wanted to be all business. Keep a poker face while I negotiated with Amos. But as soon as I walked into the diner and saw him looking my way I could feel the most enormous smile stretch across my face.

"Yeah," he nodded, "Nice, ain't it?"

"It's perfect."

*So much for negotiation.*

We were at the picnic table with coffee and pie. Amos had another cigarette burning.

"I been thinking on it some. I know I can't rightly ask for what those other places are going for because of the, um, unusual circumstances. I can promise you three months for sure. Maybe longer, depending on how much time it takes to sell the place. But then you're out on the street. It's why Donna didn't want it."

I nodded. Took a sip of my coffee. He still hadn't mentioned a figure, but if it were ten to twenty per cent less than the other rentals, I could easily afford it.

"I called my sister and told her the situation. We figured out the taxes on a monthly basis. The utilities. A little something for us to split." He took a drag, exhaled a perfect smoke ring that grew larger as it floated away into nothingness. "I think you'll like what we came up with."

"Let's hear it."

"Four hundred dollars a month."

I was expecting five hundred on the low end. This was amazing. My hand was out and across the table before I was even aware of it.

"Deal."

# CHAPTER TWELVE

I left the majority of my possessions in the storage unit. Threw my clothes into the suitcase, packed up my toiletries, and moved into the cabin that night. Four hundred a month and it was all mine. And probably because Amos was going to kick me out in a few months, he never mentioned a security deposit.

I knew I'd locate Glen before my time here was up. I just knew it.

And that would be my next—my final?—move before becoming his student.


I couldn't sleep. It was too dark out here. Every sound was magnified.

*What was that?*

I threw the sheet aside for the third time and got up. Put my pants and shoes on in the dark, then went through the place, turning on lights. I opened the front door and looked out. My car was a silhouette in front of the garage. Or was it a mountain lion? Did they even have mountain lions in Maine? Did they grow that large? Maybe a black bear? A raccoon?

I switched the porch light on. I saw nothing but felt every eye in the woodlands on me as I made my way to the car, opened the door, and slid across the seat to the glove compartment. I'd been so distracted by other events, I'd forgotten what was in there.

I emerged with the pistol in my hand. The eyes followed me as I walked to the cabin, locked up, and went back to bed. The pistol slept on the floor within reach of my hand.

I left the lights on.


I decided to celebrate my new living quarters by shaving off my beard. I'd had it for twenty years and it was more gray now than reddish brown; it seemed to represent the old me. I needed to celebrate the new me. It was gone in fifteen minutes.

I spent the rest of the week running errands. Getting a new cell phone, finding a writing chair. I visited my storage room and took *Blues By The Case* back to the cabin. It was my favorite, and I reread it eagerly. Maybe because it was the first of Glen's books, I really connected with it in more than just a good-read kind of way. The loner hero spoke volumes.


There's something unsure about the sound of one pair of shoes walking through a dark, deserted alleyway. The hollow, expectant slap of soles on cement. Every shadow could hide a danger. Every dead end could be a trap. And when two feet stepping as silently as possible is unsettling, the addition of another pair stepping slightly louder is downright frightening.


Granted, there are a lot of loner detective heroes in literature, and Glen's is just one of them. They should have a convention, maybe start a union. Be lonely together.

I could write that book. Make it a parody of all the loners in mystery fiction. And I already had the perfect title.

*Lonely Together.*

I took a pad of paper and a pen out to the writing room. Made a couple notes about loner detectives and alcohol. Loner detectives and women. Loner detectives and…? Loner mailmen?

I'd have to hit the library and the Internet, read up on the other characters. See what they all had in common. And should I count the detectives with second bananas? They weren't as lonely as the solo gumshoes, but they still didn't seem to mix well with society. Actually, the sidekick seemed to protect them from interaction with other people.

I never thought about this stuff in Cincinnati.


Work was work. The facility was newer, having been erected two years prior to my arrival, so the machines gleamed and the paint on the walls hadn't dulled yet. But they were the same machines. And the job was the same old, same old. The sole matter that kept my interest was the hope of finding a letter to Glen, junk mail even, I didn't care. A needle in the postal haystack.

I was careful in my interaction with the other employees. If anyone asked—and that first week, they all asked, usually in the lunchroom—I was a part-time flexie from Ohio. My grandparents had lived in Maine all their lives. It was my folks who struck out for Ohio.

"They'd bring me up here on visits home. I fell in love with the place. The land, the people. I knew I'd end up living here. And here I am. Looking forward to it."

"It's a great place. And you're a flexie, huh?"

"Yeah. Bottom of the barrel. Last one hired, first one fired." I knocked my knuckles on the imitation wood veneer of the lunch table. "Hope there's no layoffs."


But just maintaining at work was pressure. *Be Ezra. Do your job. Don't get caught snooping on the mail.* It gave me a sensation much like I imagined private investigators experience. You're not who you say you are, but you've got to act like you are. Remember your lies. Remember your life. Your fake life takes over your real life.

There might be a story in this. I could change the location. Make the Postal Distribution Center a high-tech arms development lab. I thought about jotting this down at lunch. Get a file cabinet for the writing room. Start a folder with all these ideas I'd been getting. I could tell people I was in a writing workshop, when, in reality, I was alone, writing *in* a workshop. Ha!

I loved the workshop. I spent more time there than I did in the cabin. It's where I was rereading Glen's books. All of them. Maybe the osmosis process would take hold on the worktable. Seep into the grain. Work its way into my mind. My writer's brain.

Simon thought he was doing me a disservice, putting me on the overnights, but it was what I wanted. No bosses other than the shift supervisor. No interruptions. We overnight elves worked until sunup and then went home. If I wanted to take an extra interest in an envelope or two, that was my business. Quality control, I called it.

And that's what I was doing at this point. It was my third week—my ankle almost ready to go to real work—and I was in a trance, watching envelopes fly by. A pattern was emerging, and that pattern snapped me to attention. Every envelope looked alike.

I checked the clock. Perfect. Walked down the line to where the envelopes were being loaded.

"Sara, break time."

She glanced at the clock.

"Thanks, Ezra. It's all yours."

I slowed the machine as soon as she was out of sight. Boxes were piled up behind me. Maine Power and Light stamped on their sides.

The monthly utility bills were going out. This is where I would find Glen Dower. He may have moved to the sticks to get away from his fans, but I don't think he'd do without gas or electricity. He was a writer, not some crazed loner like that Unabomber guy.

*"I write on a computer."*

He had said that. Was it at the signing in Dayton? Did it matter? No. What mattered was Glen needed electricity. And not just for his computer. For his lights, his refrigerator.

And I was looking at all the gas and electric bills for the state of Maine.

And they were being bulk mailed from large cardboard boxes. Alphabetically.

I hadn't been this excited since prom night, watching the windows fog in Lover's Lane. My search was nearing its climax. I slowed the machine even more. Checked the envelopes.

Chambers...Charters...Chastain...

My timing was perfect. I'd be through the D's before Sara came back from her break.

I emptied the box beside me into the machine. The last of the C's.

Czechlewski.

I hefted the next box onto the loading table. Took the blade to slice the tape. It was like opening every Christmas present in the world at once because inside the box, hidden among all the dross, was a pearl. A diamond. The pot of gold.

Somewhere in here was Glen Dower's home address.

Except it wasn't. I looked twice. Once while the bills were in the box. Again, while they moved slowly down the line. I mean slowly. I had the machine down to a somnolent pace. Any slower and there was the chance the machine would stop. Each time the names were the same.

Dowe. Dowen. Dowert.

No Dower. Had he moved? Did someone find him before I did and send him scurrying further into oblivion? Had all my planning been for naught?

"Ezra?" It was Sara, looking at me like I had my hand in the cookie jar. "Is something wrong?"

"Um...no, nothing. Not now. There was. The machine jammed up. I had to stop it and clear the problem. I was just starting it again. Slowly at first. Make sure it's okay." I adjusted the speed. "Give it a little more juice. See if it's okay."

She watched as I added increments of speed to the machine. The envelopes became a blur of blue and white again. "Seems to be fine now."

"Good." She stepped around me. Nodded toward the lunch-room. "Your turn."

I could feel her eyes on me all the way to the door.


Just before I was off break, I had remembered something. His number was programmed into my phone. I pressed the Call button.

"Hello. You have reached..."

It was still his number, but that didn't mean much. The real question was: *Was he still in Maine?*


I hadn't been in a bookstore since departing Ohio. Like a junkie needing a fix, I went into the first one I found. Maybe Glen had a new book out that I had overlooked with all my energy diverted. It had been awhile, and, if he did, maybe I could find some new information concerning his whereabouts. I went in search of the New Fiction section.

No new Glen—I would've known if there was a new book; I just needed an excuse to hit the bookstore—but there were new mysteries from several authors, and I was reminded of my lonely detective idea. I looked over the dust jackets. A couple of them sounded interesting, but I decided to wait until I had cashed my next paycheck before I splurged on new hardcover books.

I found the remainder table and picked up two books. They were first edition copies in hardback by good writers for a fraction of the cost of new paperback printings. Is this where my books would end up? Or would they go through several printings? So many that by the time they were remaindered I wouldn't even care? But to see your first-edition printing on the remainder table had to be disheartening. My understanding was that print runs on mysteries were notoriously low unless you were a superstar or a comet, burning brightly for a tale or two, and then falling to remainder-purgatory. And back to lower print runs. Or oblivion.

I was taking my purchases to checkout when I passed a display with a large placard. *Maine Authors*. Maybe Glen would be here.

He wasn't, but that made sense. He was hiding out, enjoying his solitude. If people knew he was here they'd bother him. So he stayed under the radar. There were quite a few others whose names I recognized, though. Stephen King, of course. He had a whole six-shelf section to himself. But there were also novels and non-fiction books of every genre by many names I recognized, including Tabitha King—Stephen's wife, and a fine writer in her own right—cookbooks, and travel books. There was even an area for the Kings' kids. Must be something to that genetic thing. Plus a busload of men and women who specialized in children's books. I didn't realize Maine played host to so many authors. And it wasn't just writers of recent vintage. There was a long line of literature that stretched back into history. Nathaniel Hawthorne, Longfellow, Harriet Beecher Stowe, Edna St. Vincent Millay. I was in good company.

I went back to the King section. I had read a lot of his stuff over the years, but had a special fondness for his books about craft, *Danse Macabre* and *On Writing*. They were off to the side of a lower shelf, but something above them caught my eye.

Writing As Richard Bachman.

*And then I knew.*

Glen was someone else. It was that simple, and I'd been too stupid to figure it out. I didn't think he would write as someone else. He would always be Glen Dower. But he could *become* someone else. His utility bill *had been* in that bulk mailing I had sorted out. He may have even been Mr. Dowert, but I don't think so. That was just too close.

He had assumed an alias. Maybe even changed his name legally. If that were true, there would be a record of it somewhere.


The Internet cafe in the mall wasn't crowded. I got a cup of coffee and a computer in the corner. Googled Glen Dower. There were many hundreds of thousands of hits. Most of them had to do with a Welsh hero, Owain Glyndwr, or Owen Glendower as the Brits called him. He had led the last organized rebellion against the British monarchy, trying to regain independent status for Wales. According to the article I scanned, a lot of people even today shared his sentiment.

I refined my search.

*Glen Dower, author.*

Over four hundred thousand hits.

I was going to be here for a while.


Nothing. Nada. Zip. Zilch. Nil. Bupkis. I even checked his website. It read like a tired pamphlet. No energy and nothing had been added in weeks, maybe months. Was Glen's importance dying out? Was I the only one who would keep his flame illuminated? There had to be a new book soon. He needed to prod the world. Say, "Here I am. Read me."

Or else he may be forgotten. A bright light of his generation dimmed to darkness beneath the bushel basket of his own choosing. Would he make that choice? Did he make that choice?

I couldn't see it. He had been silent too long, and writers don't retire. They keep writing. It's in their very makeup. He was still writing. I knew it. And what he was working on now might be his best book to date. Earn him legions of new fans and the best reviews of his career. A bestseller. An award winner.

I believed I could help make it so.

I only had to find him.


My attention back on the computer, I was looking for any person or thing that may have tried to contact him via the U.S. Mail.

Agents. Publishers. Anyone.

The answers to my questions would lie in the upper left corner of the envelope.

The return address.

# CHAPTER THIRTEEN

I had prepared myself with a list of likely return addresses, ranging from charities and causes I'd heard Glen supported to his college alumni office. But there were two I thought would stand out heads above the others: his agent, Al Field, and his publisher, Four Star. They were the only two I could think of who would contact him on a semi-regular business basis. The others would be quarterly or yearly correspondence. And they were both in New York City, which made a quick spot check of return addresses easier.

Of these two, he probably had more contact with his agent than with his publisher. If I understood the relationships correctly, the agent was the middleman between the publisher and the author. At least until a manuscript had been accepted. Then the publisher would assign an editor to work with the writer. Since Glen had no new book at the publishers (this was verified by the publisher's website, listing of upcoming titles), I was going to concentrate on the agent.

It would help to see one of Al Field's business envelopes. And I needed to do this without having to make a trip to New York City.

I decided to write a query letter to the Al Field Agency, asking for representation. I checked a couple of reference books on how to proceed and immediately ran into a snag.

While they accepted both email and snail mail submissions,

they requested an SASE, Self-Addressed Stamped Envelope, for their reply to the latter.

This would not do. I needed one of their envelopes.

There must be some way around this.

*Dear Mr. Field,*

*My name is Ezra Lockert. I am a writer of short stories, currently working on not one, but two novels. One is a comic mystery concerning a convention of loner detectives. The other is a sci-fi tale of alien encounters at the local laundromat, wherein a space suit of indestructible material is stolen and replaced with a lacy pegnoir. You can imagine the comic possibilities of an alien running around in such a getup.*

*I am currently seeking representation and would be glad to send you some of my short stories or chapters of the novels. If you agree with those in my writing workshop as to the value of my stories, perhaps we can together approach a publisher.*

*I am enclosing an SASE for your reply, which I eagerly await.*

*Sincerely,*

*Ezra Lockert*

I proposed a mystery and a science fiction novel to get his attention, since he represented Glen, and Glen had written in both genres. I knew the sci-fi bit sounded far-fetched, but I needed something, and I got a laugh out of it.

I wasn't expecting him to want to represent me—I just needed a response—but, if he liked these ideas, I'd write them. Again, my main desire was to get one of his envelopes with a return address on it.

And that's where the post office comes in.

Did you ever get a piece of mail that had been mangled during its delivery process? It happens rarely, but it does happen. We (that's the Postal *We*) try our best to get your mail to you in a timely and undamaged way. You know, *Neither Rain Nor Snow*, etc. Sometimes the envelope is mutilated before we even see it. It's been thrust into a pocket, put through the washer and dryer, whatever.

We take that messy envelope and enclose it in a cardboard-backed see-through wrapper. As long as the address is readable and there's proper postage attached, it will be delivered.

And just who is assigned the task of determining how badly something must be torn or degraded before it gets the see-through wrapper?

If it comes to the Maine Distribution and Processing Center in the early morning hours, I do. Which is where I was at the moment, keeping an eye out for my fellow workers as I carefully tore the envelope that held my query letter, and the SASE without messing up the address or the postage. I crumpled the entire thing in my fist then smoothed it out on a tabletop. Next, I slipped the crumpled and torn mess into the clear envelope. Added the Postal apology.

*Your mail was damaged in transit. We apologize for any inconvenience.*

This would almost guarantee that when—if?—I heard back from the agency, it would be in the form of one of their envelopes, not my SASE, with their return address in the upper left corner. I tossed the completed package into the mailbag destined for New York City.


The next two weeks dragged by. (I know, but they did.) The ankle decided to slow down its healing process, keeping me inside. My system was far from perfect and required more patience than I usually possessed. The mail we processed was moving by at such an incredible speed I couldn't really check return addresses as easily as I thought I might. The only time I could slow the machine down long enough to get a visual on the envelopes was when Sara took her break. What were the odds I'd get the envelope I needed during those too-fast-moving minutes?

And how long would it take to receive my answer from the Al Field Agency? Surely they must have received my query by now.

*"My name is Al, Mr. Lockert. Please stop calling me Shirley."*

I spent the weeks a little on edge. When I was a kid, I sent away for some toy off the back of a cereal box. A frogman. You put baking soda into a hole in his body and stuck him in a tub of water. The baking soda reacted with the water and propelled him along as if he were swimming. I waited every day for that frogman to arrive in the mail. I was a bit like that now, eager with anticipation.

Did they just throw my letter in the trash?

What if they liked my ideas? Could I write a book?

Of course I could. I'm a writer.

I just had to keep telling myself that.


I spent the next morning—it was a day off—in the workshop, trying to describe my alien being. Long and lanky. Green, but more an apple green than a forest green. I had a notebook page full of his or her personal traits. I thought about giving the creature both male and female sex organs, so, when a local earthman was confronted with the alien, he could brandish his shotgun and say, "Go fuck yourself."

And the alien would go away and do it.

*I* found the idea hysterical. I wondered what Al Field would think.

No, I couldn't think like that. I had to write the book I wanted to write. But the man's a success in his field—ha!—and I wanted him to think it was good. But if I tried to conform my style to someone else's idea of what my writing should be, it would no longer be my writing. I was sure Glen wrote what he wanted. He probably accepted input from people he trusted, but the final output was his. And that's how it has to be. Novels are not like movies. They are not written by a committee. They are written by one person. Sometimes two. A best-selling author dies and his or her name still appears on books for years to come, but with a caveat: *And*. And that *And* basically means some B-lister has taken over and written in the style of the dead superstar. Probably for a fixed wage and not a percentage of profits.

Or a best-selling author will write with their child. Or their cat. But it probably comes down to one person doing most of the work.

Unless it's one very talented cat.


I was on my noon break from writing. Had a bowl of soup and a mug of coffee standing at the kitchen counter. I washed the bowl, pan, and spoon, and set them in the rack to dry. Poured a second mug of coffee and carried it outside to check the mail.

It was a beautiful day. The kind of day when I missed not being a mail carrier. Mid- seventies. Sunny. Some artist's choice of brilliant blue—let's call it *cerulean*—for a sky with large cottony white clouds. The blue fading to a pastel on the horizon. I looked back at my cabin. The pine trees towering over it. Nothing but forest around. I was one lucky guy to end up amidst this: the perfect writer's retreat. Shut off, but convenient to everything I needed. Too bad it was all going away in a couple months.

And wouldn't it be funny if Glen lived within ten minutes of here?

I dropped the lid on the mailbox and grabbed a fistful of mail: fliers, bills, my writing magazine. I set the coffee mug in the open mailbox and sorted through the papers in my hand.

And there it was.

It must have come in during the day shift at the P.O. Or it came in on my shift and I missed it, which didn't bode well for my spotting any correspondence to Glen.

It was a cream-colored envelope with the return address I had been looking for. *The Al Field Agency*. It was in raised gold script. A Park Avenue South address.

I forgot all about the wonders of nature and made haste back into the house, tossed the rest of the mail on the couch, and took Al Field's reply out to the workshop.

*Dear Mr. Lockert,*

*Thank you for your interest in The Al Field Agency. We are not accepting new clients with incomplete manuscripts at this time. This is in no way meant to discourage you from writing. Your ideas are highly original, and, once you have completed your novels, we would be interested in hearing from you again.*

*The current market for short stories is bleak indeed. Unknown writers with finely crafted work are being ignored in favor of known names with built-in sales value. We feel the way to go is to get published first in novel form, then use that leverage to sell the short work.*

*Again, thank you for considering this agency to represent you. Good luck with your continued writing.*

*Sincerely,*
*Al Field*
*Agent*

At first I thought it was a form rejection letter, but, on a second reading, I saw it wasn't. He mentioned my ideas. Called them "highly original." He asked me to write back once the novels were completed.

And he added a handwritten note at the bottom of the page.

*Mr. Lockert, your SASE was damaged during the mailing process. We trust this is an acceptable reimbursement.*

*Regards,*
*Al Field*

A postage stamp was taped next to the signature. How classy is that?

# CHAPTER FOURTEEN

Back at work the next day, it hit me that even with the return address to go on, it wouldn't be easy. Sure, the color of the envelope was a shade darker than the common white envelope, but they all ran by in such a blur it would be hard to spot. The raised gold of the return address might help. It was different than most. But the best I could hope for would be a glint of light, a reflection of the gold return address.

"Ezra?"

"Yeah?"

I turned from watching the mail fly by. It was the shift supervisor.

"Sara's not feeling well. You think you can handle this by yourself rest of the day, or you want I should call in a flexie?"

I told him I could go it alone and slowed the machine as soon as he left the room, searched through the envelopes as I fed them onto the conveyor.

Nothing.


I got home and took a nap. I knew it would throw off my sleep pattern, but, with the excitement of the day before, I hadn't slept all that well. A couple hours might help.

\* \* \*

Four hours later I woke up feeling sluggish. I needed to move, to do something to tire myself out so I could sleep before my shift.

"What'll it be, Ezra?"

Donna brought the decaf coffee pot over and poured. I cradled my cup between my hands and thought about my day.

The framer at the art supply store suggested a simple black wood, but it didn't quite make it. The white matting set the cream-colored paper off nicely, but I felt the black was too stark, and she agreed. We ended up going with an off-white frame with tiny gold flecks. Sort of a tonal combination of the cream color and the gold letterhead.

It looked good on the wall of the writing workshop.

I was so into hanging the letter from Al Field I forgot about the mail. I went out to the box and dropped the lid. A couple pieces of junk mail were leaning up against the insides, held in place by a coffee mug. A piece of paper was curled up in the empty mug.

*Thanks for the coffee, but by the time I got here it was cold. Nice thought, though, and it is appreciated.*

It was signed *Stan the Mailman.*

Al Field's letter yesterday had made me forget my coffee. I stood there and laughed. At myself and at Stan the Mailman. I'll bet that's how he introduces himself to everyone.

"Hi, I'm Stan the Mailman."

Sara was still out the next day, but now I had a flexie with me. Jerry. I let him spot check while I loaded the machine.

No gold return address. But I think I made a friend.

"I like working with you, Ezra. You're slower than most. They'll have to give us some overtime to reduce this backlog." He tossed his head toward the incoming mail. "Smart," he tapped his index finger against his skull. "Kidneys, man. Kidneys."

Jerry was right. They asked us to stay late and keep working. It was fine with me, but I felt a little of the anxiety kick in. If this guy noticed I was slowing up the belt, how many others knew? Is that why Sara was looking at me strangely? Was she really ill or had she complained about working with me? Was this guy really a flexie or was he staff? Maybe even in management, a company spy. I knew Simon Hillacre wasn't too happy with my being here. Was he looking for some reason to fire me?

"Hey, Ezra, you wanna go get a beer after this?"

This guy was trying too hard.

"Before noon? Are you nuts?" *Add something, Ezra.* "Maybe some other time. Some *later* time. I've got a doctor's appointment today. Haven't been sleeping too well and gotta get the ankle checked." *Good, Ez. Roll with it.* "It's why I've been running the machine a little slow today. Had to be sure I could keep up, but tomorrow this baby's gonna fly."

Jerry was walking out with me when someone called from behind us.

"Maloney, see you a minute?"

He patted me on the back. "See you tomorrow, Ezra." I turned to say good-bye and there was Hillacre. We locked eyes.

"How's that leg, Lockert?"

"The ankle, Simon," I said. "Almost there, boss. On my way to the doc's now."

Jerry was trotting up to him like a kid looking for approval. I could feel their eyes on me all the way out the door.

"Hello?"

"Hey, Sara. It's Ezra."

No response.

"From the job."

"Oh."

"Just wanted to check in, see how you're doing."

"I'm...I'm feeling a lot better, Ezra. Thank you. I'll probably be back in a couple days."

"Good. The place isn't the same without you."

She was silent.

"Well, take care of yourself. Feel better."


What were my options? If Sara returned the next day, I'd be back to checking the line. No way would I be able to find any envelope from The Al Field Agency. If Jerry was there, I'd be able to spot check envelopes as I loaded them, but I would have to run the sorter full out. Maybe cheat it a bit when he's on break.

If there was no one watching me.


"Morning, Ezra." Jerry.

I was in luck. At least I got to run the machine.

"Hey, Jerry." I walked up to the loading slot, rapped my knuckles on the metal. "What ya say we see how fast this baby can go?"

"And kiss any overtime goodbye?"

I shrugged. "We'll see."

The machine started humming. I started pouring in the first load.

"How'd it go at the doctor's yesterday?"

Jerry had left his normal position and was just across the sorter from me. I stopped what I was doing. The machine cried like a baby wanting to be fed, but I ignored it and stared at Jerry.

"He said I should get a life."

"What?"

I repeated myself slowly, adding weight to each word, hoping he gets the message.

"Get. A. Life. I think it's a good idea. Don't you?"

I think it sunk in.

"Um…yeah." He retreated a step. "Yeah, it is."


I hit pay dirt just before lunch. Al Field's return address glittered like a nugget in a sea of slop. Jerry was down the line without a clear view of me. I let the mail fall from my arms.

"Aww…"

I slowed the machine down and then stopped it altogether.

"What's wrong, Ezra?"

"My leg just spasmed and I dropped a bunch of mail. Hang on a minute. We'll be up and running in no time."

"I'll give you a hand."

I leaned around the sorter. Made my voice gruff.

"Stay where you are. It's my mistake. I'll correct it."

"But…"

I fixed him with the stare again. "Jerry?"

He threw his hands in the air and went back to his position. "All right."

I could see his legs through the machine, but nothing else, so he probably couldn't see me at all. I gathered the paper up, watching for that spark of gold.

And there it was, just like the one on the envelope I had received. Addressed to a Jason Firth in some town in Maine I had never heard of. I curled the envelope, lifted my pant leg, and slipped it inside my sock. Dropped my pant leg back down. Perfect.

I stood up with an armload of mail.

"Hey, Jerry? Sorry if I snapped at you."

"Aw, that's okay."

I dropped the mail into the machine and revved it up.

# CHAPTER FIFTEEN

I went to the men's room on my break. Dropped my pants and sat down. Anyone looking under the closed door—anyone who *chose* to look under the closed door—would see my shoes and my pants around my ankles. I pulled the envelope out of my sock, took a pen from my shirt pocket, a square of toilet paper, and copied down the address.

Jason Firth lived in Purgatory, Maine. Hard to believe there was such a town, but shows you what I knew. If I had missed the envelope, it would have gone through the regular chain of connections until it ended up where it was addressed to end up. *In Purgatory.* It sounded like something out of a weak horror novel or a spaghetti western. But the more I thought about it, the more it fit in with Glen Dower's sense of humor. Someone asks him where he lives, he says, "Almost Hell."

If indeed Jason Firth was Glen Dower.

I needed time. A few days at the least. If this sense I had of being watched was not some kind of job-related paranoia, I needed to get Simon Hillacre to take a step back. To call off his dog.

It was time for me to go on the attack.

\* \* \*

"You been talking about me, Jerry?"

"What are you saying, Ezra?"

"I think we both know the answer to that one." I shut down the machine. "Quitting time. Make sure you inform your keeper how much work we burned through today. We might have broken some kind of record."

I didn't wait for a reaction. Just walked away.

"Ezra?"

And I kept walking.


I had reinserted Jason Firth's letter from the Al Field Agency into the regular flow of mail. It was on its way to Purgatory, and I hoped soon I would be, too. But right now I was back in a stall in the men's room.

I gave it about fifteen minutes. Enough time for Jerry to think I had left the building. Then I washed my hands and left the bathroom.

I had to walk by Simon's office on my way out.

"Is Mr. Hillacre available, Elizabeth?"

"I'm sorry..." She searched her brain for my name.

"The name's Ezra."

She nodded. "He's with someone at the moment, Ezra."

"That's okay. I'll wait."

But instead of taking a seat, I walked to the office door, knocked, and opened it quickly. Simon Hillacre had a visitor; he turned from his visitor to look at me. His visitor did not.

"Mr. Hillacre, just wanted to pop in and tell you what a great job Jerry Maloney did today. We must've set some record for pushing pieces through the process. Do you keep track of those kinds of statistics?"

Simon's eyes flitted to his guest—maybe *his* supervisor?—then back to me.

"Thank you, Ezra. I'll be sure to let Jerry know. Now, if you'll excuse me."

I pretended I had just noticed that the chair across from him was occupied. "Oh. Sure. Sorry." I started to back out the door. "Oh, one other thing. The doctor says my ankle's almost back to normal. Another week or two and it'll be good as new."

I closed the door.

"Thanks, Elizabeth. You have a great day."

I knew I would. I whistled some happy doggerel tune all the way to the car.


I had two stops to make. The first one was in downtown Portland, a phone call had to be made and an appointment scheduled for tomorrow, immediately following my shift.

The second stop was the bookstore I had discovered at the mall. I went to the travel section and spread a map of Maine out over a small table. I checked the list of towns, found Purgatory and its coordinates, and let my finger follow my eyes. I knew I could have used the web for this, but I was feeling old-fashioned.

Purgatory was north of Portland, just off Highway 95 between Lewiston and Augusta, the state capital. Looked to be quite a jaunt up the highway, but, when I checked the driving distance inset, it wasn't bad at all: thirty-two miles from Portland to Lewiston and then another thirty-one up to Augusta. So Purgatory was maybe forty-five, fifty miles from where I was sitting. I didn't know if it was large enough to have its own post office, but, if it didn't, I needed to know whose jurisdiction it came under: Lewiston or Augusta.

Because that's where I was going to live.

And work. And study.


Sara was back at work the next day.

"Hey, Sara. Good to see you."

"Thanks."

She didn't know where to look, but wherever she chose, she looked uncomfortable. No, guilty was the better word.

"What was it, some kind of flu?"

"Yes."

She got the machine going. Ignored me.

"Lots of toast and tea?" I asked. "Soups?"

She shrugged and looked around to see who might be listening. She was watching the machine, but she spoke to me in a barely audible whisper.

"I can't talk to you, Ezra."

"Oh? Why not?"

"I've been told not to."

"By…?"

She shook her head.

I nodded and said, "Okay," and walked to my place on the line, all kinds of conspiracy theories running rampant in my head. Who was involved and why? I wondered if I was going to end up next to… Was I about to meet Jimmy Hoffa?

What had I done? Not much.

I had just come in from out of the Midwest to trample some postal fiefdom. Let some guy know he's not the head honcho he believed he was.

But I thought it had been clear I wouldn't be staying long. So why the spy mentality? Was there something going on here that I didn't know about? Did Simon think I was a plant in his facility, sent to uncover some scam he was working?

I started to see a pattern. I needed to worry the loose plank in the fence until it broke off and gave me access. I waited until Sara was about to go on break.

"It was Simon, wasn't it?"

She kept watching the mail.

"You weren't even sick, were you? What did he do, give you a couple days off so Jerry could spy on me?"

That got her to raise her head, but she wouldn't look at me.

She looked everywhere else, but not at me.

"A couple days off with pay? There's got to be some regulation against that somewhere, Sara. He put you in deep doo-doo. And himself, as well. You could both be fired."

"He said you complained about me, Ezra." Tears started to flow. "That you called me...a lazy bitch."

"I never did that, Sara."

She sniffled. "I think I realized that when you called me at home. To see how I was." She ran her sleeve across her nose. "But then it was too late." She inhaled more tears. "He told me we were gonna...fix your wagon."

"Well," I smiled, "Let's see how he enjoys riding with a flat tire."


I found an empty business-size envelope, folded up a few blank pieces of typing paper, and stuck them inside. Scribbled some words on the front of the envelope.


My visitor was waiting when I walked into the office outside Simon's. Jerry Maloney—the "flexie"—sat across from him. Elizabeth picked up the phone and poked a button.

"They're all here."

Faster than I would have thought possible, Simon was opening the door, a huge smile on his face. "Gentlemen, please come in."

My union president, Carl Johannsen, let Jerry enter first. He and I followed and sat down.


I said I feared for my job.

Simon played nice, admitting nothing.

"I think Simon wants to...fix my wagon."

His eyes widened at that direct quote, but he remained calm.

"There's nothing wrong with your wagon, Ezra. You are one

of our finest workers."

"That's good to hear, Simon," said Carl. Carl was a large, light-skinned black man. He had told me on the phone yesterday that he had been a carrier for twenty years before winning a position in the union office. "The thing of it is, Simon," Carl continued, "Ezra's paranoia may just be new-job jitters, but if it's not, you've replaced one part-time flexie…"

"Sara Newcombe."

"…who has worked at that position for two years, with another part-time flexie…"

"Jerry Maloney."

"…who happens to be the next flexie on the list, to move up to staff, to seemingly spy on a permanent staff employee."

"That's nonsense," Simon said. "Honestly, Ezra, I think you should see someone about this…this persecution you feel."

Carl ignored this. "And what flexie next in line for a staff position wouldn't dress up his reports a bit?" He cast a cold glance at Jerry, who started to squirm a bit. "Seems I remember a similar case. What was it, Simon, maybe twenty-something years ago?"

"Gentlemen," Simon said, doing his best to sound calm. "This is all nonsense. Sara was ill and took a couple days off. Two days. Jerry simply filled in for her as a willing—and flexible—flexie."

"Who met with you after each shift," I contributed.

"As he should. I had to let him know if Sara would be back or if he should continue with the shift."

"Let's cut to the bottom line, okay?" Carl stood up. So I stood up. Simon remained sitting. Jerry looked frozen to his seat.

"I don't really give a rat's ass about Ezra Lockert." He looked at me and winked. "He's told me he hopes to transfer out of this facility as soon as his ankle is better. I think that's what you want, isn't it, Simon?"

"I think it would be best for everyone considering his mental state," Simon said. "Let him be someone else's problem."

"That type of comment—and unfounded accusation—is unprofessional and not necessary. But I will make note of it." Carl put both hands on Simon's desk and leaned in. The chair squeaked as Simon hunched back. "What I do give a rat's ass about is some flexie reporting on a staffer." He turned his head slowly toward Jerry. His voice dripped venom. "You are a postal employee, true?"

"Yes, sir."

"You are a union member, true?"

"Yes, sir."

Carl stood up and turned to Jerry. His left arm shot out, finger pointed to Simon. "What this man may have asked you to do is a firing offense. For both you and him. You are not a company stooge. If anything like this happens in the future, you report it to your union, and we will take it from there. Do you understand?"

"Yes, sir."

"Good." Carl turned. "Simon. Ezra." Then he left the room, not closing the door.

It was quiet in Simon's office. The air was heavy with revenge.

"You won't be transferring anywhere soon," Simon said to me now that it was just him, Jerry, and me. "You will remain at this facility and you will do whatever shit job I have you do."

Jerry snickered as I took out my cellphone and said, "Did you hear that?"

Carl stuck his head back into the room. "Yep." He walked back in, holding his phone. "You know, Simon, when Ezra here told me about this, I thought he was full of it, and you almost had me convinced. But I remembered what you were like once. I had hoped you'd changed, maybe grown a bit of wisdom over the years. Then you had to go and say something stupid like that." He turned to Jerry. "And you're just like he was. You'd probably sell your mother down the river for a staff job."

Jerry looked as if he were going to cry.

"Well, this union is a brotherhood. One for all and all for one, that kinda crap. We don't need someone out for himself at the expense of others. It's bad for morale. It's bad for the union." He paused for emphasis. "I can pull your card for this."

Jerry broke. "He made me do it. And he told me Ezra was a flexie, like me."

"Jerome," Simon said.

Jerry looked to Simon. We all looked to Simon. Simon said nothing else.

"Please, Simon, continue," Carl said. "We're all ears."

"Never mind."

I stepped up to the plate. "Look, this is all because of me. I understand Simon's loyalty to his workers. It's admirable, but I think we can resolve this without too much pain."

Carl sat. "Proceed."

"First of all, Sara Newcombe. Where is she on the flexie seniority list?"

Simon opened a drawer. Consulted a piece of paper. "Third."

"She moves up to second," I said. "Jerry drops behind her to third."

Jerry almost jumped out of his chair. "No way!"

I turned to him and very calmly said, "Then Carl pulls your card."

"And unless Simon can find you a managerial job," Carl added, "you're unemployed."

Jerry looked to Simon, who kept his eyes on the seniority list. "Okay."

I continued. "Secondly, none of this goes upstairs to Simon's superiors." Simon raised his eyes to me. "*Yet*. Carl?"

"I'm cool with that."

"Third...Jerry writes up a statement saying exactly what happened from his perspective."

"Now wait a minute," Simon said, "Nothing in writing."

I removed the envelope with the blank pages from my pocket.

"I already have Sara Newcombe's statement." *No, I didn't.* "Jerry's gets added to this. It stays on file in the union office. No one sees either one of them." I handed the envelope to Carl. "But if anything like this ever happens again, the union will forward them to Simon's immediate superiors."

Carl was opening the envelope. He glanced at the pages.

"Good work, Ezra." He winked. "Simon?"

He was defeated and he knew it. "Yeah. Okay."

Carl turned to Jerry. "Jerry?"

"I'll have it for you by Monday."

Carl was not having that. "You'll have it for us before you leave here today. And it's on your own time."

"Yes, Carl." Simon wanted us all to leave. It showed in his voice. "Is that all?"

"Almost," I said. "If, at any time, any action is taken against Sara Newcombe, Jerry Maloney, or myself, these reports will be made public. Not only to your immediate supervisors, but to the local media, also. Are we understood?"

Simon nodded.

Carl smiled. "I can't hear you."

"Understood."

"Then I guess we can say this meeting is adjourned."

Carl insisted on taking me to lunch on the union tab. "Man, Ezra, that was beautiful. We've been trying to catch Simon at this for some time now. We know he uses that staff position as a carrot. He dangles it at the senior-most flexie and they dance whatever step he calls. Maybe he'll think twice about it now."

"I hope so."

"You oughta stay here and work your way up to shop steward. Keep an eye on that shithead."

"I wouldn't be that useful. It's just that I felt threatened, and I would have been the one without a job. No one would know. Or care."

"True, but you had the balls to face the ogre, and you planned an attack. It was positively...Machiavellian. A thing of beauty."

I thought about telling Carl I recognized what was happening because that's how I had gotten here. Would I still be the hero of the moment? Everything he had said about Jerry being out for himself was true of me. Maybe it does take one to catch one.

"All I want, Carl, is a delivery route in a small town. Someplace where I can live a simple life. Deliver the mail, have a few friends, a hobby or two. I miss being a carrier. I was one before I hurt my leg, and I'll be one again. Soon, I hope."

"When you figure out where that is, Ezra, let me know. I'll make a couple calls."

"Thank you. I appreciate that."

Carl started laughing.

"What?"

"Simon would, too. He'd love to see you outta here. Me and Simon backing the same man. Who woulda thunk it?"

I could only think of one person.


By the time we finished our lunch, it was too late and I was too tipsy to drive up to Purgatory. I probably should've taken a cab home, but I drove myself, slow and careful. Anyone seeing my car on the road would've thought it was a ninety-year-old lady driving. I made it home and crawled into the sack.

Tomorrow I'd go to Purgatory.

# CHAPTER SIXTEEN

The phone rang not five minutes after my alarm went off. I was conscious, but not out of bed. I caught the phone on the third ring.

"Hello?"

"Ezra?"

"Yeah."

"It's Sara. Sara Newcombe."

"Hey. How you doing?"

"Fine. I just wanted to call and say thank you."

"For what?"

"You know for what. I had a long talk with Carl this afternoon."

"From the union?" I asked, playing slow.

"He's still laughing about my statement."

"I found it kinda funny, too."

"Well, thank you for keeping me off the record," she said. "And for the move up."

"You'll be staff in no time."

"And thanks for caring about me when you thought I was sick."

"You're welcome." There was silence on the line. "Sara?"

"Yeah?"

"You know what to do if Jerry or Simon make things rough for you?"

"I do now."

"Good. Thanks for the call. I'll see you at work."

"Thanks again, Ezra."

The overnight shift was a breeze. No Jerry, nor Simon. Sara and I had some laughs and tore through our work with ease. Quite a difference from the tension of a couple days ago.

After work I changed into street clothes, jumped into the car, and headed north on I-95. A little less than an hour later I was walking into a place called Sarge's, a diner about five miles shy of Purgatory.

They've franchised burger places and coffee places, pizza joints, and pubs based on defunct sitcoms. If they ever franchise diners, I think I'll just eat at home.

I took a seat at the counter. A muscular man in a tight T-shirt and blue jeans stepped out of the kitchen. A faded Marine Corps tattoo stuck out from under a sleeve.

"Coffee?"

"Black. Thanks."

I picked up a menu. It was as thick as a deck of cards.

"Whoa."

"Problem?"

"No," I said. "It's just I've never seen some of this stuff on diner menus before. Where you from?"

"Astoria."

I must have looked confused. He smiled.

"Queens," he explained. "New York City. Where you from?"

"Cincinnati."

"Ah, the great Midwest. Home of the two-page menu."

He set a heavy porcelain mug down and filled it full of thick darkness.

"Thanks." I lifted the mug and inhaled. "Smells good."

"Tastes even better." He disappeared into the kitchen as soon as I closed the menu. He spoke to me through the cutout in the wall. "Lemme guess…eggs and sausage, side of grits, and whole wheat toast."

"I'm a creature of habit," I said. "But let me start with a tequila straight up with a scotch on the side."

He crossed his arms over his chest, giving me a clear view of his inked arms.

"We're gonna get along just fine."

"How long were you in?"

He scrunched up the side of his face in thought.

"The Corps? Or jail?"


The cook eyed me like he was trying to figure out how my face would taste with a slice of cheddar on a hamburger bun. Sometimes I ask one too many questions. This might have been one of those times.


The diner door opened and the new arrival said, "Hey, Sarge. Let me get two breakfast burritos and a large gasoline to go."

"Sure thing, Jason."

*Jason?* Could I be this lucky this quick? I watched Jason take a seat farther down the counter and tap out an old drumbeat on the Formica. He caught me watching and nodded.

"Morning."

"Morning."

He tilted his head, narrowed his eyes. I'd never actually seen Glen's eyes, or hairless face, but that voice was his. I'd bet my life on it.

"Do I know you?" he asked.

*Oh, Jeez. Did he remember me from the book tour?*

"No," I said. "Don't think so."

"You look familiar."

I tossed off a small laugh. "I get that a lot. And it's always somebody who owes me money." Man, I was glad I'd gotten rid of my facial hair. It would have made it much harder to convince Glen I was not me.

He shrugged. "Eh."

I turned back to my coffee, picked up the menu, and studied it like my life depended on it. I could feel his gaze, its heat making me blush.

Sarge slipped my plate onto the counter. I was gnawing on a piece of toast when he handed Jason a paper bag and a go cup.

"Keep the change."

"Thanks, Jason."

I watched him turn to go.

"See ya," he said.

I nodded.

*Yeah. You will.*


"Everything okay?" Sarge asked.

"Great." I was dipping my last wedge of toast into my grits, my spoon helping to coat the bread. "So, how long?"

"Twenty years in the Corps. Three in the joint."

"Mind if I ask what happened?"

He smiled.

"Most people never do," he said.

I gave him the once over.

"Most people like to live," I said.

He laughed at that one.

"Yeah, I guess I do scare some people a bit." He took my empty plates away. "But I'm just a big softie inside."


When he finished sizing me up, I got the distinct feeling he had decided to let me live. For now.

\* \* \*

It was all I could do to keep my car between the lines. I had seen Glen Dower. Sarge had called him Jason. Had to be Firth. How many other Jasons could there be in this area?

I passed a small roadside sign.

Welcome to Purgatory.

I let out a long cowboy yell. "Yee-haw!" They should have pearly gates on each side of the road because, while this may be Purgatory, it sure feels like Heaven to me.

Now, if they only had a post office.


They did. I was one of two people in line, waiting to buy stamps when I realized Sarge had never told me what he was in for. And I had been wise enough not to inquire further.


At the start of my next work week, I dropped in on Simon.

"Morning, Elizabeth. Simon in?" I kept walking.

"Ezra!"

I opened the small door and saw he was with someone. I went over to the small couch where Carl had sat a little over a week ago and plopped myself down, lengthwise.

"It's okay, Simon," I said. "I'll wait."

I put my feet up over the end of the couch. Simon scowled at me.

"Could you excuse us for a moment, Harry? I had forgotten about this appointment."

Harry got up from his chair. "I'll just wait outside."

He nodded at me on his way out. When the door closed, Simon fixed his angry eyes on me. His voice sounded like air escaping from a flat, all slithery and pinched.

"What is it, Ezra?"

"I know where I want to go, and you're gonna get a real kick out of it."

"Where?"

I waited two beats for dramatic effect. "Purgatory."

Simon leaned forward, picked up a pen and made a notation on a little pad of yellow paper. He tore it off and stuck it on his computer screen. "Why stop there?" he said. "Why not take the full trip to Hell?"

I stood up with a smile. "Work your magic and let me know when it's possible."

I left the door open on my way out. Smiled at Harry, and jerked a thumb over my shoulder. "He's all yours." I kept walking. "Have a great day, Elizabeth."

"It's a beautiful area," Carl said. "Simon knows?"

"Yeah."

"I'll make those calls. See what we can do for you, Ezra."

We shook hands.

"Thanks, Carl. I appreciate it."

"You hiring movers?"

"No. I'll rent a truck. Conserve my resources."

"You need help, give me a call. I can probably get a couple young guys to give you a hand."

It's the anticipation that makes it all the more thrilling. Once you know you want something, you work your way to the goal. You get so close you can almost taste it, but it's still just out of reach. You've gone as far as you can go; now it has to come to you.

And someone else usually ends up pushing it your way, which means there's a price tag attached to it. And that's not good because the man who said it knew what he was talking about.

"Payback's a bitch."

But you don't care. You're blind to that particular bitch. And she'll take you down eventually, but right now you're riding the high and the night makes you feel cool and free.

And you're waiting for it to happen.

The teasing tantalizes.


I closed the book. I knew just how the detective felt. Only he was waiting for Blue, and she would ride him into his own personal oblivion. Leave him a shattered husk of a man.

I was waiting now, too. But my waiting was real. Palpable. Not some fictional vampire curse. My human husk would fill in, fill out, grow into a new shell over a new man.

I was waiting to become the writer I knew I could be.


Simon stopped me on the way out and handed me an envelope.

"Don't come back."

"What?"

"Last night was your last night."

I opened the envelope. There was a paycheck dated for that day. There was also a fact sheet about Purgatory.

I started in two weeks. As a carrier. Replacing a retiree. I looked at Simon.

"If you weren't such a jerk," I said, "I'd hug you."

"Yeah." The sarcasm dripped. "I love you, too."

And then I knew I'd have to do it. So I did. I threw my arms around Simon and held on, laughing and jumping up and down until he screamed.

"Security!"


I had to laugh. Everybody thought Simon was being an asshole by letting me go without warning. If I didn't have a job waiting down the road, it might be scary, but this felt like a vacation. Not a real go-somewhere-and-see-the-sights vacation, but close enough. I had two weeks to find an apartment, empty the storage room, and truck it up to Purgatory. Settle in and start work.

And prepare myself for school.

That's what it was.

The University of Glen Dower in Purgatory, Maine.

# CHAPTER SEVENTEEN

I was in line at the Purgatory post office. I probably could have gone right to the counter and announced my presence, but that would have felt like cutting.

"Next?"

I stepped up. "I'm looking for Helen Allen."

The man leaned back and spoke up.

"Helen!"

"Yeah?"

"Someone to see you."

"What do they look like?"

Counter Guy gave me the once-over. "Pretty safe, I guess."

"Send 'em back."

Counter Guy nodded to a door on the side. I heard it buzz as I approached, turned the knob, and walked through.

"Back here."

I followed the sound of the woman's voice. She was sitting behind an old desk covered with papers. She was wearing the postal uniform and looking up at me with thick glasses. A photograph hung behind her in which she stood holding a pitchfork in front of the *Welcome to Purgatory* sign, a devilish grin on her face.

"How may I help you?"

"I'm Ezra Lockert."

"Well, good for you. What's that mean to me?"

"I'm your new mail carrier. I start in a couple weeks. I'm in the area looking for an apartment and thought I'd drop in. Say hi."

She started to get up. "Oh, *that* Ezra Lockert. I thought there was something familiar about that name." She came around the desk and shook my hand. "Welcome to Purgatory."

"Thank you."

"You'll be replacing Roy. Roy Kerther. I'd introduce you, but he's out on the route."

Without a word, she started walking. Without a word, I followed.

Over the next hour, I met everyone in the place. There weren't many. It took an hour because they all engaged me in conversation, and they all began with the same question—the same question Helen had asked as we left her office for a quick lunch.

"What are you running away from?"

"I'm not."

That stopped her. "Really?"

"Really."

I could have told her I was running *to* something. That might have thrown her off a bit.

"It's just that people here wanna go to the bigger cities. Bangor, Augusta, Portland. Some of 'em even made it to Chicago or New York. Rare we see someone wantin' to transfer up here."

I told her the same thing I'd told Carl. How I was burned out on the big cities. Looking for quality of life. So on and so on and scooby dooby doo. She seemed to buy it.

The others did, too. Some of them had trouble understanding it, but the rest of them welcomed me as if I had just converted to their religion.


"There's gonna be a slight hitch, Ezra."

We were eating lunch in some place called Paulie's. Huge burgers. Her treat. You ever notice how food always tastes better when it's on someone else's tab?

"Oh?"

"Roy doesn't retire for another month. He gave me a date and I started the hunt. I didn't consider they'd find you so quick."

"A month, huh?"

"Yeah. You'll still start in two weeks when you're supposed to. Just that you'll be a clerk and fill-in carrier for that time, then, when Roy leaves, you'll take his route. Ankle's all good?"

"As good as it's gonna get. And the wait's okay by me. I'll get to know everybody."

She nodded her agreement as she put the last part of her burger into her mouth and chewed. Took a sip of iced tea.

"How about a slice of pie? They got good pie here."


I found an apartment easily enough. The third floor of an old Victorian just off the town square, maybe a five-minute walk from where Helen and I had eaten lunch. It was smaller than my cabin, but it would more than suffice. Carl had a couple of union members help me load the truck, follow me up to Purgatory, and help me trudge my life's possessions up the stairs to the attic apartment.

I led them out of town to Sarge's diner and bought them all lunch. We could have walked to Paulie's, but it was a little more expensive. I was grateful for their help, but I wasn't going to blow my budget showing it.

I had lots of time to travel around. Get to know the area. I felt a bit like a tourist, and, as tourists do, I was going to sightseeing. And the first place I wanted to go wasn't listed on the map of the stars' homes in Purgatory.

But I knew how to get there.


I had the address memorized. The local map I picked up in a deli showed it out west of town. Jason Firth lived on a dead-end street at the top of a hill. I could drive up like I'm lost. Sit there awhile and then turn around. Is his house even at the dead end? Maybe halfway up the hill.

Only one way to find out.

A two-lane highway with a few houses scattered about led to Jason's road. When I got there, I stopped. The location was all woods, and small *No Trespassing* signs were nailed to trees on each side of the entrance. I had no intention of tramping through those woods—yet—so I pulled into the hard-packed dirt-and-gravel road and eased up the hill, raising a small cloud of dust as I drove.

There were no houses.

This was the road. I was sure of that. Was Glen the only person who lived here? Were all these woods his? Something started whispering in my head, telling me to turn around. Don't go any farther. I stopped the car and looked around. Something felt off. Was it my imagination or was I being watched?

It took a couple minutes to make the turn in the narrow road, but I was soon back on the highway and heading for town.

I had gone maybe a mile when I passed a small mail truck. Not much more than a cart really. The driver—a man of some girth and more than a little perspiration—had finished putting mail in a box and was driving up the wrong side of the road to the next box. I made another U-turn and went after him. I parked twenty or so yards in front of him and walked back.

"Help you?"

"You wouldn't be Roy Kerther, would you?"

"That I am. Who's asking?"

I put my hand out.

"Ezra Lockert. I'm replacing you after you retire."

We spoke for fifteen minutes.

Roy was giving me the best welcoming gift I could ask for. He was handing me the route that included Purgatory resident Jason Firth. And in just over a few weeks it would be mine.

Good things come to those who wait.

# CHAPTER EIGHTEEN

I had a brand-new set of keys. To a brand-new United States Postal Service "truck." *A mail truck.* A real delivery truck is a big boxy thing with windowless sides and a door that opens by sliding or pulling. What I would be driving could only truly be called a cart. It was small and had an opening in the back and on the sides. Slots for the mail. A roof overhead. A glorified golf cart, really, but judging by the way everyone proclaimed their love for Roy at his retirement party, they were probably going to bronze his and put it out front of the main branch. Would they do the same for Roy himself when he passed on? I could see them shaping his body just before rigor mortis set in.

"Get it so he's sitting."

"Yeah. Now raise an arm. Not that straight. He may've been a Republican, but he weren't no Nazi. Put a little bend in it."

"Good. Good. Now fold the fingers. So it's like they're holding some letters. We can add 'em later."

"Tilt the head toward the raised arm. Like he's lookin' at someone on the roadside as he drives past. He's sayin' hello. Salutin' 'em with the letters."

\* \* \*

A bit overboard? Maybe, but I was having fun with it. Exercising my imagination. Letting it flow. Isn't that what I came up here to do? I was having a good time. My first day back as a carrier, and the weather was impeccable. I had driven the route several times in my car in anticipation. Had it down cold. Now it was for real.

But I had yet to drive up that final hill to Glen Dower's home. That would have been a bit much. The road ends there. That's the way Roy had explained it. If I had driven all the way up to the house in my car, I would have had to turn around at the end, and that might have drawn Glen's attention. The one thing I didn't want.

Yet.


Now I scootered—carted?—out of town, imagining everyone I passed as a bronze statue caught in mid-stride. Bending over. Mowing a lawn. But the game got real old, real fast.

It was a twenty-minute ride before I had to make my first delivery, and it felt weird. The mailbox was on the wrong side of the road, and I would be facing oncoming traffic, as if I were delivering mail in Europe.

I looked ahead. Nothing.

I looked behind. Nothing.

I signaled anyway and crossed the road.

*Why does the postman cross the road?*

What was it with me this morning? I was positively giddy, giggling at the slightest silly witticism. Had I thrown back too much caffeine? Or was it just getting out of the mailroom, enjoying the freedom of being out in the world?

Could it be I was more nervous than I thought, anticipating my meeting with Glen Dower?

\* \* \*

I put my hand out and now it was almost as sweaty as his.

"Roy. Congratulations." I looked around the bar. "Great party. Thirty-five years is really something to be proud of."

"Thanks, Ezra. Appreciate it." He pulled me in closer. "Let's grab ourselves a beer."

"Sure thing."

We navigated our way through the crowd. Well-wishers. Back-slappers.

"Way to go, Roy."

"Sleepin' in tomorrow?"

"Call me. We'll go fishin'."

"You got some big shoes to fill there, Ezra."

"Don't I know it."


We were on our second beer. I had never seen a man sweat so much. Maybe it's the beer. Drinks it down. Sweats it out. Roy's face was beet red. He hadn't said much since the first beer.

"Whatta ya think of the route?"

"Think I got it."

"Good."

I wanted to ask about Glen. If he had met him. What was he like? But I'd have to wait until he gave me some kind of opening. The second beer got him talking.

"You know, I lost Martha a few years ago."

"Your wife?"

"My dog." I must have looked lost. He exploded laughing. "Yeah. My wife."

What do you say to something like that? Sorry? He put a meaty arm around my shoulder, leaned in, and looked me dead in the eyes.

"I can joke about it now. Couldn't then. Don't mean no disrespect. Martha was a marvelous woman. Too good for any man. Don't know how I got so lucky."

This would have been touching if he hadn't been spitting half his words.

"What I'm tryin' to say here, Ezra, is...the people on my route. They became my family. Martha and me weren't blessed with children, so you can imagine how lonely it was after she passed." He tilted his beer. Drank it like water. "But word had gone out. My first day back at work? Every one of them people I delivered mail to was waiting at their box for me. Some had food. Roasts. Pies. Tomatoes. You name it. Some just had a kind word. Or a hug. Like Widow Higgins. She knew Martha." His voice broke. Gained a rasp. "They used to quilt together. She gave me a hug. Tears runnin' down her cheeks. We just stood there. Holdin' each other. Sharin' our pain. Our loss." He ran a sleeve across his face. A thumb wiped away tears. "When I turned to go, she put a big box in the back of my cart. Soon's I got home, it was the first thing I opened. Even 'fore I put the food away."

He wasn't with me anymore. He was at home. Alone. Opening a package from a widow lady given to him years ago.

"It was a quilt. I knew it would be. But...it...it wasn't finished." He sniffled. Set his beer down. Used both hands to pull tears away. To part the watery veil. "I sat down and cried like a baby, holdin' that quilt."

He took a minute to compose himself. I hadn't noticed before, but the room had gotten kind of quiet. A somber tone was creeping in.

"I keep that quilt on my bed. And, one night, good Lord willin', it'll be complete. Martha and me. Back together again. Like we belong."

He threw his arms around me. Hugged me hard. I hugged him back.

"I been watchin' you, Ezra. You're good with people. That's half the job. You'll do fine."

"Thank you, Roy. Thank you."

We parted. He held me at arm's length. His hands on my

shoulders.

"You take excellent care of my people, Ezra. You may not see 'em much, but they're there. And once they get used to you? You'll be family, too."

The next day, it seemed like my new family was off on vacation. No one was greeting me with anything. Except for Widow Higgins. I saw her from a long way off. The land around her place is cut back from the road. Farmland once. Now just a big yard.

I thought she was a scarecrow at first. Tall. Thin. A yellow dress with a full skirt catching the wind. Big straw bonnet pulled down. Stuck in one place. It wasn't until I got closer that the scarecrow raised a hand and waved at me.

"Mornin'."

"Same to you, ma'am."

"Rosa Higgins."

"Ezra Lockert."

"You're Roy's replacement. I met you real quickly at the party last night."

"Yes," I said, pretending to recall our encounter.

She remembered she was carrying something. She pushed the pie plate forward.

"This is for you. Welcome."

"Thank you, ma'am."

"Hope you like cherry."

"It's one of my two favorites."

"What's the other?"

"Pumpkin."

"Well." She stuck her veined hands into hidden pockets. "If I'm still around in the fall, I'll see if I can't help you out there."

*Still around? Was she talking fall vacation or something more permanent?*

"I'll look forward to it. Thank you." I set the pie plate carefully in the back of the cart as a thought came to me. "Ma'am?"

"Yes?"

"Do you use lard? You know, in the crust?"

She raised one eyebrow. Studied me a moment. "Why? You one of them good health people?"

I laughed. "No, ma'am. Just that lard makes the best crust."

Her smile was a passing grade on my test. "Yes, I do."

"You've got me salivating already, ma'am."

"Rosa. You call me Rosa."

"It's a good thing you didn't give me a fork with this, Rosa. It'd be gone by the time I get to the next mailbox."

I gave her a couple of toots on the horn. Moved on down the road.

I didn't know if Glen had been Roy's last stop, but I had set it up so he'd be mine. The road started uphill as a gentle slope, then got steep, and leveled off at the top of the hill. Glen's front fence was maybe fifty yards on. The house another twenty. The only house on the road.

I had decided I was going to walk it. Not the entire way. I didn't want to leave my government-owned vehicle on the highway. I would use it until the road got steep. There was a little level indentation where I could park. If anyone asked, I'd say I wanted the exercise, but I had to be consistent. I couldn't walk one day, ride the next. It was going to be walking. Every day.

The whole idea was to give myself time at the top of the hill. With Glen, I hoped. If I rode the cart up, it would be a quick stop, pull the lid down, put the mail in, lift the lid up, and ride away. Walking gave me a reason to take it slow, lean against the fence, catch my breath.

It gave me time for Glen if he came out. To get him used to seeing me. Maybe come out and say "Hi." That would be the start. The trust, the friendship that would come later.

I was halfway up the hill when I realized something: This was hard going. I was starting to sweat like Roy. It was a good thing I had hustled through my route. That was another thing I'd planned. I worked an eight-hour shift. If I delivered all my mail in less time than that, I was free to go home. Just so I was back to swipe my timecard at the shop at the end of my shift.

So I had two, two-and-a-half hours before I had to be back. Plenty of time for the hill, even if I crawled. And if crawling made it any easier, I would do it.

One foot in front of the other. Make it to the fallen tree.

Good. Now the yellow bush. The white tree. What is that? A birch? An aspen? Who cares. You just passed it. Way to go.

It was cinematic the way the house allowed itself to be seen. I was crunching up the last steps of the incline. I could see where the road leveled out. Each step raised my head a bit higher, revealed a bit more. Gradually the hill was replaced by the straightaway. The fence. The house.

To be honest, I was a bit disappointed with the non-descript nature of the house. I guess I had hoped it would be an impressive, two-storey Victorian, something out of a Hitchcock film, worthy of its occupant. In truth, it did have two storeys, but the only distinguishing feature were the wooded steps that led up to a front porch, which was maybe big enough for two chairs and a small side table.

The rest was just...I don't know...a house?

The garage door was closed. Curtains were drawn across the windows. I walked to the mailbox, checked out the location. It was my first trip so there wouldn't be anything wrong with looking around. It was natural. Not looking would have been strange.

So I looked. I stood at the mailbox. Admired the house. Looked at the yard. The woods. Put my hand in the bag and took out Glen's mail.

*Jason Firth's* mail.

I stretched, the correspondence high in my hand. I put the mail into the box and raised my head to the house.

Was that a curtain closing? Or was I wishing it were?

I closed the lid. Walked back down the hill. No problem. Downhill is always easier.

The front of the house was definitely out for my purposes. Even if I could find a decent perch, there was nothing to see. Drawn drapes. Not really conducive to your average, everyday Peeping Ezra.

I had to face the truth: Peeping is an ugly word, but that was what I was to become.

No. I took that back. I was to become an observer, a learner.

The garage took up the right side of the house, so there would be no windows there. I'd have to come back. Check out the left side of the house and the back. But now that I knew where the house was situated, it would be easier to find my way around it.

# CHAPTER NINETEEN

Preparation is a major part of success. Just ask any Boy Scout. Or a chef. You can't be halfway through making a meal and discover you forgot the most important part—the ingredient that sets the finished dish apart from the merely mundane.

And preparation was equally important in my endeavor. I couldn't go walking through the woods in bright colors. I needed to blend in with the trees and bushes. Do that Zen thing. Become one with my environment.

I drove a couple towns over and found an Army surplus store. They catered to everyone who wished to thrive outdoors: hunters; survivalists; kooks. Who else would wear a baseball hat with moose antlers on it? Or a helmet with holders above the ears for two cans of beer, a plastic tube extending from the cans to the wearer's mouth?

It made for moments of amusement, but I had some serious business to conduct. I had to assume a persona. Become a character, which was cool because I could write about myself later. Use the Shopping Man as a character.

"Camouflage?" I asked.

"Woods, desert, or snow?"

"Woods."

"Third aisle," he said, giving me a suspicious look. "Past

camping." As an afterthought, he added, "Let me know what kinda weapons you're looking for."

The place was huge. Concrete floors. Corrugated steel walls. The ceiling must've been thirty feet high. They had an above-ground swimming pool filled with water and several fish. For a couple bucks, they gave you a pole and you tried your luck.

I bought a half-dozen camo shirts. Long sleeves. Matching pants. Camo hat. Bunch of black T-shirts. Couple pairs of black pants. Took them to the checkout.

"You a hunter?"

*I guessed I kind of was.* "Yes."

"You got a vest already?"

"Yeah."

"Okay. We got a sale..."

"I've got a vest."

"Just checkin'. Wouldn't want you to take a bullet."

Interesting phrase: *Take a bullet.* "Me, neither. Thanks."

I felt rather conspicuous, driving around town in camouflage clothing. The exact opposite of why I had purchased the stuff in the first place. I was trying to blend in.

I followed that thought, getting more and more uncomfortable. When I gassed up the car, I went to the bathroom and took the shirt off. The black T-shirt looked more regular. I'd wait until I found my spot, then put the shirt back on.

One thing in my favor was that these back roads were dark. I drove the main road past Glen's turnoff. Took the next street left, and that was the last streetlight I saw. The road coiled around the hill. Climbing. I couldn't see any lights through the trees.

I figured I was close to Glen's place when the road started to dip down again. I pulled a U-turn and started looking for a place to leave my car.


I couldn't pull all the way off the road. There just wasn't room, but I managed to get most of the car over to the side. I didn't know how long I'd be gone. How long it would take to find Glen's house. I locked the doors and left the flashers blinking with the hood up. I had brought a cardboard sign for the windshield.

*Gone for gas.*

I stepped into the woods, ignoring the *Private Property* sign.

*No Hunting, No Trespassing, No Public Access.*

Put my camo shirt on and pulled a small flashlight out of my pants pocket. Held it, pointing the beam straight down. I tried to be as quiet as I could. I was not alone in these environs. Small animals scattered at my approach. Bugs chirped and buzzed. It was difficult following the small beam of light and finding Glen's house.

But I did.

I was maybe thirty yards away, obscured by a large tree. Some small, tangled brush. There it was. The backyard lit up like daytime by two powerful floodlights, one at each corner of the house, mounted just below the eaves. Their beams met mid-yard.

And there he was. It had to be him.

Glen Dower.

Sitting on a bench beside a picnic table, a book in his hands. He had been reading, but now he was looking up at the woods behind his house.

Had I made too much noise? Would he call out? Would he walk into the woods?

A rustling to my left drew his stare. A doe and a fawn exited the woods and crossed a corner of his yard. Then disappeared into the darkness.

Glen stood, the book in his hand. He scanned the woods again, then turned and went inside. The lights went out in the backyard. In the house, a light came on behind a curtained window. A shape stood there, and then moved on.

I was back at the car, quietly closing the hood. No sense in pushing my luck. I had achieved what I had set out to do. I had found the place.

My seat in the class taught by Glen Dower.

I was on the main road into town. A police car passed me going the other way. Moving fast. I watched him in the rearview mirror as his brake lights pulsed once. Was he stopping? Had Glen called the police? Just because he heard some noise in the woods?

What if the policeman turns around and stops me? What do I tell him?

```
"Yes, Officer, I was in the woods."
  "Any particular reason, sir?"
  "No, Officer. I was just out for a drive
and…"
  "Answering the call of Nature?"
  I grinned. "When Mother calls…"
  "You have a good day, sir."
```

The brake lights dimmed. The police car moved on.

This whole thing could really play some tricks on my head. I'd better check and double-check everything.

Like the car. How many times could I leave it out like tonight before somebody drives by and stops? Maybe even the policeman? And what was I thinking, putting the flashers on? I may as well stand there and yell, "Look at me! I'm hiding in the woods!"

I needed something I could move off the road and into the vegetation.

A bicycle. No. A bicycle would take forever to get there. And to get home. I needed something faster.

A motorcycle? Too heavy. Too bulky. Too loud. It would leave a trail when I took it off the road into the woods.

I thought of my official vehicle. From there it was an easy leap. I needed a small motor scooter like the hipster kids use to zip around in Europe. Something quick. Something lightweight. So I could pick it up and carry it. Leave no tire tread on the earth.


I thought I'd done enough walking to limber up my leg muscles, ease the hurt the hill to Glen's house had put on them, but I hadn't. My calf muscles cramped up during the night. Twice I awoke, my lower half contorted. My hands clutching my calves. A moan held back in my throat. I stood and stretched the leg, the muscle, until the pain subsided. Then I returned to bed, the sheets soaking up the sweat from my skin.

# CHAPTER TWENTY

I put Widow Higgins' mail in the clean pie plate, a thank you note on top. Slid the plate into her mailbox. Got back in my cart and tooted the horn.

Most postmen couldn't give a damn about what they deliver, and for the most part, that's probably just as well. But some of us do take a personal interest in the people on our route. Like Roy said: We look at them as family. And, since they are like family, we keep up with them by perusing their mail. I'm sure Roy did it. He hadn't said so, but he was one of the ones who cared. He'd want to know.

Don't get me wrong. We don't open the mail, but we'll note the bills. The book clubs. Junk mail. Read the occasional postcard. Just our way of keeping informed, so we can have that family feeling. Share the love. The knowledge. Feel closer.

I could care less about most of the people on my route. There were only two whose mail I reviewed daily. Widow Higgins and Jason Firth. I'd kind of adopted Widow Higgins, ever since she gave me that pie. I just kept an eye on her bills like a good son. Made sure she wasn't spending too much. No extravagance.

Just the normal utilities. Phone. Electric and gas. TV. I thought she was on a fixed income. Government check. Something from some brokerage account over in Augusta.

I'd even helped reduce temptation by tossing the occasional credit card offer. The magazine come-ons. The stuff she didn't need to be bothered by.

Glen was another story. I'd pull my cart over to the side of his road, check around me. Make sure no one was hiking through the woods. Coming up or down the road. Then I'd scrutinize every envelope. The return address. The content, if I could glean that from what may be written on the outside. I was tempted once or twice, but I never followed through on the urge to open a flap. To unseal a package. I'll admit I had shaken some, tried to figure out what was rattling around inside. Hopefully without damaging anything. Being the one who placed his mail in the box is a major responsibility. I kept him in touch with the world. While I would have liked to share more of that world— *his world*—it would have been the supreme violation of his privacy to open his mail. So I sat. Took a short break, looked over his mail as I ate my lunch.


The walk to Glen's house took even longer than the day before. My leg muscles were stiff, complaining at every step, but I focused on my landmarks. Took my time. Made it, only to be greeted by the closed-up house again. I didn't even see a drape move, but the previous day's mail had been removed from the box. I took my time refilling the box, giving Glen an opportunity to interact with me, but it was like he wasn't home. I closed the lid securely and walked back down the hill. Head down. My eyes just ahead of my feet.

# CHAPTER TWENTY-ONE

As soon as I was off work, I changed clothes and rounded up all the loose change I could find around the apartment, dropped it into a gallon jar, and ran it through the coin counting machine at the supermarket. After they took their cut, I had just over ninety-eight dollars.

My first bicycle—a sweet three-speed—had cost me fifty bucks, and that was how many years ago? I knew a hundred bucks might get me a no-gear, pedal-it-yourself bike, but that was not what I needed. I needed something motorized, gas or electric.

I bit the bullet and took four hundred dollars out of the ATM. I realized I was still acting like I was hurting for cash, but old habits die hard, you know? With what cash I had in my wallet, the coin money, and the new bills, I was looking at close to five-hundred-and-fifty dollars. I felt pretty sure that amount would get me what I needed.

I remembered passing a huge place just off I-95 a couple exits north of Portland called *Wheels*, so I got back into the car and headed south.

"It's a beauty, isn't it?"

I had to agree. "Yeah."

It was as if all the other machines in the shop were paying homage to it. Motorcycles, scooters, and bicycles genuflecting their unworthiness as they spread out around the four walls.

I had walked through the doors and there it sat, atop a riser covered in black marbleized linoleum, in the center of the showroom. It was black and it was beautiful. Powered by your legs or an electric motor. The placard on the easel beside it claimed twenty miles on a charge at a top speed of twenty miles per hour.

And it folded in half.

The twenty miles was good, but the folding was even better. I could keep it in the trunk, drive out to the mall, park and pull it out, and then ride to Glen's. Only five miles. Ten, round trip. If it was a nice day I could even pedal, a cyclist out for an enjoyable day.

He held out his hand.

"I'm Bob."

I pointed at the placard where *See Bob For More Info* had been printed in red.

"You must be the man to see for more info."

"That I am." Then he blinded me. "Only twenty-five hundred dollars."

"Twenty-five..."

Bob beamed. "Plus tax." He could see the sale fading away, waving bye-bye, *arrividerci*, Bob. "Hey, it's the only one in the state. The Bentley of bicycles." Then he totally blew it for me. "Everyone will be looking at you as you ride by."

I could not afford to have everyone looking at me. "Have you got anything a little more...average-guy? Day-to-day?" I walked over to the cycles lined up along one wall, did mental calculations as I moved, feeling like Goldilocks measuring beds.

This one's too big. This one's too heavy. This one's too expensive.

Bicycles would be too slow, and a bike rack on the car might draw unwanted attention.

But the small scooters looked just right. And they were.

"Do I need a license for one of these?"

"With the motor scooters, yes. With the electrics, no."

"I got that." I pointed again. "And I'd like that."

"Then you're good to go," Bob informed me.

I settled on a shiny, black two-wheeled electric scooter with a top speed of just over twenty miles an hour. It had a thirty-mile range on a single charge, and it could be fully charged in just under five hours. A small luggage case was attached to the back of the driver's seat. The scooter folded in half.

And it was on sale. Only three hundred and fifty dollars.

Bob wheeled it out to the car for me, showed me how to fold it, and together we put it into the trunk.

I didn't realize how heavy it was until I tried to get it out of the car by myself. I managed, but it was awkward and I was a sweaty mess when I opened it up, sat down, and read the scooter's manual. It weighed more than ninety pounds. There was no way I could haul it up and down three flights of stairs. I needed to talk to my landlord. Maybe he'd let me keep it in the garage. Charge it there, too.

Landlord said sure. For an extra twenty bucks a month. I found myself missing Amos.

A little later, and careful of my back, I worked the scooter back into my trunk and drove to the mall, where I bought some pens and a couple of small notebooks. I opened the luggage case on the scooter, put the pens and the notebooks inside, and hit the road.

I was in position, standing behind a large oak, watching the house, waiting for my teacher. My transportation was hidden in the bushes some distance behind me. Close to the road—and pointed in the other direction for a quick getaway—but not close enough to be seen. I had made sure of that. Shiny metal could reflect car lights. I had to make sure it wouldn't. I had thought of painting it flat black, or covering it with some black electrician's tape, but both of those would call attention to the thing. I didn't want that. So I covered it with an old greenish-gray towel and checked from the road. It was practically invisible.

Glen's backyard was dark. No bright floods this time, but there were lights on in the house, in the curtained room where I had seen the shadow. And at the other end of the house. The kitchen. I could see cabinets. The top of the refrigerator. Small checkered drapes pulled back.

The room between them was dark, just a soft wash of light across part of the back wall near the kitchen. I couldn't tell whether there were curtains there. They could be hanging inside, on both sides of the window, where I couldn't see. I hoped not, but that wasn't up to me. I'd have to be flexible. Work with what I had.

The light went out in the curtained room. Shortly afterwards, Glen entered the kitchen, having walked through the darkened room. Would that room ever be lit? What kind of room connected the kitchen to the curtained room? Was the curtained room the bedroom? That was my guess, but if this was where he wrote, and he kept the curtains closed, I was going to be angry.

Glen was at the refrigerator. I could see him from the shoulders up, wearing a blue T-shirt. He opened the fridge, bent down, reached in and then closed the door as he straightened up. He walked out of the kitchen into the dark room, a silhouette.

A light came on. Not a ceiling light, but a small lamp. Brass, maybe. On a wooden table. He sat down at the table and set a two-liter bottle next to him. I could see him plain as day under the lamp's light. And then half his face disappeared.

He had opened a laptop computer. His hand reached out and lifted the bottle. He took a long drink, set the bottle down and raised his arms over his head, interlocking his fingers. I could see his hands bend. Then his head lowered so all I could see was laptop and a blue-gray light across his forehead.

He had turned the computer on.

Glen Dower was writing. This *was* his writing room.

I had an urge to kneel. As if I were confronting the holiest of shrines, but I also felt a little unwelcome. Like I shouldn't be there. This was something very private for him. The work. The process. The public part was when he was finished writing. Had made all his changes. Corrected his mistakes. It's why fiction was created. So we could correct our mistakes. The ones we couldn't correct in real life. Glen had said that. Written it in *Pay The Piper*.

I took out my notebook and scribbled, sharing the time. Writing time with my teacher.

All my work. My time. Effort. Planning. It had paid off.

I was where I wanted to be. Where I needed to be.

School had begun.


The bottle was half empty, and Glen was showing no sign of slowing down. But I needed to get home and sleep. Get in at least a few hours before work. I had to admire the man's stamina. Persistence. There were times he would look up, his hands flailing through the air, conducting a silent symphony of words. Ideas bouncing around inside. The smile. The frown. The hands slowed a bit. Refitting. Reworking. Then the forward dive into the computer. Face down. Fingers I couldn't see pouring out words. The same words I used, but in a different order.

My notebook had been forgotten after the first page. I could describe the scene only so much. It was a man behind a computer in a room with a light. All the life was in his head. The action. I didn't know how to get in there. I returned my notebook to my pocket and watched.

How do I translate it to the page? That was what I was there for. To watch. To learn. From a distance now. Soon, hopefully, close. In conversation.

With Glen.

* * *

The scooter worked fine. Quiet down the hill. Then just a long electrical squeal in the dark, but by then, I was well away from Glen's place.

What bothered me was the notebook. It was hard to write in the dark, and I had to take my eyes off the window, away from Glen, my teacher, to do it. I might miss something.

Then it hit me. I needed a camera. Something basic that would take good pictures. I could build an album. The photos would inspire verbal responses and I'd write them down like essays about Glen and the writing process.

There might even be a book in it.

# CHAPTER TWENTY-TWO

I had been grabbing lunch at the Quik Mart a few times a week since starting my route. The sandwiches were good. Not too pricey.

"Hey, Ezra."

"Tom. Roast chicken. Some lettuce. Mustard."

"Whole wheat?"

"You know me."

I went over to the magazine stand while Tom made the sandwich. Nothing really interested me until I saw a photography magazine. The cover said it had an article Fate had written just for me.

*Natural Light In The Day And Night.*

I picked it up and carried it over to the counter.

"You into photography?" Tom asked.

"A little. I'd like to learn more, but my camera's kinda beat. Cost too much to repair."

He slipped the magazine and my wrapped sandwich into a brown paper bag.

"You gettin' a soda?"

"Yeah."

He rang it up.

"My daughter just got a camera from the shop over in Robbinsville. They were cheap as the ads in the magazine you got here."

"New?"

"Yeah."

"Might be hard to afford it. It took most of my savings to move up here."

Tom handed me the bag. Smiled.

"Hell, Ezra, what you need's The Tradin' Paper." He pointed to my left. "In the stand next to the dailies."

"What's that?"

"Things people got for sale. And they're usually cheap. TV's, guitars. Washing machines, cars. I'm sure they got a section for cameras."

"Put one on my bill."

"I wish I could. It's free."

I was sitting in my cart eating lunch, looking through The Tradin' Paper. There were half a dozen cameras advertised, and they were within my range. I recognized the names of the cameras from the ads in the photo magazine. Some of them came with an assortment of lenses, but they were a few hundred dollars more than the others.

I pulled a pen from my pocket. Circled one ad. It was a good brand with an extra lens. A good zoom. And the price was right. A little more than three hundred bucks.

I finished my sandwich, put the empty soda bottle into the paper bag, and stuffed it under the seat. I curled the paper and slid it into a mail slot in the back of the cart. It was time to get back to my day job.

I stepped out of the cart and shouldered the mailbag. My leg muscles didn't scream half as much today on my way up to Glen's, but there was still no sign of anyone living in the house, except that, again, the mailbox was empty.

"I'm calling about your ad? In The Tradin' Paper?"

"Yeah?"

"Is the camera still for sale?"

"It is. Works real well. It's all cleaned up. Got a new battery. You interested?"

"Oh. Yeah. Sure. How do I get there?"

The guy pegged me for a beginner right away, but he was patient. Showed me how to work the camera and review the pictures I'd taken.

He said he was something called a "stringer." He worked for some papers in other cities. Anything happened up here, he took the photos. Sent them in. Turns out he made enough to buy some newer equipment. Getting rid of all his older stuff. He made me offers on all kinds of stuff, but I stuck to the one camera with the added zoom lens.

I took a few more shots and he checked them out through the viewfinder.

"Hey, you've got a good eye."

"How do you mean?"

"You take good shots. Nice composition."

"Oh. Thanks."

He was probably appeasing me, trying to finalize the sale. I tried to haggle a bit.

"No. The price is firm. It's a good deal. Take it or leave it."

I took it, but he did throw in the camera's user manual and a book of photography basics.

I stayed home that night and studied the manual. Got so I could work the controls easily. The zoom. The focus. I could go manual or automatic. Since I had to be comfortable with the camera in the dark so I wouldn't waste any time out in the woods, I focused—ha!—on the automatic settings. Didn't wanna miss any shots of Glen.

The camera would now be my notebook, my pen and paper, and it needed to flow as smoothly as the pen did. Learning to think visually might even help my writing. I could frame an entire scene and then select what I wanted to portray. Alter the mood by choosing something hidden in a shadow or sitting out in the open. *A picture's worth a thousand words.* And what's a book but thousands of words? I could string a whole series of photos of Glen into a book. Or I could go somewhere and take pictures. Then come home and make up a story from what the photographs said to me. It would be so much easier with all the ideas right in front of me.

I got so I could work the controls while looking at them. Thinking through what I was doing. The hard part came when I turned off the lights. The camera became a different beast. My fingers forgot where they should go. I fumbled. This would take some time, but I had to learn it. It was just a feeling, but I knew my best pictures would happen at night.

I had been dreaming. One of those fragments. Not a complete anything. There was nothing, and then Glen's face, a gentle smile. And he said my name. But it sounded harsh. Questioning.

"Ezra?"

And I woke up. It was so real.

"Glen?"

Of course, he wasn't there.

# CHAPTER TWENTY-THREE

I crested the hill. Still no sign of life from the house. I took Glen's mail from the pouch and approached the mailbox.

The flag was up.

My heart started doing a little dance. I projected an outward sense of calm, like this was nothing out of the ordinary. What if he was watching me? I wasn't supposed to know who he was. Any abnormal action on my part could let him know I was onto his secret.

I opened the lid. Took out the envelope Glen had placed there. It was addressed to Al Field in New York City. It was thin, so it must have been just a letter, no new writing. Was this what he had been working on night before last? Did this thin thing take that long? He had been hunched over the keyboard for hours. He had consumed most of a two-liter bottle of...something. All of that, for this? A letter to his agent?

I shook the envelope and then remembered where I was. I quickly put the envelope inside my mailbag, then took out Glen's regular mail, put it into the box, lowered the flag, closed the lid, and walked back down the hill.

I had never known one thin letter to carry so much weight.

I was pushing myself in two different directions. As a postman, I had to respect Glen's right to privacy. Just send the letter along its way. But what if it contained information that could benefit me? Something I could learn about writing?

The letter had all the electricity of a note sent from a teacher to my parents. Was I being chastised? Was I being praised? Would my parents beam with pride or slap the shit out of me? I could see the belt sliding out of my father's pants.

The car horn brought me back. I had been lost in my thoughts and crossed over the white line. I jerked the wheel. Took the mail cart back into its lane. The car passed. Some teenager flipped me off. I ignored him. Put the letter out of my mind. But the daydream had been so real I could feel the sting of the belt across my backside.

It was one of the hardest decisions I've ever had to make, but I posted the letter. Respected Glen's privacy. It would have been easy to take it home and steam it open. Read it, reseal it, and send it on. But I didn't.

I felt good about it. Proud of myself. I wasn't a snoop. I was a student. There would be other lessons to learn, and I would be ready.

My day off. Laundry in the morning. Pay some bills. I left my apartment, intending to drive out to the mall. Leave my car in the lot and take my scooter from the trunk. Ride out to Glen's. See what was going on.

But something felt off. Like I was the one being watched. I walked past my car, hearing my scooter in the trunk. Its solid squeal calling me. I ignored it and walked to the corner. I was looking both ways when I crossed the street, but I was really checking around. No one was there, but still, the feeling was strong.

Was I feeling guilty?

What for? For learning? For studying at the feet of a master?

Granted, he didn't know I was there, but how many other people study someone from afar? Every kid with a guitar watches his hero play licks on video over and over until they get it right. What was so wrong about observing an artist firsthand?

Was it wrong? Was it guilt? Is that why I felt watched?

*Was* someone watching me?

I turned to a store window and checked the reflection of the street behind me, just as Houston O'Halloran would have done. No one. There was no reason I could see for feeling this way. It made me shiver.

And then the feeling was gone. As quickly as it had come upon me. It just vanished like I had walked out of a sniper's sights, or he had eased up on the trigger, waiting for a better shot. That's a good thought. A good image. There may be a story there.

Just because I didn't see anyone didn't mean there was no one to see. The last time I'd had this feeling someone was watching me, only one of us had walked away unscathed.

Paulie's Bar and Grill served the best burger in town, and they had no problem with a thick slice of raw onion. Most places, you ask for that, you get pieces of onions. Rings piled high. Hardly anyone just slices through an onion anymore and puts the savory slab atop the meat, but the cook at Paulie's did. And there's a huge difference. The crunch of the simple onion just makes the meal. Those damn loose rings just pull off and hang. From the burger. From your mouth. It's just awkward eating.

Even a cold beer doesn't help it much, but it's like fine champagne with a thick slice of fresh onion. Sweet Vidalias, when they're in season. They're the best. I'd eat them at home, too, like an apple. Take the skin off and bite into them.

But any onion cut thick makes a better burger.

\* \* \*

There were crumbs on the plate as I finished my second beer.

"Good?" Orlando asked.

"The best."

"Dessert?"

"No. Thanks, anyway."

"Another beer?"

I pushed away from the bar. Stood. "Not today. Just the check, please." I made a show of raising my arm and looking at my watch. "There's someplace I've gotta be."


I was starting to become like that onion I admired. Layered. An object of depth. I was learning about all sorts of new things, thanks to Glen. Scooters. Digital cameras. Camouflage clothes. I was becoming a more well-rounded individual with greater resources to call upon for my novels.

But it was also a hassle. I guess anything worth learning is worth suffering for. Isn't that what they always say about artists? They suffer for their art? Peeling back the layers to get to the writer underneath hurt. It would take time, and the longer I studied, the more layers I'd uncover.

I drove to the mall, parked the car, and removed my scooter. I put the camera in the storage compartment alongside my camo shirt, and rode out to the woods behind Glen's house. I hid the scooter, donned the camo shirt, and, with the camera in hand, treaded carefully up to my tree.

This was now my routine, much like Glen's stretching and knuckle-cracking. My camera was like his laptop. Once I had learned enough from Glen, I could forego all this. I could just go to a writing place like Glen's table and write. The time I saved would be invaluable. My word output would increase tremendously. Pages would grow into piles of paper.

I raised the camera to my eye, zoomed all the way in and

focused on the window to Glen's writing room. Even with the long lens, the image wasn't as close as I would have liked. And it was a little awkward, holding the camera steady. I snapped a picture. The shutter raised and light entered the camera. An image was recorded on the digital card.

It didn't matter that the room was empty. This would be a test run. I needed to acclimate myself to the camera in these surroundings. I had less control than I did in my apartment, and I wanted to be as comfortable as I could with the equipment and the area. I turned to the far end of the house. The back of the garage.

*Snap.*

The shutter sounded louder than I remembered in my apartment. Or was it just my perception out here in the darkening woods? I swung the lens over to the next room. What I figured was the bedroom. A slight change of focus.

*Snap.*

The writing room. I could see much more of it in the daylight. It might actually be a nice still life. The front photo on a book jacket.

*Snap.*

The kitchen window. Focus.

Glen was standing there drinking a glass of water. I almost dropped the camera, but something said push the button. So I did.

*Snap.*

Then I dropped to my knees. Had he seen me? Had he heard the camera? I wanted to know, but I couldn't stand up. If he had heard the camera, and I stood up, he might see me. Then all my planning would be ruined. I wouldn't become a writer. I'd be a postman with a route.

Maybe not even that, if he recognized me as his postman.


"Ezra? Boss wants to see you."

The Author was there. With my supervisor.

"That's him."

I had to play dumb.

"What?"

"Ezra, this gentleman says you were hiding in his woods, taking pictures of his house. Is this true?"

Deny. Deny. Deny.

"Not me. No. Why would I do something like that?"

The Author was studying me. He pointed at my face.

"It's him. I know it is."

"Ezra?"

"I didn't do it."

"I'd like to make a formal complaint to a higher office."

"Ezra, could you leave us for a moment. Wait outside, please."

I turned to leave.

"And close the door."

I couldn't hear the words, just the voices. It got quiet until the door opened. The Author walked out, looked at me.

He stepped toward me. "I know it was you. If I see you around my place again, I'll call the police."

He left.

"Ezra?"

I walked back into the office.

"I'd like to think the gentleman is mistaken, but, in order to forestall any problems, I'm reassigning you. You and Bridget will switch routes starting immediately."

Cradling the camera in my hands, I used my elbows and knees

to crawl through the brush back to my scooter.

At home, I reviewed the photos I'd taken. All the close-ups were blurry. Out of focus. The wider shots in town were all sharp. Some of them even looked good with the late afternoon sun and shadows playing across the buildings.

I didn't even notice the blur on the other close-ups until I found the shot of Glen drinking the glass of water. He wasn't even recognizable. I thought maybe my shock at seeing him at the window had caused me to mess up, but that wasn't it. The close-ups were blurry.

It was me. I didn't hold the camera steady enough. I needed another piece of equipment I had seen in the photography magazine. A tripod. So the close-up shots would be as steady, as in-focus, as the wider shots. But a tripod would be too big, too cumbersome, in my small space in the woods.

Especially if I had to leave in a hurry.

"Sure, I remember you."

"Got a question. Is there anything like a tripod, but smaller? To steady myself? The camera?"

He was quiet on the other end of the phone for a moment.

"You need a monopod."

"What?"

"Monopod. All the photojournalists use 'em. One leg. Mono. They're quick. Expandable. Steady."

"Do you have one for sale?"

"I got an old one around here somewhere. You want it?"

"Yes."

"Come on over. You remember where I live?"

I said I did.

"How much?"

He named a price, and I agreed.

\* \* \*

The monopod made all the difference in the world once I got used to it. And it collapsed to a little more than a foot long. I attached rope to each end and slung it over my shoulder. Put on a long jacket. It felt like I was carrying a small rifle. There was a bulge, but it was a guess as to what it was. I adjusted it, and let it hang from my side, the rope over one shoulder like a rifle. This worked better. There was just a slight rise in my jacket above the shoulder, hardly noticeable.

I had consulted the camera manual about the proper setting to use for nighttime. I had wanted to check with the photographer when I bought the monopod, but I decided not to. It was something he didn't need to know.

"Why do you want to learn about nighttime shooting?"

"So I can take pictures of someone in their home without their knowledge."

I did talk him into letting me use a longer lens for a day. If I liked it, I'd come back and buy it.

I was starting to get into technical territory, no more just point, focus, shoot. The longer zoom needed more light to make an image, and that meant more adjustments, which meant more grain in the enlargements if I blew it up bigger than eight by ten.

I could see a huge photo of Glen's face covering one wall in my living room, across from the couch, an eye cut out to allow me to look out the window. Like I was looking into his mind.

Like I'm trying to do now as he sits at his computer. The kitchen light is on. The lamp on the writing table is on. It is an exercise in depth of field. There was a section about it in the manual. The magazine had mentioned it, too. It was basically about how much of the frame you wanted to keep in focus. The background would be blurry, but Glen would be in sharp focus. It was a combination of the depth of field and the length of the lens.

And then there was the light source to consider. The lamp was bright enough, but I didn't want to chance it. I wasn't sure how bright the bulb in the lamp was. I needed to make sure I got an image.

This was kind of cool, all this figuring and science. Maybe I should take some lessons. The photographer might be able to point me in a direction.

Glen seemed to be on a roll tonight. Other than the occasional grab-and-drink from the bottle, he kept his head down, working like a man lost to this world. He was finding his way in a new reality. A reality I couldn't share until he had finished.

I took my eye from the viewfinder and just stared at the house, at Glen, sitting there writing. The notion occurred to me that I was there, at the beginning of something being created.

A new book was on the way. The letter to his agent was probably to confirm that. Maybe I should have read it.

No, that would ruin the surprise. He may have outlined the whole plot. It would kill the story for me. The journey. I could wait until the book came out. Or until we became friends. Writer friends, discussing our work. Playing ideas off each other.

It was getting late. I stayed for another ten minutes, even though all the pictures would look about the same. Packed up and went home, knowing I'd have to buy the longer lens.

I wondered if he'd take the first lens back in trade?

# CHAPTER TWENTY-FOUR

I had just parked the mail cart off the side of the road and was about to begin my afternoon repast when I heard the sound of a car engine approaching. I glanced up and observed an old dark blue car speed by, crunching over the gravel, heading up the hill toward Glen's. I couldn't see the driver. The windows were tinted.

Was it Glen? His agent coming to visit after receiving the letter about the new novel? No, couldn't be. The letter had gone out only a day or so ago. He wouldn't have gotten it yet. Do agents even make house calls?

It had to be Glen. Had he seen me? I stowed my sandwich back in the bag, tossed the bag into the back of the cart, and got out. I trudged up the hill, feeling lighter than usual.

My mailbag. I had forgotten it.

I went back and hefted it onto my shoulder, started walking again.

What would Glen think of me? Sitting on the side of the road? Eating lunch just down the hill from his house? Would it be an invasion of his space? Or would it look like what I hoped it looked like: a postman taking his lunch hour before completing his assigned route.

I picked up my pace—I wanted to run—and hoped I would get to the top of the hill in time to get a glimpse of Glen.

This might be the day we officially met. A new beginning. My entry into the writers' world.

I heard the solidity of a car door closing. Then a loud metallic squeak of a garage door badly in need of oil. I was almost at the top of the hill, where the road straightened out near the house. I had to slow down. I didn't want Glen to see me practically jogging into view.

That was probably why I missed him. The squeal stopped just as I crested the hill, and I watched the garage door meet the concrete. I saw the screen door close on someone's back as he— Glen?—disappeared into the house. He didn't turn around to close the door. He stepped around it and disappeared inside.

The door shut.

I was caught flat-footed, staring at the house.

*Act, Ezra. You're a character. A postman. Do your part.*

I shrugged like I had been hoping to meet the owner of the house. Took the mail from my bag and put it inside his box. Brushed my hand across the top, clearing imaginary dust.

I couldn't help but steal a glance at the door. At the curtained windows. And I felt it again, like back in town. That feeling of being observed. Was it just my anxiety? Or was Glen looking through the peephole in the door? Watching me? Wondering about me? Did he want to come out and say hello to the new postman?

I gave him an opportunity to make up his mind. I bent to tie my shoe. When I straightened up, there was no opening door. No parted curtains.

No more feeling of being watched.

I walked back down the hill and finished my sandwich. Drank my pop. Headed back for the post office, disappointed.


The post office was quieter than usual when I got back. Some people were crying. Tear stains were drying on makeup, mascara trailing.

"What happened? Somebody die?"

"Yeah. Roy."

"My route Roy?"

"Yeah."

*An unfinished quilt. Roy and Martha lifting it and carrying it out to a couple of rocking chairs. Finishing it. Completing the pattern. Just as Roy had wanted.*

"What happened?"

"Heart attack. He was splitting kindling. Bridget found him."

"How's she doing?"

"She's a mess. Couldn't finish her route. Helen sent her home."

It was front page on the local weekly. "Beloved Postman Passes." Nice picture of Roy as a young man just starting out in his postal uniform. Mailbag over his shoulder. Beaming at the camera. Next to it, a shot after the body had been taken away. A tree stump with a log standing atop it. Roy's axe buried halfway through it. Nice story. No mention of bronzing him to stand in front of the shop, though. Details of the visitation. The burial.

Most of the people on my route subscribed to the paper, but some didn't. So I stayed home that night and wrote out a short note about Roy's death. Service times. The locations. I took them to a copy shop and had them print it out on nice paper. I made enough copies for everyone on my route. I'd put one in each person's box along with their mail.

I spotted Rosa Higgins from a long way off. She looked more like a scarecrow than ever before, standing tall and still at the end of her driveway, dressed all in black. One with the world. Dark grey storm clouds rolled over the woods and across her fallow fields, threatening to lose their mourning at any moment. The wind whispered and howled as it tossed her skirt. She put a hand on the mailbox to steady herself.

"The whole world is sad today, Ezra."

"Sad news travels fastest."

She nodded. "It's a small town."

"You okay?"

"Better than I thought I'd be. Roy and Martha are together again. That's God's will."

"Yes, ma'am."

I handed her the mail with my note on top. She read it.

"You do this, Ezra?"

"Yes, ma'am."

"Rosa."

I nodded.

"It's kind of you. Not just me?"

"Everybody on my route."

"That's good. It's right."

Then she spread her arms and leaned into the cart. Hugged me hard. She smelled like roses. The scent lingered as she stood. I hadn't been embraced like that since my mom.

"You're a good boy, Ezra. Thank you."

"Welcome, Rosa."

"I'll see you at the service?"

"You will."

She smiled and turned to walk back up the drive.

"Rosa?"

It seemed an effort for her to turn around. I saw fresh tears on her cheeks.

"Yes?"

"You need a ride to the service?"

"I do. Thank you. Call and tell me when."

"You got it." I'd get her number from work.

I sat for a moment, watching her walk back to the house, the weight of one less friend heavy on her shoulders. Then I turned the cart and slowly drove away. I didn't sound the horn. It didn't feel right. Not today.

\* \* \*

The thought came as I was riding up the gravel road: Maybe I could use Roy's death to meet Glen. Don't put the note in the mailbox. Take it to the door. Knock.

I knock, wait for the door to open. It doesn't take long.

"Excuse me, sir."

The postal uniform puts me past any suspicion, close enough to reach out and touch The Author, but he still eyes me a moment before he answers.

"Yes?"

"Sorry to bother you, sir. Your former postman? Roy?"

He nods.

"He's passed on, sir." I hand him the note. "From the way everyone's taking his death, I thought you might want to know about the plans. The service."

He takes the note. Glances at it. Looks at me.

"You write this?"

"Yes, sir."

"It's good. Honest."

"Thank you, sir."

He puts his hand out. I accept it.

"Ezra Lockert."

He doesn't give me his name. I guess he figures I knew it already from his mail. We shake hands.

"Good to meet you, Ezra."

\* \* \*

But the house looked even more shut down today. Set back farther. Unapproachable. As if the dark clouds rolling overhead were scolding it and the house was cowering in the corner, afraid of Nature's wrath.

It was an optical illusion. A trick of the eye, but it helped me make up my mind. That and the crack of thunder. I put Glen's mail in the box. The note went on top; an orphan pulse of lightning broke loose from the sky and the rain poured out, like Roy's axe had opened its belly.

I closed the lid, slung the empty mailbag over my head, and hurried back to the cart.


Two days later, I was standing over the casket at the visitation. Roy still looked like he was going to start sweating, even with all the powder the funeral home had caked on his face.

Everyone from work was there. The night shift came on their dinner hour. Lots of folks I didn't know until Rosa took me around and introduced me. She said some nice things about me. I recognized the names from the mail I delivered. Every one of them dressed like it was Sunday church time.

*Everyone but Glen.*

He didn't show.

"Ezra? You mind taking me home now?"

"Not at all, Rosa."

We said our farewells. I let them see me take Rosa's arm as we walked out the door.

Me, the good surrogate son.


Lots of people spoke the next day at the burial. The minister was smart. He just stood back and let people reminisce. A local bluegrass group sang *I'll Fly Away.*

In my head I rewrote the lyrics: "*Roy fly away.*"

The musicians raised their heads toward the sky, arms up,

hands waving. The rest of the mourners joined in. The whole congregation waved to the clouds. I looked around. There were smiles and tears everywhere, even some guy wearing a tuxedo, standing on a rise a good twenty, thirty yards away. His face was up, his arm raised, hand flapping back and forth. It was when he lowered his head and looked at the crowd below that the sunglasses came off. A handkerchief blotted away some tears.

It was Glen Dower. At Roy's funeral. In a tuxedo. Crying. Something I never would have expected.

And I hadn't brought my camera.

The minister was saying a few words in closing.

"I'll be right back, Ezra."

I watched Rosa walk away with a couple of other people. They went up the hill to Glen. They all hugged him, but he held on to Rosa the longest.


"The man you went over to? Don't think I know him."

"He's on your route."

"He is?"

"Jason Firth."

I let it dawn on me.

"My last stop. Top of the hill."

She nodded.

"How do you know him?"

"Martha—Roy's wife—and I made quilts together. He bought one at the hospital bazaar."

Oh, my God. *The Hospital Quilt* from his book of short stories. I was riding with one of Glen's inspirations. Was she aware of it?

"What's he do?"

She shrugged. "Don't really know. He moved up here some years ago. Keeps to himself."

"Standoffish?"

"No. Not really." She looked out the window where the

woods ended and her fields began. "I can see how you'd think that the way he stayed off to the side. It just takes him time to get to know people."

"Maybe I should knock on his door. Introduce myself." I signaled a turn. Rosa was quiet until I stopped the car in front of her house.

"Don't do that, Ezra. Let him come to you."

"What?"

"Jason. Let him be the one to do the introduction."

*Why? What did she know about Glen?*

"If you say so."

I started to open my door and get out of the car. Rosa's hand stopped me. She spoke slowly, considering her words as she talked. "We're a small town, Ezra. You know that. A lot of us were born around here. Never left. But some people, like you, like Jason, you come here for other reasons. Yours might be the job, but it might not. It's none of my business. But you're a good fit."

She patted my arm like someone else's grandmother would, then took her hand away.

"Thank you, Rosa."

I waited. She was going to say something about Jason. Glen. I knew it, but it didn't come. I had to ask.

"And Jason? Mr. Firth?"

"He's good, too, but he's different. A mite skittish. Like a mistreated dog might be. You accept folks, Ezra. Face value. Like you did me. He doesn't. He picks people carefully."

"Why do you think that is?"

"Not sure, but I think part of it's why he moved up here. To get away from people. Maybe certain ones, maybe just people in general."

*From people like me?* No. From the others, the ones who kept approaching him. Barging in on his life. I kept my distance. Respected his space.

"Too bad Roy's gone. He might have been able to explain it

better. They really got along. It surprised me, Jason not being at the visitation, but it was probably the crowd. The small space. He wouldn't be comfortable."

"Sounds like you know him pretty well."

"As well as most around here. Once he accepts you he's a lot of fun, but there's always something…"

She trailed off, searching for the right vocabulary.

"What?"

"Removed. Like he's standing outside himself, watching how you react around him. Roy's the only one I know got past that. They were real good friends."

Fat, sweaty, beer-spitting Roy? I couldn't believe it. What could the two of them possibly have in common?

"How'd Roy manage that?"

"Books, I think."

*Books? Did Roy know who Glen was? Did Glen let Roy get that close?*

"Books?"

"They were both big readers. Always talking about it. They passed books back and forth. Martha and I used to laugh about it and carry on with our quilting."

Carry on with your *inspiration*. I needed to reread the book of short stories. Maybe Roy would…*The Unknown Reader*. I could see it. It was Roy. The working man who was so much more than the picture he presented to the public. He was real and right in front of me. I had missed it, but Glen hadn't. I needed to keep my eyes open. Become more aware.

*Lesson learned, Sir.*

Even when I was not watching him I learned from him. Maybe everything in life is an opportunity to study, to learn.

The flag was up on Glen's mailbox. I opened the lid. My note about Roy's death was there. He had written across the bottom *Thank you*. Signed it with his initials. *JF*. No punctuation.

Contact at last. And it made sense we'd meet this way, through the written word.

I knew he was watching me. I could feel it, but I remembered Rosa's warning: *Let him be the one to do the introduction.* I didn't look up, just put the note into my bag, his mail inside the box.

I celebrated with an all-Maine dinner. Lobster, of course, and a side of something called red flannel hash. Plus a bottle of the Pine Tree State's own Winterport wine. Lobster in Maine is like steak in Kansas, except it's not corn-fed. Or grass fed, for that matter. I'm surprised some restaurant hasn't listed it on the menu as being saltwater infused. The hash gets its color from beets. They're chopped up and mixed in with leftover bits of almost anything. Potato, cabbage, ham. Other stuff, too. Tastes better than it sounds.

I ordered seconds.

And the wine. White. Local. Cold and crisp. A little heavy on the fruit, but good. I raised the glass to toast my good fortune.

To Glen. And to Rosa. And, "Thank you, Roy."

I finished the bottle, washing down dessert. A huge black bear paw. Dark chocolate, maple caramel, and pecans for crunch.

I had been watching for more than an hour. Glen shone brilliantly this night. The two-liter bottle sat on his table untouched. He hadn't even looked away from the keyboard. Maybe my note had something to do with it. An inspiration. Like the quilt.

Could he be writing about me? Like he did about Rosa and Roy? *The Thoughtful Postman.* Not a very good title, but workable. If he didn't write it, maybe I would.

He got up once while I was there and went into the kitchen. Stood at the sink and drank a glass of water.

I snapped a shot. His eyes shifted to me. Did he hear the camera? The windows were open. How good was his hearing? It couldn't be that keen, could it? But I was in the dark. Dressed in black. And the outside lights weren't on. If he did hear the camera, he couldn't see me. It was just a deer, stepping on a twig.

I wanted to take another picture, but I didn't. If he had heard the camera, it may be too much and cause him to illuminate the backyard. Come out and chase down the sound. I regretted it. It would have been a good image. He would have been looking right at the camera.

Right at me.

He went back to the writing table and sat down. Kept writing. I watched for another hour before I left. Whatever was urging him on was strong. He didn't drink from the bottle at all.

Why water? Is it something about the writing rhythm? Was water what he drank when he was on a roll? Was it something subconscious, or did he think something else would warp his words? The artificial liquid versus the natural flow of the water. Maybe that was it. Water, the writer's sports drink. Something to keep him on a steady course. Not a sugar high where you get a burst of energy and then crash. Lose your train of thought. Derailed.

I was still mulling it over on the scooter as I made my way toward my car and then home.

# CHAPTER TWENTY-FIVE

How should I approach Glen? According to Rosa, I shouldn't. But what would I do when he lets me in his life? How would I react? If I went for well-read and erudite, would it be too much like Roy? He was a postman. I am a postman. This had been Roy's route. Now it was mine. If I started spouting off about books, would I seem a mere facsimile of Roy's original? I needed to be something else. My own person. Something unique to make an impression on Glen, so he'd remember me.

Maybe the opposite. Pretend I'm not a reader. Let the relationship develop from shared experiences, starting with Roy's death and my friendship with Rosa. I didn't even plan *that*. It's just one of those lucky coincidences. If I put it in a book, no one would believe me, but in real life that's what it was. A stroke of luck.

And I get some damn good pies in the bargain.

Was there some way I could get Rosa to invite Glen over for dinner to meet me? How would he react? She'd have to tell him I'd be there; otherwise, he may walk in, see me, and turn around and leave. Would he even accept the invitation?

I couldn't *not* be a reader. Everybody reads to some degree. Magazines. Books. Internet sites. I'd have to be an occasional reader, I just couldn't focus on fiction; too close to Glen's world. It might make him suspicious if I just started spouting off about some character in a book.

I could read non-fiction. Biographies. Histories. Travel. And only a couple books a year. What did I hear once? The average American only reads one or two books a year? Out of the thousands published. It's a crapshoot for the publisher. And think of the writers. All the unwritten books that never make it to an agent or publisher. Glen's already been published. He wouldn't be my competition. Some guy or gal I never heard of, and probably never will, that was my competition.

It was a good thing I had my postal job. At least until my books take off. Hopefully, they'd find a broader readership than most. Maybe not as large as Glen's readership, but look at the authors who aren't as good as him. Their houses, their bank accounts, their sales figures. It's not a fair world.

Maybe I had a shot, and maybe Glen would only come into his proper acknowledgement after he was dead. A Van Gogh of the literary world, his first editions commanding huge sums he'd never see, never share. An autographed first edition? The price would be even greater. But I could never sell them. Still, it might be tempting to at least know what they're worth.

So that was going to be it. I was a reader of non-fiction. Two or three books a year. Fiction is off-limits.

Until Glen recommends something.

# CHAPTER TWENTY-SIX

I was camouflaged to the hilt. I don't think my own mother could have spotted me. I had become a chameleon, my color shifting to suit my environment, one with the woods. If Glen looked up from his writing table and stared right at me all he'd see would be nature. The sun—if it came out from behind the clouds—would be at my back, so I didn't worry about reflections off the lens of the camera. And its body was a flat matte black, blending in with the bushes and branches. It was like I didn't exist.

At this moment, Glen didn't exist, either. The bedroom curtains were drawn. The writing room was empty, the laptop closed. No movement in the kitchen. But it was still early on my day off. Six a.m. I was hoping to observe his morning ritual. Would it be coffee and eggs out on the patio? Or would he sit down at the writing table with his bottle and get right into whatever had him so occupied of late?

I was feeling quite satisfied. It was a beautiful morning. A bit cloudy, but warm. No breeze. The sun kept threatening to make an appearance at any moment. The occasional echo of a woodpecker sounded from what could have been a mile away.

*Rat-a-tat. Rat-a-tat.*

It could have been mistaken for small arms fire; like a .22. I should have taken it as a warning, because shortly after I heard it, a cloud of evil descended upon me in the form of Maine's chief mischief maker: the black fly. I had heard the jokes about declaring the pesky thing the state bird, and seen cars carrying the bumper stickers: *We breed 'em. You feed 'em,* but so far I had evaded their attention. I had been so intent on viewing the house, lost in my meditations, I hadn't even realized they were around.

Until the first bite.

I wanted to shout, but I didn't. I slapped at the back of my neck and checked my palm. There was a black Rorschach blot and some blood. My blood.

"Unh..."

*Forget this, Ezra. Get out of here. But be quiet. Don't draw any attention to yourself.*

I let the camera drop to my chest, the rawhide cord holding fast. I made my retreat slowly, the dark swarm staying with me. When the house was no longer visible, I turned, swinging my arms about my head, trying to create some space between me and the invading insects. *Who's invading whom?* I walked quickly back to the scooter, leaving the buzzing cloud behind. I flung the branches covering the scooter aside and kept moving. It seemed instinctual. A moving target is harder to hit, and maybe the motion itself would keep the damn things away.

"Black flies, huh?"

It was the same salesman who had sold me my camouflage outfit.

"Yeah."

He was trying to hide a smile. It came out as a condescending smirk.

"Surprised you weren't back before this, but then it has been a tad windy lately."

"They don't like the wind?"

"Nope."

"What else don't they like?"

"Rain. Cold. I've seen 'em at night, but not too often. The temperature's usually too low." Now the smile came. "Do know one thing they like, though?"

"What's that?"

"You." He must've used the same lines a hundred times or more. They came out rapid-fire, pauses for effect, the whole bit. "Black flies just like a tourist," he told me.

"How so?"

"They arrive after Memorial Day, usually leave by Labor Day, sometimes earlier. I love 'em."

"You do?"

"Yep."

"Why?"

"Tourist or black fly, makes no never mind to me. Both put money into my pocket."

He helped me find some netting that went over my head and tucked into my shirt under my collar, but it made using the camera unwieldy. The net pressed into my eyes.

"Yeah. That happens."

"What do you do?" I asked. "When you're out birding?"

"Depends."

"On what?"

He rubbed his nose with his forefinger and thumb, weighing his words.

"How silly you want to look."

He went into the back and came out with a sample. He even helped me slip it on. It seemed like it would satisfy my needs. It might even help me hide in the woods better, but he was right, it was silly looking, and I felt foolish when I put it on.

"It's like a one-person tent," he explained. "It goes over your head. It's got a lightweight aluminum frame that holds the netting away from you and gives you enough room to maneuver inside. Raise your arms. Use your binoculars or camera."

"You sure it'll keep the bugs off me?"

"Don't forget to close off the bottom tight as you can. You

don't want none of them critters getting inside. They definitely don't like to be confined."

If not for the aluminum frame, it would have folded up small enough to fit into the compartment on the back of the scooter. I ended up buying what they called a courier bag, not unlike the one I had for work. They didn't have it in camo, but they did have it in olive green. It slung over my shoulders and rode across my back. It had a big flap over a large deep pocket with a Velcro closure. I could fold the netting up and adjust the aluminum poles so they were completely hidden, once the flap was flipped.

Lots of people wished they would win the lottery. I wished I had been the one to invent Velcro. But I also wouldn't have minded winning the lottery.

Wishes might be a good subject for a book. At least a short story, or maybe a children's book. The title could rhyme like the rest of the book.

*The Dish With A Wish.*

I spent my afternoon—like the writer I was—with a pad of paper and a pen. I soon realized a dish is not a real active lead character. What's the most it could wish for? To be cleaned lovingly? Not to be dropped? Maybe it could get thrown away or left behind only to be found by someone and end up in the circus spinning dizzily upon the end of a stick with a group of likeminded dishes, while an audience of thousands roars its approval. But would my dish be a plate? Would kids relate to a plate?

*Relate to a plate.* I jotted that down.

And what do I name it? D names for dish. Donny? Debby? Doris? Denny? And P names for plate. Peter? Paul? Pam? Polly? Is it a he or a she? I could start with a boy plate or dish and see where that goes. I can always change it to a girl later if I have to.

How do you tell the difference between a boy plate and a girl plate?

There's got to be a catchy punch line there somewhere.

Pee Wee. Pee Wee the plate. I like that.

But maybe he'd be a bowl. Bob? Barbara? Boris? Brenda? An ice cream bowl? Kids would love that. They'd eat it up. *Ha!* He could start out way in the back of the cupboard, neglected because his color didn't go with the other bowls. And then his lucky break, pun intended. One of the normal pastel bowls gets damaged beyond use, and he's pressed into service until Mom can buy a new one. But the kid loves him. Demands to use him all the time. He's different, but in the kid's eyes he's just as good as the other bowls. Better even. Because of his difference. A nice little story, but, applied to a larger canvas, an allegory for racial inclusion or accepting others even if they are different, and what it can bring to the group as a whole.

But I had trouble with the rhymes, and the title didn't scan right for me. *An Ice Cream Bowl's Dream.* It should be *An Ice Cream Dream*, but I couldn't write about ice cream itself. Well, I could, but how long a story would that be? My hero would melt away if he were outside a freezer for any length of time. He could wish to travel, be put in a bowl and carried. But then he'd be eaten. What kind of a message would that send? Stay at home, shut up in your room? Be careful what you wish for?

I could place him in a cold climate. Siberia, Antarctica, Alaska. But do kids eat ice cream when it's cold outside?

Maybe I should rethink my lead character.

I went back to the alphabet. I didn't have far to travel.

F. F is for fish. And a couple lines leaped out from the depths of my streaming consciousness, and they were good.

*Trish was a fish.*
*A fish with a wish.*
*She wanted to find*
*Her very own niche.*

Would kids comprehend what a niche was? How do you tell them without obviously instructing? What do kids' stories have in common?

Repetition.

I could explain niche with a line meaning the same thing.

*A place to fit in.*
*A place to begin.*
*So she swam to the Gulf*
*And stuck out a fin.*

Not too shabby for a beginner. And writers don't have to be limited to one area. I could write adult novels as well as kiddy lit. Get the little buggers hooked on my stories at a young age and carry them with me throughout their lives. My own production line with a waiting mass of consumers.

*"Mommy, look. New Ezra book. Me want it."*

*"Yes, dear."*

Kah-Ching!

And, years later...

*"Hey, man. A new Ezra mystery. Cool."*

Kah-Ching!

A few years later...

*"Happy birthday, honey."*

*"Oh, wow, the new Ezra Thriller. Just what I wanted. Thanks, dear."*

I could do it. Look at Glen. His books were all over the landscape, including outer space.

Could I get Trish the Fish into outer space? Oh my God, could Trish be a series character? That was something Glen didn't do. Why not? In all the interviews I'd read, no one had ever asked him that question. Isn't that where the money is? Where the real fan base lives? The support, both from readers and from publishers? Maybe I could mention it to him once he lets me in on his real identity.

I reread what I had written. Damn, is it pronounced niche to rhyme with fish? Or is it pronounced neesh to rhyme with...what? Sheesh? Or *neech* to rhyme with leech? Or beach? Peach? Reach? Teach?

I closed the pad of paper around the pen and laid it down on the kitchen table. All this thinking about fish had made me hungry. I'd hit Paulie's for fish and chips, maybe a pint or two, and then home to bed. Tomorrow was another day off, and I had bigger fish to fry. *Ha!*


Paulie's was slow, but then Paulie's was always slow except for Darts Night and probably whenever there's some big sporting event like the World Series or the Super Bowl. I'd learned that the real Paulie had retired last year and sold out to some Texas transplant named Orlando. Building and all. Orlando kept most of the same food, but a couple of Tex-Mex dishes made their appearance on the menu. I didn't know how much the bar and grill brought in, but Orlando lived upstairs, and the two apartments over his probably took care of the mortgage.

"Evenin', Ez."

"Orlando. How fresh is the fish?"

"I had to slap it."

"Is there an extra charge for the humor?"

"None at all."

I placed my order. Orlando set a pint glass in front of me, and we talked about nothing in between watching an aging actress on a talk show and eating bites of my dinner.

# CHAPTER TWENTY-SEVEN

Trying to put on my netting outfit in the woods felt like putting on underwear in front of an open window. Even though I was obscured from the road and Glen's house, I felt I had to keep an eye out to make sure no one saw me wriggling around.

I did it, but at first I thought it was all for naught. No sooner had I raised the camera to my eyes than I heard the sound of a car engine turning over. Was Glen going somewhere? By the time I could have gyrated out of my black-fly fatigues, there would have been no way to catch up and follow him. So I stood there feeling like an idiot. A well-disguised idiot.

I knew I wasn't really an idiot because an idiot would never have had the thought I had. I could turn this disappointment into opportunity. If Glen were gone, the house would be empty. I could approach it from the back. Even if someone were to drive up the road to the house, they wouldn't see me. And I'd be able to hear them in time to get back into the woods.

At first all I wanted to do was look in the window, but as I gathered my intestinal fortitude for the approach, I began to wonder if the back door might be open. Folks out here didn't always lock their doors like they did in Cincy. I could walk through the entire house in a few minutes. Even if Glen had just gone to the store, I'd be a ghost by the time he returned.

It was awkward walking in the netting, but I didn't want to waste any time. I moved away from my tree and took my first cautious step toward the house.

The back door was my best bet because—Shit! Glen had just slid it aside and stepped out onto the patio. It's a good thing his attention was focused on balancing the oversized mug he cradled in his hands, otherwise he might have seen me. I froze in place for several seconds so my movement wouldn't catch his eye and then retraced my steps as he set the mug on the picnic table and took a seat on the bench.

I was safe behind my tree again, but my body and mind were in adrenaline overdrive. I was shivering nervously, reacting to my near mission-ending mistake. Had Glen been returning from somewhere? No. The sound I had heard was definitely a car leaving, the motor and the sharp crunch of gravel dissolving into the distance. A delivery? At six in the morning? I don't think so. Had he had company? If whomever had to be at work before the normal nine to five, it would make sense for them to leave at this hour. But who could it have been?

I was angry with myself. Why had I wasted my time trying to scribble some kid's story when I could have been here, discovering the identity of this mystery person and their relationship to Glen? They seemingly had spent the night. They had to be a good and trusted friend.

Was it Rosa?

No. She doesn't drive, and why would she spend the night?

Who could it have been?

Glen was tipping the mug, downing the last of whatever he'd been drinking. He took the mug into the kitchen, stood at the sink for a while, and then crossed through the writing room and disappeared.

My heart rate was just about back to normal when I saw him step out of the sliding doors again, carrying a walking stick. He set it on the table and began to do some stretching exercises.

He was going for a walk in the woods, which meant I had to get out of there.

I slowly backed away from my tree until I could no longer

see Glen or the house. Then I turned and walked as quickly as I could to my scooter. If I thought walking in the netting was awkward, trying to move with longer strides was nerve-racking. I was sweating stinky fear by the time I reached the scooter. How would I explain this to Glen if he found me? I tossed the shrubbery aside and lifted the scooter. I could hear my heart pounding in my head. I didn't worry about leaving a trail now and made the road in seconds.

Several cars passed me on the way back to the mall. I must have looked like a tourist: a grown man in full body netting riding a small electric scooter. At least the netting would keep folks from recognizing me. I made my mind up then and there to only watch Glen at night. It was cooler, so there would be less chance of being bothered by those damn black flies, and, as I pondered and reviewed what I had already observed, Glen seemed to work more in the stillness of the evening hours, as the darkness was not conducive to hiking. He could have the woods in the daytime. At night, they would continue to serve as my classroom.

I knew I was going to have to start napping after work.

Before school.

# CHAPTER TWENTY-EIGHT

I liked watching him work at night. I could be more relaxed, just another shape in this region of shadows in the woods.

And he was so much easier to see.

In the daytime, he worked with the natural light from the window, but at night he turned on a brass—I imagined it to be brass—lamp on his writing table. It sat a bit higher than his head, throwing a soft circle of light across the table on one side, and his head and computer on the other. The rest of the room was dark.

It was easier to take pictures at night, too. In the daytime, the monopod and camera were too cumbersome—I had to be away from the tree and above the surrounding shrubbery. Plus, there was always a chance the sun would reflect off them, calling his attention to me. At night, they were just another abstract shape in the darkness. A bush. A vine.

Obviously, I didn't use flash. Talk about calling attention to yourself. Luckily, the room light was bright enough. Since all Glen did was sit there and write, it was almost like he was posing for me. His fingers would be a blur, but I couldn't see them much.

I had just taken a great shot, perfect for the author photo on his next dust jacket. I caught him when he was thinking about his story. He was sitting straight up, hands on hips, not hunched over. The light illuminated most of his face. The window made a natural frame.

If I submitted it to the website, I could probably make a lot of money, but he'd find out somehow. Then I'd have to stop and disappear.

Did he look at the website? He must know about it. Sometimes I think his publisher feeds the fire. Some of the things written on it sound too professional, like some public relations flack was dishing hype to keep the man's name out there.

He'd like the shots where he's hunched over the keyboard, just his forehead and the top of his head showing; they would add to his mystery. But that could be anyone, some model in a photographer's studio. No one would believe it's him.

I was just about to go home when he got up from the table and left the room. I looked at my watch. It was too late for a sandwich. He didn't normally eat after ten. I could see the bottle through the camera lens. It was still half full.

He came back with a cell phone to his ear. I clicked a couple of frames of him standing behind his chair, but his head and shoulders were in darkness. He was wearing a green T-shirt with a picture of a typewriter on the front.

Then he sat down. His head bent to his shoulder, holding the phone in place. As I was taking the shot, he closed the computer. Beautiful. A full shot from the table up. These would be the best shots I'd taken. He was sitting up straight now. One hand on the phone, his neck erect. I couldn't ask for much more. The shadow was across his forehead, slanted down across one eye like a fedora slipped low.

Oh. Oh. He was slouching in the chair. Talking on the phone. His entire face was in the light. The digital camera was great for this. Hundreds of photos on a chip. I'd delete most of them and just keep the best ones. Make me look like I knew what I was doing.

I had my camera packed up and took one more look before leaving. He was still on the phone, walking in circles around his writing table, his free arm gesturing wildly. I couldn't tell whether he was thrilled or agitated.

He leaned over and turned off the lamp. I waited.

Minutes later I heard a door slam. Then his car started. Bright beams swept past the side of the house into the trees. I took my flashlight out of my camera bag, turned and started running through the woods to my scooter. It was a good fifty yards or so to the road, and there was really no path, not that anyone could see. But I knew my way, and I was at the scooter pretty quickly, cramming the camera bag and flashlight into the carryall.

It took a minute to carry the scooter through the brush and onto the narrow road. Then I was on my way around the curve and down the hill, hoping to pick him up where this road and his meet. My blood was racing, my heart drumming, but when I got there, the only light was the streetlamp, hanging high up on crossed wires.

I slammed my palm against the handlebars. The horn honked weakly.

What was that phone call? Could it have been a fan? Had some-one else managed to track him down? I didn't see how, but if I had been able to do it, I guessed someone else could have, too.

And where had he gone? My first thought was the police. If I were being harassed, that's where I'd go.

Once my senses calmed down, I rode to the mall, put the scooter back in the trunk and drove slowly into town. I took a detour a few minutes out of my way and went by the police station. His car was not in the well-lit lot.

I had no other ideas, so I pointed the hood toward home.

I had little desire to go straight home. After all my time in the woods, my apartment was feeling smaller these days. Because of the dormers, I could only stand up in the center of the room. If I moved to the perimeter, I was always stooping or bending. I'd have to consider looking for a new place after the first of the year when our raises would kick in, but at that moment, I was where I was. At least I didn't have to stand up straight to sleep.

I was about to turn the corner when I saw his car—I was pretty sure it was his car—outside Paulie's Bar and Grill. I continued with the turn, parked my car in front of my apartment and walked back to the park bench across the street from the bar. I sat there and watched. Waited. I couldn't make up my mind. Should I go in, or not? It would be the closest I'd ever been to him, other than the book tour and that quick encounter at Sarge's diner.

A blonde woman walked out of the bar, fishing in her purse for her keys. Her heels clicked solidly on the concrete. Her shoes sounded angry. I watched her get into her car, a silvery sporty thing, and drive away.

What the hell? I could use a beer before bed anyway. Just one. See what he was doing. If he was even in there. Just because his car was outside didn't mean he was in Paulie's. He could have been visiting someone in one of the apartments on that side of the street.

Maybe I should have stayed on the bench. I debated less than a minute, got up, and crossed the street.

The place was darkened, but I saw him as soon as I walked in. He was sitting at the bar, under a small, fake Tiffany lamp that hung from a ceiling covered in baseball caps. I took a seat several stools away. Nodded at Orlando as he approached.

"Evenin', Ez."

"Hey, Orlando." I pointed to one of the taps. "Pint."

As he drew my regular beer, I looked in the mirror behind the bar and caught Glen shifting his eyes away from my direction. Orlando set my beer down. I put a ten next to it. Orlando picked it up and went to make change. I turned to look around the place. My movement drew Glen's attention. We made eye contact. I nodded.

"Evenin'."

He nodded and turned back to his drink. There was a half-empty pint glass in front of him.

I couldn't believe I had been so cool. It must have been something about neutral territory. Outside his house, I was nervous. In here, we're just a couple of guys.

Still, I was jittery. Afraid I'd miss something. Here, he was just a man like me. And not a particularly interesting man. Maybe that was the persona he had cultivated. Slumped over. Arms resting on the bar. Both hands wrapped around a small glass. I'm sure Orlando had no idea who he was. The couple playing darts didn't know or seem to care. And Patsy Cline on the jukebox was too busy weighing in with her judgment about her own sanity.

He tipped his drink. Finished it and slid the glass across the bar.

"Another?"

He nodded. Orlando poured some vodka. Added lime juice and stuck in a swizzle stick. He gave it one quick stir and pushed it back across the bar.

"Put that one on my tab."

I couldn't believe I'd said that. Glen looked over at me.

"Do I know you?"

I shook my head. "We kinda met the other day at Sarge's. I'm Ezra."

He nodded and jerked an ear toward his drink. "What's this for?"

"Bein' neighborly," I said. "And you look kinda pissed at the world."

"Not the whole world. Just a small part of it." He smiled. Raised the glass to toast me. "Thanks."

I nodded my pint his way. "Welcome." Turned back to my drink. Glen Dower just toasted you, Ezra. I bit my tongue to stay calm and stared into my glass. Act like it's an everyday thing. No big deal. But somewhere inside me a little man began dancing up and down my spine screaming "Contact!"

There was an old TV hanging from the ceiling at the far end of the bar. An infomercial for some physical fitness machine was playing with Close Captioned praise. A studio audience beat their silent hands together. Orlando picked up the remote from the back bar and ran through some channels until a baseball game came on. He set the remote back down. Now thousands of hands clapped in silence. Shook their fists. Typed out on the screen: (*Organ music. Charge!*)

Glen turned away from me and watched the screen. I turned to the TV, but studied his reflection in the bar mirror. I might never be this close again.

The years had been kind to him. His hair was gray around the temples, but still full. His face had thinned from the roundness I remembered on the book tour. A small flock of crow's feet walked out from his corners of his eyes. He hadn't shaved, but he looked comfortable in his skin.

Every now and then I'd catch him glancing my way in the mirror. Could he feel me looking at him?

It was after a couple more drinks when our eyes caught again. Glen motioned to Orlando.

"Next round's on me."

I smiled. "Thanks."

"Don't mention it." He turned back to the game.


I'm not much of a drinker, so I nursed the beers, but he just kept ordering those gimlets. Don't know what he was trying to do, but by the end of the game he had put a sizable dent in a large bottle of vodka.

It didn't help that the game went into extra innings.

As soon as the last batter lined out to short, Orlando hit the remote. The screen closed in on itself.

"Last call." He laid checks in front of us.

Glen stood up and put a hand into his pocket. Pulled out a fistful of wrinkled bills, extracted a couple, and dropped them onto the bar. "Night, all."

Orlando eyed the mangled money. "You're not drivin', are you?"

Glen stopped. "I was thinking about it." He looked at his reflection in the mirror and had to steady himself. "You're probably right. Thanks. I'll call a cab." He pulled a cell phone from his pocket.

My voice leapt up. "I could give you a lift." I think I managed to throttle it back a bit. Not sound too eager.

He looked at me and the crows' feet deepened into a squint. "No. Thanks, anyway. I'm a few miles outside of town."

"No problem."

"I'm too tired to give directions. I'll just let the driver get me home."

"I know where you live."

*Nice, Ezra. Why not show him your camouflage suit while you're at it?*

He got that deer in the headlights look I had seen on the book tour. His voice had an edge to it. Almost evil. "And how might you know that? I don't know you."

The hate—fear?—in his eyes froze me. I couldn't think of what to say.

"Hell, Mr. F," Orlando said. "Ezra's your mailman. He knows where everybody lives."

His eyes still held mine. "That so?"

I nodded. "Not everybody. Jimmy and Sara cover the town. Bridget's got out east. I got out west. I replaced Roy. Roy Kerther?" *Say something here. You're going to lose him.* "Tell me your name and I'll tell you if you're on my route."

He barked a short laugh. "I knew Roy well." That thought stopped him, but the storm in his eyes had passed and he offered his hand. "Jason Firth."

I accepted his hand. "Ezra Lockert." We shook. "And I do

know where you live."

*Yes, indeed, Mr. Jason Firth. I know that quite well.*


We rode in silence. I couldn't find a way into an easy conversation. Everything sounded forced to me like I was some damn reporter trying to scoop his life. It was only when we were crunching over the gravel up the hill it came to me.

Concern. Caring. And I was concerned. And did care. My emotions were genuine.

"I know it's none of my business, but what set you off tonight?" He just kept watching the headlights fuse into a late evening fog. "I'm kind of a regular there. Haven't seen you there."

"You're right. It's none of your business."

The silence grew, tried to push its way out of the car. I stopped in front of his gate.

"Give me your keys," I said.

"No. I can get myself in. Thanks for the ride."

"Your *car* keys. I'll drive it up tomorrow on my rounds."

He looked at me. Those eyes again. The questions in them. "Oh," he said after a few seconds. "Good idea. Thanks."

He took his keys from his pocket and gingerly worked a key off the metal hoop. Handed it to me. "Good night. Ezra."

"G'night, Jason."

He got out of the car. Closed the door. I watched him walk away as if I were a high school kid making sure my date got in the door okay. At the fence he turned and came back to my car. I hit a button and the window slid down.

He put both hands on the door. Leaned in. "Look, I'm sorry. I didn't mean to snap at you. It's just that...well, I value my privacy. I'm not good with people. They always seem to want something from me, and I never seem to be up to the task."

"Hey, I apologize. I didn't mean to pry."

"It's okay. It's been awhile since I've talked with a

stranger...someone I haven't known for a while." He looked to the woods, like he heard something. Then he looked back at me. "You're right, I don't go to that bar much. Orlando's got a good memory. For names and drinks." I could barely make out his grin in the darkness. "And I'll pay for it tomorrow."

He just stood there a moment. He seemed to be wrestling with a decision. "I was meeting an old friend. I thought we might be able to see each other again. She felt differently. That's it. A sad, overdone story. I'm sure you've heard it before."

I nodded and almost said something. My mouth was open. A voice inside told me to let it go. *He shared something with you. Don't cheapen it with false sentiment.*

"Well, see ya."

I put the car in reverse. He let go of the door and took a step back.

"Yeah. Goodnight. Thanks again for the ride."

"Don't mention it."

I put the car in reverse and made the turn. Watched him walking to his door in the rearview mirror.

It had to be the woman I had seen earlier, walking out of the bar. It would explain the half-empty pint glass on the bar in front of him when I sat down. What was she thinking? Any woman should be honored that a writer of Glen Dower's talent would be interested in her. Why had she walked away?

She had hurt him. That was obvious. Oh, God. I hope not enough to keep him from writing. It could happen. Or maybe it will fuel his imagination. Maybe he'll write a whole novel about her. Or maybe just one really good scene.

A murder scene.


I had just hit the bottom of the hill when nature called. All those beers. I parked off the road and stood in the vee of my car door. A cabbie's piss is what a friend in New York City called it last time I visited him. Before we lost touch.

There was a crunch in the woods. I snapped to attention. I must have startled some animal. I peered into the darkness, imagined animal eyes looking back. What were they thinking? Was I issuing a challenge? Was I marking my territory? Leave this writer alone. He's mine.

Was it an animal?

"Hello? Who's there?"

There were more sounds. A shuffle over dried leaves and branches. Then the sounds receded as whatever it was made its way deeper into the woods. I listened to the last of my waterfall flowing noisily onto the earth.

I should have gone home. I was tired, maybe a bit drunk, and I had to work tomorrow. When I got to where I had to turn onto the main road back to town, I stopped. The dashboard clock was glowing red. One-thirteen a.m. I sat and watched as the three mutated into a four.

I turned away from town and back toward my spot in the woods.

I had to be sure Glen was okay.

# CHAPTER TWENTY-NINE

I could hear the house before I could see it. The music moved through the trees, replacing the night wind with melody and words. Something about a man who loves to rhumba. I didn't worry too much about making noise as I walked to my perch. The music was that loud.

There was light pouring from every window. Glen was on the back patio. A backlit silhouette. I didn't know what the rhumba looks like, but I didn't think it looked like the dance he was doing, jerking all over the concrete. One arm extended, its hand holding a bottle of clear liquid. More vodka? The other hand waved, conducting the band. His sloppy feet moved up and down. Back and forth.

The music stopped and so did he. He tipped the bottle moonward. Drained a good portion of its contents. As the next song began, he gripped the bottle by its neck, pulled his arm back, and threw it into the woods. The glass caught the light from the kitchen, then fell, making a hollow thud somewhere a little too close to me for comfort.

The song continued as he struggled to stand, weaving back and forth. Something about a couple getting out of L.A. before they got killed or caught. Then his eyes racked across the back woods and he screamed.

"Fuck you! Fuck you!"

He didn't seem to worry about his voice carrying. I didn't

think he had any neighbors close enough to hear him anyway. He looked to be staring straight at me. Gooseflesh peppered my skin. I froze and became just another part of the woods. He couldn't see me. The light did not come this far. I was safe.

*The woman.* He was mad at the woman—another connection to his process. I had guessed he would do something about her, and this primitive dance was his opening salvo. This would fuel his rage and it would not be long before it would boil over onto the printed page.

He stood there a while longer, then went into the house and turned off all the lights but one. Turned off the music. He set a two-liter bottle on his writing table. Then he sat down, opened his laptop, and began to write.

*Composing while drunk. A misdemeanor at most.*

I kept glancing at the empty vodka bottle all the way home. I was thrilled it hadn't broken. It rested on the passenger seat Glen had so recently occupied. I had wrapped it in an old towel and it was going nowhere now. Just home. And I would find a place for it. A place of honor. In time, long after each of us was dead, his work would last, and my collection would be in a museum, maybe back in the very same house he was writing in now. The Glen Dower Museum.

Future writers would visit his home and look over his artifacts.

That was what rode beside me now.

An artifact.

I was so excited by my acquisition I couldn't sleep. There was something knocking at my mind. Something I was overlooking. I cursed myself. Like a detective who knows he knows something in a badly written mystery, but he can't remember what it is until just before the end of the novel. Until just before the bad guy finishes him off or gets away.

Then he remembers. I ran over the events of my evening, and there it was.

*The car.*

I got up, threw on jeans and a T-shirt, shoes, and picked up Glen's car key.

I started with the exterior, making notes in a small notebook. Registration number. Expiration date. License plate. Tire treads were a little worn. I'd be sure to mention that.

I popped the trunk: jumper cables, a jack, some windshield washer fluid, and a spare tire. Normal car stuff. Nothing to give away who owns the car.

There wasn't much inside, either. Nothing in the back seat. Nothing under the seat. In front, on the seat, were some music cassettes. The old car had a cassette tape player. I found some things in the glove box: a spoken word CD of poets reading their own stuff, and the insurance card. Made out to Jason Firth. The address matched the one where I delivered his mail.

Had he legally changed his name? Or was Glen Dower an alias? A pen name? I don't think so, or someone would have discovered that bit years ago. Back when he first started writing.

I made a mental note to check it out.

I was tired, but I hurried through most of my rounds the next morning. Then, before returning Glen's car, I drove over to the Robbinsville Photo shop, and handed in my camera's memory card, which held the fruits of my photographic labors.

"Be ready in a couple hours," the young girl—Sally Anne, according to her employee ID card—informed me.

"Great." Then a thought popped into my head. What if they looked at the pictures after they were developed? That was a connection to Glen I did not want someone else making. "Hey,"

I said in as light voice as I could manage. "What's the strangest photo you've ever seen someone hand in?"

Sally Anne smiled. "Mister, we don't have time to look at them. I put your card in the machine, your pictures get processed and placed in an envelope."

"So you never get curious about what people are photographing?"

"No offense," Sally Anne said. "I got enough to do, keeping up with my own life."

"I hear that," I said.

I stepped outside and used my phone to find the next business I needed to visit.

I knew the guy in the third frame shop was my man. He was already wearing cotton gloves. The previous two stores had high school kids fronting their counters. Lord knows what they had on their fingers.

"It might seem a bit silly to you..."

"Don't worry about it. If it's important to you, it's important to us."

I nodded. Peeled the tape back. Unrolled the bubble wrap. His eyebrows rose.

"Vodka bottle, huh?"

"Yep."

He tapped his fingers on his chin. "I don't think a frame is what you want."

"No?"

He shook his head. A hand approached the bottle. "May I?" Respect.

"Be my guest."

He put one cotton-clad finger in the bottle opening. Rotated it. Tilted it.

"You want to display this. So anyone can see most, if not all, of the glass. A frame would hide the sides and the back."

He steadied the bottle. Removed his finger. Held that cotton covered finger up. "Be right back." I had found my conservator.

He returned, pushing a small cart. Resting upon it were two glass cases, some squares and rectangles of wood in assorted stains, and thin strips of black metal.

"Won't glass break?"

He corrected me. "Lucite. Museum quality. How high up do you plan to display this?"

"What do you mean?"

"Will it be at eye level? A mantle or shelf? Or will it be lower? On a desk, perhaps?"

There was more to this museum stuff than I realized. "Um. Lower. Table height."

"Then I suggest this one." He lifted the larger case. Set it on the counter next to my bottle. "Pick a base. I suggest a contrasting color from where it will end up. It sets the *objet d'art* apart from its surroundings."

Art object. In French. He was definitely on my wavelength. I pointed to a lighter shade.

"Good choice." He picked up the metal strips. "This is just to give you the general idea." He contorted the metal into the base making a stand about four inches wide. "I'll have to adapt the base so the cover fits securely." He picked up the bottle and situated it onto the metal stands. Set the Lucite cover over the bottle so it was resting on the wooden base. The bottle was tilted slightly, lying back as if reclining, its label looking up for all to see.

I bent over and looked through the clear plastic on all sides, nodding the entire time.

"I could have it for you by next week. Say Thursday?"

My smile was all the answer he needed.

"Very good. Now, would you also like a small brass plate? To identify the work?" He pulled a book from under the counter. Opened it. "We could engrave it in any style you like. Something that captures the character of the piece."

I hesitated. No. No names. Not yet. "Maybe later. Thanks."

I was nervous when I went to collect my photos. Not just because I'd taken the risk of handing them over to someone. What if I'd moved when I snapped the shutter? They looked good on the viewfinder, would they be blurry when enlarged? But I was also excited, like I was when I had lined up to meet him all those years ago. I paid, went to the car, and opened the envelope.

There he was. Glen. A phone to his ear. The laptop closed. A full head-on waist-shot portrait. He was bathed entirely in the light from the table lamp. No shadows, except for the side of his face away from the lamp. I mentally patted myself on the back. It looked artistic.

Too bad his eyes were closed.

But the second one was just as good. And his eyes were open, staring straight ahead, as if he were looking right at the camera. Next time, I'd delete the ones I didn't like and just develop—process—the ones that looked good. A little self-editing.

I put the packet of pictures on the seat beside me and drove away. I had a couple more errands to run.


I parked Glen's car in front of the fence and hit the horn. A couple of jaunty toot toots. Waited. No response from inside the house. Maybe he was still sleeping off the vodka. If he had written most of the night, maybe he was more tired than I was.

I killed the engine, removed the key, picked up Glen's mail and got out. The key gave me a good excuse to open the gate and approach the house. I knocked on the front door.

"Gl—" I caught myself. "Jason? You home?"

No answer. I tried the doorknob. It was locked. Now what was I to do? I was counting on Glen to give me a ride back into town to my own car. The walk would take forever. I stepped over to a window. The drapes were drawn, but I knuckled the glass. Stepped back.

"Jason?"

Clutching the mail and the car key like a passport, I walked around back to the patio. The picnic table was empty. I went to the door and knocked. I leaned against the glass, cupped my hands and tried to see inside.

"Help you?"

*What the*—? I must have jumped two feet in the air. The mail went flying. My scream startled some doves and they broke noisily through the leaves, seeking the safety of the sky. When I turned around there was Glen, walking toward me from the woods.

"God, you scared me."

"Sorry." He squinted at me. "Who are you and what are you doing here?"

I had managed to hold onto the key. I thrust it toward him like a talisman. "I brought your car back."

He looked at me like I was from Mars. Or worse: a fan who'd tracked him down. "What?"

"Last night? I drove you home. From Paulie's? I'm Ezra."

I gave him time for that to sink in. When it did, he said, "Oh. Oh, yes." He took the key. We stared at each other for a moment; I stooped down and started collecting his mail.

"Sorry for the mess," I said.

He bent over. Picked up a magazine. "Sorry for the scare."

We were quiet as we gathered the rest of the mail. When we were done, I handed what I had to him. He set it down on the picnic table.

"Last night..." he began. Then paused. "That was the first dose of alcohol I've had in three years. And, other than...some ball game...I don't remember too much."

"That's about all there is. We had a couple drinks and watched the game. You were a bit tipsy so I gave you a ride." *Connect, Ezra.* "I think it was some woman started you off."

Again, it took him time to remember. "Hope we didn't make

too much of a scene."

Let him think you were there. Share his anger. If he's embarrassed he might explain more. "Not too much. You got a little loud. Then she left."

"And I hit the bottle."

I nodded. "You were a decent drunk, though. You don't remember?"

"Nope. Shit. Guess I blacked out. Sorry."

"Gee, and I thought our kiss was special."

He stiffened.

"I'm joking."

"Bad joke."

"Yeah." I smiled. "Sorry."

"God, is sorry all we can say? Look, it happened. It's over. I hope I make at least another three years before it happens again."

"I'll drink to that."

Glen cocked his head and looked at me. He didn't exactly smile. "You've got a dangerous sense of humor. At least I didn't put my fist through a wall like last time."

He was a violent drunk? I never would've known from the previous evening. And blackouts? Not drinking for three years?

"What were you doing out in the woods?"

"Just walking. When I get too cooped up, I walk. It helps me think." His arm swept across the area. "Why have all this and not use it?" He jumped off the table.

I backed up a step.

"Let's go get the car. I'll give you a ride back to town."

I was buckling my seatbelt when I noticed my envelope photos on the seat. I picked them up and put them in my shirt pocket.

"What's that?"

"Some pictures I took." *Don't give him a chance to ask.* "People at work. Retirement party."

"Roy's?"

"I wish. He was in rare form that night." I tapped the photos. "Someone else back home. But Roy is missed."

"Yeah, he is. He was a good man."

We rode in silence until we hit the main road, then he surprised me by saying something that made me feel like someone special.

"How about after you get home, I buy you dinner to thank you for getting me home?"

I controlled my enthusiasm and said, "Sounds good to me. Thanks."

"But let's stay away from Paulie's. I might still be a little susceptible. How's Myrna's No Lobster?"

"Don't know it."

"Great comfort food. Southern. Out on Route 73, over toward Robbinsville." He gave the car some more gas. "And they don't have a liquor license."

# CHAPTER THIRTY

We drove right by the photo shop. The girl who had waited on me was helping some man pull down a metal garage door over the front of the store. They closed early.

"I can't believe you don't know this place. How long you lived here, anyway?"

I thought about lying, but why make too much of a habit of it? "Couple of months."

He looked at me. "Really? I would have pegged you for a local."

"Why?"

"Just figured postmen...excuse me, postal people..."

"Postal American," I said, and then when he didn't get it, "Postman's fine."

"I just figured they grew up where they worked."

"Most do. I transferred up."

"From where?"

Again, I thought of lying. But why? "Cincinnati."

"Why?"

"Cost of living. Life style." I shifted in my seat and faced him. "Cincy was too much of a city. Too expensive. Too much stress. Post office pays the same everywhere, so it made sense to me to go somewhere smaller. Someplace where life's a little easier."

"I can understand that."

He flipped on his blinker and turned the wheel. We left the main road for a hard-packed dirt road with some gravel worn into it. Little rocks danced under the car. Trees stretching branches into each other above. I looked out the back window at the dust we stirred up.

"You try Myrna's once, I guarantee you'll make the drive over again. It's that good."

"Southern, you said?"

A single-level cinderblock building appeared at a break in the trees with a big wooden sign out front. Myrna's. Painted on the front window in large white capital letters: NO LOBSTER!

"Yep." Glen turned the car into the parking lot and started looking for a place. "How's your cholesterol?"

The screen door slammed behind us. Some people looked up. Most just kept eating.

"You mind eating at the counter? Service seems to be a little quicker."

"Your place. Your treat. Your choice."

We walked past the usual Formica and chrome tables to the empty counter and sat down on red vinyl rotating stools. Mine had a slash of gray duct tape holding a rip together.

A woman with bottle red hair, wearing a tight yellow dress and white apron, came out of the swinging doors to the kitchen. She saw Glen and smiled.

"Jason! Two times in one week! Joe's gonna think we got somethin' goin' on."

"Hey, Myrna. This is Ezra. He's my mailman."

*And soon to be friend,* I thought.

Myrna held out a chubby hand. She was definitely an advertisement for comfort—all round and pillowy.

"Hey, Ezra. Welcome." She looked me up and down. Turned to Glen. "I don't know, Jason. Looks a bit peaked to me." Then she looked at me. The smile got even larger. There was lipstick on a front tooth. "We gonna fatten you up, skinny." She let go with a laugh that I'm sure could be heard in the parking lot.

"Doctor tells me I'm carrying too much as it is," I said, hand on my belly.

"Balderdash! Not by our standards. You're a beanpole." She leaned in close. Her forearm on the counter shook like a Jello plate. "I got two words for you, Ezra." Her hand cupped around one side of her mouth. She stage whispered: "*Mashed potatoes.*"

Glen laughed. "With the gravy. You have got to have the gravy."

I looked from Glen to Myrna. This was fun. I was having fun. "You don't mean the thick white stuff, do you? With chunks of sausage?"

Myrna looked at Glen and put a hand over her heart.

"Where you from, boy?"

"Originally, the Midwest. I lived in St. Louis for a few years."

"Well, welcome to your new home." She reached under the counter, pulled up a menu, and set it in front of me. "I know what Jason's havin'. Take a gander."

I put on a big smile. "If you're cooking, I'll leave it up to you."

Myrna straightened up. Waved my comment aside. "Honey, I don't cook. That's for Joe, my husband." She looked over the crowded restaurant. "You two still here after it slows down, he'll come out and eat a pie with you."

A girlish voice squeezed out of the swinging door. "Myrna, I'm sorry. We got a rush job. It just..." She was tying an apron around her waist. When she looked up, we were staring at each other. We had just done business together.

It was the girl from the photo shop!

"Hey, Sally Ann. You called and I 'preciate it. Gave Brenda a little extra time. Whyn't you start with these guys? I'll go tell Bren she can hit the road."

"Usual for me, Sally Ann." Glen stood up. "Gonna go wash my hands, Ez. Be right back." He took a step away. "Oh, the chicken fried chicken is killer."

Myrna went off to find the other waitress. Sally Ann just stood there. A drop of sweat trailed down my side. I had to think of something. She didn't know we weren't friends. We were here together. I could build on that.

"Hi, Sally Ann. I'm Ezra. But you know that. You get around, huh?"

"Have to," she said. "Only way I can afford college is to work two jobs."

"About the photos," I began. "I'm putting together a surprise gift for Jason. So if we can keep our business to ourselves..."

"No worries, Ezra."

"Oh, good. See, he and I just met and I thought a gift like this would be a great way to break in a new friendship."

She nodded slowly. She looked over my shoulder and said, "Here he comes." Sally Ann zipped her fingers across closed lips.

"Thanks," I mouthed.

Glen's hand on my shoulder. "So, what's it gonna be?"

"I'm going with the chicken fried chicken."

Sally Ann raised her order pad and started writing.

"You won't be disappointed. Mashed potatoes?"

"Of course. And some black-eyed peas."

Sally Ann looked up at me. "Anything to drink?"

"Iced tea." I winked at her. "Just a little less sweet than you." Her cheeks flamed red. She finished writing and headed for the kitchen.

Glen laughed. "Ezra. Are you flirting with Sally Ann?"

I shrugged. Looked up at his smiling face. "You wanna split some catfish strips?"


Glen dropped me off in front of my house.

"That was fun, Ezra. Thanks again for getting me home last night."

*Glen Dower had fun with me. Me!* "You're welcome," I said.

Why did I feel I had to invite him in for a drink? It's not a date, what we were doing. Did I want to tempt Fate? Bring about my downfall? If he came up, he'd see my books. *His* books. He'd know I know. Then he'd be gone. Forever.

"I'd invite you in for a drink, Jason." Checked my watch. "Catch the last of the game, but the place is a mess. And I got to work early tomorrow."

"I'm not big on sports anyway. Some other time. G'night."

"Night."

I stood and watched him drive away. Walked into my house, counted to thirty, and looked back outside. The street was deserted. Should I go upstairs? Get my camera? There was no way I'd get a better shot than I already had. It took me almost an hour to make up my mind.

I went to my car. Got in and turned the key. I wouldn't stay long, and I'd use the car. No scooter to load and unload. It was dark and most folks would be home. I still had the *Gone For Gas* sign in the trunk. I'd put the hood up, too. That should be enough, and it'd be quicker getting home, and that meant more sleep for Ezra.

# CHAPTER THIRTY-ONE

I had been pretty good about my clandestine trail. It wouldn't be obvious to anyone who happened to be walking these woods. I could only hike it one foot in front of the other. If someone had chanced upon it they'd think it was made by an animal. A small deer, perhaps. Nothing as big as a human being. Well, not as wide. As lumbering. Although, that could be a bear. So either way I was pretty safe. I wore flat-soled shoes. Nothing with any identifiable tread, and every time I left, I remembered to kick some leaves around. Cover whatever marks I did leave. I was thinking about getting a branch and dragging it over the area, like the Indians—Native Americans—used to do. But I kept my trail so compact I'd just end up dragging it behind me, or walking backwards, and drawing a straight line. Then what? What if I put the branch in my car and got stopped by the police for some reason? How would I explain that?

"What's this?"
  "It's a branch, Officer."
  "I can see that, sir. Why do you have it?"
  "I work for the post office."
  "And this is…?"
  "My local branch."
  "Sir?"

"I use it to cover my footprints, Officer, after I finish spying on a famous author. Watching him write. Would you like to see some photos I've taken of him?"

So I just used my feet to hide any indications that I'd been there.

But this night gave me pause. I had stopped my car well short of my entrance, the headlights just touching it. And it looked like an opening. Maybe I had gone in there one too many times. Granted, I knew what I was looking for. I don't think anyone else would notice it, but I needed to change it. Add some foliage or something.

I put my *Gone For Gas* sign on the dashboard. I didn't put the flashers on. Coming back to a dead battery would not be a good thing. Locked doors and reflective tape on the bumpers would have to be enough.

I followed the small penlight beam, holding it straight down. I'd build up the entrance on my way out. Right now I just wanted to see if Glen was working. We had had a good conversation at dinner; maybe it had triggered the creative urge, jumpstarted an idea. But, when I got to my usual spot by the tree, the house was entirely dark.

This was not his normal routine. Glen never turned in before eleven. Sometimes I could hear the news show theme music when he left the windows open. News anchors' voices. A late movie. But tonight, nothing.

He hadn't seemed that tired to me. Well, win some, lose some. At least I'd get a bit more sleep tonight.

I went back to the trail opening. As quietly as I could, I pulled fallen branches over the opening I had created. I was looking for a new exit to get to my car when I heard a motor. Wheels kissing the road. I killed the penlight. Froze.

A set of bright headlights probed the woods. Seeped into dark crevices, stirring the nocturnal creatures. I heard the muffled wings of an owl, its silhouette black against the night sky. A squeal of brakes. A car sliding on the gravel drive.

Glen had gone out again and was just coming home. The light retreated, arcing as he turned into the garage.

Why do sounds seem to carry farther in the night than in the day? Obviously, there are fewer sounds competing with them. Even out here, though, they seemed to ring much clearer. In the daylight hours, I would hear Glen's car door shut, but it'd be a dull *thunk*. Now it was a solid *chunk*. The garage door screeched as it made its trajectory downward, louder than that owl ever could. The garage door muffled any other sounds I might have heard.

But a light came on in the kitchen. Glen walked through. A moment later there was light in the basement. Well, as much as there could be. The windows seemed to be some dark opaque glass. At least from the outside. I never would have noticed the difference in the daylight.

There he was again in the kitchen. Without a shirt. The window was high. Above the sink. I couldn't tell if he had totally disrobed or not.

What was he doing?

I didn't have to wait long. He came back through the kitchen with a large green plastic laundry hamper in his arms. He was doing laundry. At this hour?

Great. When I was a successful writer I'd still have to do laundry. Nah. I'd drop it off. Let somebody else do it. Pay by the pound.

"Good night, Glen." I mouthed the words. Softly.

Then followed my penlight back to the car.

\* \* \*

I was going to go home and go to bed until I drove by Paulie's and saw a small silver car parked outside. It looked like the same one from last night, but...What were the odds there'd be two of those vehicles around here? Curiosity got the best of me. I rolled slowly by, looking for a place to park. Any other night would be no problem, but there must be something special tonight, every spot was taken.

I parked in front of my building and walked the five minutes back to the bar. Two cars were pulling out, right in front. A line from *Blues By The Case* popped into my head. Glen had pulled it out of a real blues song. Credited the writer in the acknowledgements.

"If it wasn't for bad luck, I wouldn't have no luck at all."

Half a dozen men poured out of Paulie's door, smelling of beer and testosterone. The last guy was sober enough to hold the door for me.

"Thanks."

"Welcome."

The place was packed. Darts night. League play. A couple teams were still at it. Everybody else standing around. Drinking. Laughing. Reliving the evening. Lots of men and women. But I didn't see the driver of the silver car. I did see a seat at the bar and claimed it.

"Hey, Ez."

"Orlando. Nice crowd."

"You missed the fireworks."

I looked around. Everything looked normal. As normal as Darts Night could.

"Points at ten paces?"

"Nah." He tossed a coaster in front of me and placed a pint on top of it.

"Thanks."

"Man/Woman stuff," he said. "You know the guy."

"Yeah?"

"Gave him a ride home last night."

*Glen?*

"He still here?"

Orlando shook his head. "A couple of the guys took him outside and threw him against his car."

"What happened?"

"He had a few quick hits like last night. Then he just sat there and watched the league. The same woman comes in, and they talk. She orders coffee and tries to get him to have some, but he has a couple more drinks. Last night? Where he was kind of mellow? Tonight he gets loud and grabs her arm. Tries to take her outside."

"She still here?"

Orlando jerked his head toward the bathrooms.

"Took a half hour for her to calm down. Then *she* had a couple. Been in there awhile."

Orlando moved down the bar. Freshened up a couple drinks. I kept a watch in the mirror and sipped at my draft. I had just ordered a second round when the bathroom door opened. It was Her: the owner of the silver sports car. She came over to the bar. Her makeup had been retouched, but her eyes were rosy red. Alcohol and tears will do that. She leaned across the bar to put a folded bill in Orlando's shirt pocket. He backed up a step.

"No. Not necessary."

"Thank you." She tossed the bill on the bar anyway.

She straightened up. Adjusted her bag on her shoulder.

"He shouldn't be drinking, Landy," she said. "When he comes in again, tell him so."

I had to get into the conversation. Talk to this woman. She knew things about Glen. I hoped Orlando would play along.

"You guys talking about Jason? Jason Firth?"

She looked at me like I was some slug that had just crawled up onto the barstool.

"What's it to you?"

Orlando helped me out.

"Ezra gave him a ride home last night."

"Oh." The ice didn't melt much. "How was he?"

"Quiet. A little sullen."

"You were lucky. He can be a real bastard."

"I didn't see that side of him. You see that, Orlando?"

"Not until tonight."

She was going to say something, but she held her tongue just a bit too long. I drew blood for the boys' team.

"Maybe it's got something to do with you."

She didn't take the bait. Just nodded.

"Yeah. Could be me. Or the alcohol. Depression. Self-esteem. Pick your poison." She tossed the bill on the bar. "Good night."

Orlando and I watched her walk out the door. It was as if all the energy in the room went with her. I raised my glass. Toasted her leaving.

"You should pay her to sit at the bar during a heat wave, Orlando. She'd save you a fortune in air conditioning."

He picked up the bill she had thrown on the bar, put it in the tips jar, and then moved a towel over the bar in ever widening circles.

"She's all right, but you didn't see Jason, Ezra. I thought his arteries were gonna pop."

So Glen had a temper. Maybe it comes with being an artist. He invested so much of himself in his work. Writing. Honing. Rewriting. And every character has to be different. In manner. Speech. Attitude. Emotion. It's got to take a toll. He depleted himself creating these characters. Giving them various aspects of his personality.

Who provided for him? Who filled his empty moments? There was no one close by for him that I knew of. No one I'd seen. That woman. And me. And Rosa. That was basically it around here. And I was with him more than she was. He just didn't know it. I wanted to be with him. She didn't. But it seemed he wanted something more from her.

It was like some high school soap opera.

I wondered if Orlando knew her name? Where she lived? I needed to know more about her and Glen. Maybe she'd talk to me. How could I melt her icy façade enough to get myself in? So she'd trust me enough to talk about Glen.

Glen could be my way in. She cared about him. That was obvious. No one gets that upset unless they love the other person. What if she knew I cared about him, too? Maybe she'd teach me what she knew. So I could help him.

I wondered if she's a good kisser. Sometimes the cold ones are the hottest. At least in Glen's books. Is she the basis for any of his women? I should find that out. But how? Does she even know he's not Jason Firth?

"Her name's Darla," Orlando told me after a while.

I wanted to know more, but Orlando was too smart for me to push it.

"She works at the hospital," he added. "I think she's a nurse or something." He pointed at my near-empty pint glass. "You want another?"

"Why not?"

# CHAPTER THIRTY-TWO

I needed to find her. *Darla.*

"Maine Presbyterian Hospital. Hold, please."

I was on hold so long I could recite the commercial they played on a loop for the hospital. Who knew so many words ended with—oscopy?

"Thank you for holding. How may I direct your call?"

"Darla, please."

"Patient or employee?"

"Employee."

"Do you have a last name, sir?"

"No. Just Darla."

"I need a last name. Sorry, sir."


I checked the hospital's website. Called each department as listed. How long could this take? It's not a common name. Darla.

"Oncology." *Nope.*

"Renal." *Nada.*

"Labor and Delivery." *Zilch.*

"ICU." *Zero.*

"Cardiac." *Hey!*

"Darla, please."

"The doctor or the nurse?"

What are the odds? Two Darlas in the same department?

"Nurse."

"Hold, please."

"...for your baby. Neonatal care is so important. And here at..."

"This is Darla. How may I help you? Hello?"

I hung up. I knew right away it wasn't her voice. So she wasn't the nurse. She was the doctor. That would help explain her gruffness. Her condescension among the common folk. Orlando. Me.

And it also would explain that car. A nurse couldn't afford a machine like that.

Why would a doctor even go to Paulie's? It's strictly blue-collar. There were a couple places closer to the hospital that were more upscale.

It had to be for Glen. Had he called her?

But she had walked out on him the night before. Why would she come back? Subject herself to more abuse? Some people are like that. But not her. I could see that. She wouldn't even put up with my barbs. She just left.


I supposed I could go to the Internet café and find out the information I needed. Keep it off my own computer's search history.

I could just imagine what would come up if I typed "Darla?"

Everything from fictional characters to tennis players and anything in between. I needed to make contact with this doctor, not get sidetracked for an hour or two by photos of some blond in a short white skirt.

Then it hit me. A town this size, she'd have to have a private practice, too.

Doctors. Doctors. Doctors.

See Physicians.

Found it. Physicians. Divided into specialties.

Cardiac.

And there she was. The only woman among three men.

Dr. Darla Anderson.

I made an appointment for after work. The postal uniform would be the right signal to send. Professional. Concerned. Much better than showing up in jeans and a T-shirt.

Glen's house was somnolent as I finished my route. I slipped some junk mail in the box. No bills. I had noticed that. He got very few bills. Normal ones. Phone. Utilities. Taxes. Occasionally, a credit card. Was he doing well enough to have an accountant? How did that work? I know from my reading that agents get the check first. Take their fifteen percent and send the rest to the writer. Can you have them pay your bills, too? Like a Christmas Club? Slot the money to different accounts. They get paid. The writer doesn't worry.

Unless there's no money in the account. Then it's Debt City.

Does Glen handle his own money? Are there checks in the envelopes from his agent? How big are they?

Maybe he pays all the bills online.

"I know you." The ice shifted as she closed the examining room door and took my chart off the counter. Checked my name. "Mr. Lockert."

"Doctor."

She looked over my information.

"Why me?"

I stood up. Took my shirt off the chair where I had hung it. The postal emblem prominently displayed.

"I didn't know it was you. Sorry if this is awkward. It is for me, too." I put an arm through a sleeve. Another. "I'll go." Worked the buttons. She was quiet. Studying me. Come on, this is where your professionalism kicks in. I'm just another beating heart.

Nameless. Faceless.

"Sit down, Mr. Lockert."


She spent maybe five minutes with me. Never mentioned Glen. Jason. She asked questions about my heart. My routine. Did I smoke? Drink? She knew the answer to that. Amended it. Did I drink to excess? *Hell, I'd drink to anything.* Family history. Stroke? High blood pressure? Eating habits. Cholesterol.

She stood up.

"Wait here."

I was trying to figure out how to turn the conversation around to Glen when the door opened. It wasn't her. It was some big guy with bulging muscles. He pulled the leg extension out of the bed-like apparatus. Patted it.

"Lie down."

He attached things to me using some gelatin substance.

And that was just the start. They stuck needles in me. Made me walk a treadmill. I was there for two hours.

I never saw Dr. Anderson again.

That day.


I might have been weaning myself from Glen. How much more could I learn standing in the woods watching a silent figure work? There were other places to gain knowledge. Footnotes. Oral history. Like tracing a blues song back to its creator. You start with the rock band. Most people stop there, but if you desire more information you explore. Learn to read the record label. The songwriter credit. Then you find that songwriter and hear the way the original sounds. That leads you off in sometimes wondrous directions. A voyage of a discovery which could affect your entire life.

Come to think of it, I had learned that from Glen, also. In a couple of ways. The acknowledgements and thank yous in his novels.


I found no home listing for Dr. Darla Anderson. Office only. Both address and phone. It occurred to me she might live in the building that houses her office. It's an old Victorian type house. Close to the hospital. It made sense. Convenient. No long commute. There was even off-street parking. The side yard had been paved over. Gated. Electronic entrance. Parking for tenants of the building only, according to the sign. She would save a small fortune in gas and wear and tear on her car.

She could just walk from home to office to hospital and back.


The home idea didn't pan out. There were six units in the building. All were medical. It said so right on the brass plaque beside the door. A quick walk through the building confirmed it.


I felt like I was in a movie, following the silver car as it pulled out of the hospital's parking lot. I stayed back far enough not lose her. The woods were easier. There were all kinds of things to hide behind. Trees. Bushes. I couldn't hide behind things here on the road. If I used a large truck or bus as cover, I had a good chance of losing her. I had to keep her in sight.

But I had to observe my surroundings, too. I almost hit someone crossing the street because I was looking two blocks ahead. It's so much easier in the movies. When the prey is unaware they're being followed, the good guys figure out how to do it.


She lived on a lake. About a half-hour drive from her office and the hospital. It was an upper middle-class neighborhood. Large lots. Big houses. All fairly new. It was landscaped, but it was such a new community the trees they'd planted didn't offer a lot of cover.

Why didn't they just leave the old forest? Build the homes amongst the trees? They had leveled the natural landscape and started from flat land. Maybe it had something to do with the golf course. Maybe politics. I thought people in Maine were supposed to be more concerned with ecology, but I guessed it was just like Ohio or any other state. It's who you know. Who you grease. I was sure this place would look good in twenty or thirty years, but right now it was a blemish on the face of the earth.

There were not a lot of places to hide. I had more girth than most of the trees here. There were houses across the street. Next door. Lots of eyes.

I found a side street. If I parked close to the intersection, I could watch her house. And I was on the side of another house with a stockade fence. She could have seen me sitting here from her top floor, but not from yard level.

It was the best I could do.


She was at home. I had followed her all the way to her house. Saw her point her remote at the garage door. Let it open. Drive in.

Now I just sat.

And waited.


This was worse than Glen's. I couldn't see anything. I got out and walked around. Smiled at a couple of ladies pushing strollers. Just another guy in the neighborhood.

I even thought about walking by Dr. Anderson's house, but that could be too dangerous. She might see me, and that would be the end of that doctor/patient relationship and the start of a more contentious one.

I went back to my car and watched.

\* \* \*

I could have pretended to be the postman here. Use my mail cart. Wear my uniform. It was kind of a mask. People see the uniform, they go about their business. Pay no attention to the one wearing it. *Or would they?*

No uniform then. No mail cart.

I didn't need to observe her. I needed to talk to her. I didn't care about her life except for where it intersected with Glen's. She had information. That's all.

How should I approach her?

The garage door was going up again. Maybe she was going to the store. I could bump into her in the aisle. Then what? I hadn't thought this through.

A little dog was running out of her garage. She was following, using one of those extending leashes. She was turning my way. She knew I didn't live around here. She had my address on the forms I filled out at her office.

I got out of there.


"Two scoops, please. Chocolate and peanut butter. In a cup."

I took my treat outside to the picnic table at the shoreline of the same lake Dr. Anderson lives on. This was a possibility. After they closed, if I sat on the grass, the picnic table would hide me.

I looked around. Exterior lights. I wondered what time they closed. Did they leave the lights on? Was there a place close by I could leave my car?

I would need binoculars.

The ice cream was good.


Closer to home, I went back to the place I'd bought my netting.

"May I help you, sir?" A different salesman.

"Yeah, I'm new to the area. Moved from the city."

"Bangor?"

"Cincinnati."

"Ah. The *big* city."

We laughed. "I'm finding I love it here," I said. "Much more than I thought I would. I'm relaxing. I'm enjoying my life again."

"Good. We think it's got lots of plusses. What can I help you with?"

"I was thinking about getting into birding. I was wondering about binoculars."

"We've got just the thing. I'm a birder myself."

Birding is not an inexpensive hobby. Some of those binoculars cost more than a used car. There's proper clothing. Almost like army camouflage. There's furniture. You can buy a blind. Like duck hunters use.

"Our reason is much more humane, though," the guy felt the urge to tell me.

"This is amazing," I said. "I had no idea." How do I deflate this guy's vision of a huge sale? "But I'm just getting started. Is there a...an entry-level pair of binoculars?"

The ice cream store closed at ten. By ten-thirty all the garbage had been bagged. Doors were locked. Employees gone. But the lights were still on. At eleven, the lights over the picnic tables along the lake went out. The lights in front of the store stayed on.

I pulled my car into the lot. Drove around to the back of the shop and pulled the car up close to the wall. No one would see it from the street.

One thing about night up here: It was dark. I know that sounds obvious, but it was darker than I remembered it being in Cincinnati. Pinpricks of light were strung out over private docks. Lights burned in houses. Other than that, I could have been hiding in some closet somewhere.

\* \* \*

I was a shadow among shadows, dressed all in black. I spread my dark green blanket-size tarp on the ground, a picnic table at my back to make it harder to see me, and lay down. Brought the binoculars to my eyes. Aimed where I thought Dr. Anderson's house would be. Focused.

A couple was climbing into a hot tub. One of them must have said something hysterical; I could hear their cachinnation from across the lake.

Somewhere a door slammed.

A motor roared to life. Twin spots of color sped across the lake. The motor died. The boat bobbed. Snatches of conversation.

"This is the life."

"What a night."

Some splashing.

"I got one already. Get the net."

"Whooo-hooo! That's a beauty." And it was. I had the fishermen in my sights. One was shining a light on the fish. It shook. Shivered. A flash of silver.

"Breakfast."

I played with the focus and aimed back in the direction of Dr. Anderson's house. This time I got it right—she was on the back deck, reading a book. A glass of wine on the table.

Why hadn't I thought about binoculars for Glen's place? These get much closer than the camera lens. I'd be able to read his smallest frown. An inquisitive raising of an eyebrow.

Doesn't Dr. Anderson sleep? It was going on midnight. I'd have to leave soon. I needed to sleep. At least a couple hours.

# CHAPTER THIRTY-THREE

Glen was leaning against the fence when I trekked over the hill.

"Hey, Ezra," He tilted his head. "You all right?"

"Just tired. Didn't get much sleep last night."

"I slept like a baby. I've decided to alter my diet. No red meats. Cutting out caffeine. Alcohol. Lots of vegetables. You should try it. That stuff will kill you."

"Vegetables?"

He laughed. "The rest of it. I'm not so young anymore. Can't live forever. I gotta take care of the old ticker, maybe postpone the end."

"So you can keep paying these?"

I handed him his mail. There was a utility bill. A phone bill.

"Ah, the bearer of bad tidings."

"Just don't kill the messenger."

"Couldn't do that. You may bring bad news, Ezra, but it's always a pleasure to see you."

"Thanks, Jason. You, too. Take care."

I walked back down the hill, trying not to let my grin inform my feet.


I drove by Dr. Anderson's office after work. Her car was not in the lot. I stood outside her door. It was locked. The sign on the door said she only kept office hours three days a week.

And by appointment.

Some people had all the luck. I wondered what her staff did the other four days.


I'd had enough for a while. Tonight would be just for me. It had to be. I was running out of clean clothes. Laundry was a necessity. Then a nice hot bath. Just soak. I thought about the couple climbing into the hot tub. Their laughter rolling across the lake.

I almost fell asleep in the tub. That would be good. I'd make the local weekly.

*Writer Drowns In Bath.*

I put on a pair of jeans and padded around the apartment. Antsy. I had to do something.

I fixed myself a chicken breast and some broccoli. Had water with the meal. Maybe Glen was right. Eat right, live longer.

You are what you eat.


I awoke before my alarm went off. My subconscious had dredged up a concern. Popped it up right into the conscious. Loose ends. Loose ends. The phrase lay there. Bobbing up and down like a floater, a bloated body pulled from the river or lake. A drowning victim. I needed to bring this one to shore. Turn it over. See its face.

Loose ends. The phrase pushing against my skull. Trying to get out. What loose ends? *Think, Ezra.*

I lay there. The last few weeks of my life rewinding in my mind. I was missing something I needed to do. What do you do with loose ends?

You tie them up. Make them whole. A part of the fabric.

I was afraid of what had frayed.

The alarm rang harsh, like someone had snuck up beside me and shouted in my ear. It was something to do with Jason. Glen. I needed to do something. To make those loose ends meet.

* * *

It came to me in the shower. Dr. Anderson. But what could she say to Glen?

*"You shouldn't go drinking with that postman."*

From what she had said so far, he shouldn't go drinking with anyone. And Orlando had backed her up. She couldn't say squat about me. She didn't know I was watching him. Or her.

But it wasn't just her. My subconscious had kept going. Worrying over the problem. And, while I was sidetracked down the wrong road, it had delivered again. Tapped me on the shoulder. Pointed me in the right direction.


"I don't know how I got on this list, Ezra. But I never ordered any of this."

"That's why it's called junk mail, Rosa." I was slipping. She never should have seen these things. "You don't have to order it. It just shows up. It's like spam."

"Spam? I ate Spam during the war. Still do." She waved her unwanted mail at me. "You can't eat this stuff."

You can't write this stuff, either. It just happens. Sad, in a way. Most of the time Rosa seems solid, but she's been getting these erratic patches.

"There's a place," I told her. "Let me give you an address. You write them. Tell them to take your name off their list. It may not stop all this, but it'll cut out a lot of it."

I made a mental note to renew my watchfulness and get rid of all the junk mail from Rosa's deliveries.

I considered telling Glen about my talk with Rosa. I probably could have, but how? I wanted to present it to him as a writer. An example of humor growing out of the character, not just as a joke. I knew he'd get it right away, but I didn't think he would want to talk about it. It might give away too much. Open a door he doesn't want to open to me. Not yet.

I tucked it away. It could always happen later. After he was more comfortable with me. After he told me his secret.

He was a writer. Just like me.


"Hey. Sally Ann? Right?"

"Yeah?"

"Ezra. We met at Myrna's."

"I remember you. Whatcha got for me?"

It was like I was outside my body. Suspended high over the strip mall. I saw the two of us in the little photo shop doing our business while the rest of the world drove by. Did their jobs. Ate their sandwiches. Whatever they were supposed to do. Needed to do. And I was here because there was something I needed to do. Enlarge.

"Size?" Sally Ann asked.

"Eight by ten."

"Finish?"

"As soon as you can."

She stopped writing. "No. What *kind* of finish. Matte or glossy?"

"Oh." I'm such an idiot. *Make her smile, Ezra. Say it out loud.* "I'm such an idiot."

What she gave me wasn't really a smile. It was more one of those teenage looks. *Like yeah, whatever.*

"Matte. I think matte looks good. More professional. What do you think?"

"Whatever. It's your choice."

She put a big X through the little square. Matte.

But didn't publishing houses use glossy for their author photos? And this one would be perfect if Glen ever did go back to using a picture.

"Tell you what, Sally Ann. How about one of each?"

"You sure?"

"Hey, he's my friend." I remembered my previous fabrication, so I added, "Remember, it's a surprise gift. So no telling and spare no expense."

I wasn't sure that registered. She just put an X through the other square. Glossy. Changed the top of the order form from one to two. Frowned.

"Something wrong?" I asked.

"I don't know if our enlargement guy will understand this." She reached up. Tucked some loose hair behind her ear. Set the eraser against her teeth. "Ah, got it." Brought the pencil down to the paper. *Customer needs 2 8x10's. One matte finish. One glossy finish.*

"That should do it, Ezra."

"Great. Remember, not a word."

She winked at me—*humor the old man*—as she put the negative into a protective sleeve. Dropped it into the envelope.

I mended the fray. Tied up the loose end. No way would Sally Ann tell Glen about a surprise Christmas present now.


I was almost home when I realized: What do I tell Sally Ann after the holidays? I know Glen will eat at Myrna's. Sally Ann has to wait on him sooner or later.

*Most lies have expiration dates.*


"Hey," the waitress said to The Author. "How'd you like your Christmas present?"

"What present is that?"

"You know. The one your friend gave you. That photo he took of you through your back window."


I decided to worry about that later. I could always come up with another lie. Maybe come up with a real photographic gift. Or blame it on her frantic teenage mind.

\* \* \*

The night before had actually been relaxing. Just doing personal stuff. I hadn't realized how full my life had become. How busy I'd become. I decided to do a repeat.

I ordered a pizza. So much for that low-cholesterol lifestyle. Watched some action movie. The guy at the store had told me it was good. Something blew up every ten minutes. You could almost set your watch to it. Fifteen minutes after it was over, I couldn't remember much about it at all.

Just that somebody probably got rich writing the thing.


I couldn't sleep. I kept playing it through in my mind. Ways to get closer to Dr. Anderson. And every one of them had logistical problems. She didn't strike me as the trusting type, and I needed her to trust me. As a mutual friend of Glen's, maybe she would open up. Confide in me. It would go no further. Almost like doctor-patient privilege, only in reverse.

But what difference would her opinion make? It may offer me a little more insight into Glen's relationships with women, but I could glean that from his novels. From the women he created. I didn't really *need* Dr. Darla. And maybe Glen would think I was trying to move in on his friends in an effort to get closer to him. He might have a negative reaction to that.

Shut me out entirely.

And every hour I spent trying to get closer to the doctor was one less hour I spent with Glen, learning my craft.

I felt my mind relax. It was that easy. No more traipsing around trying to get information from Dr. Anderson. Just let her go. I probably knew more about Glen than she did anyway.

I could feel sleep coming on. I drifted down with it. Softly falling. Reminding myself to reread Glen's women characters. Were they his feelings about women? Or were they just characters he created? Gave life to? Totally anathema to how he really felt?

Now there's a ten-dollar word. *Anathema*. Where did that come from? The loose wide-open range of the exhausted mind? It was a real writer's word, and it gave me a sleepy nod of recognition. A tip of the authorial nightcap.

I slept the sleep of a real writer.

# CHAPTER THIRTY-FOUR

"Hey, Ezra. We got the new issue of that photography magazine in."

I didn't need it, but appearances must be kept.

"Thanks, Tom. Make it a chicken burrito today."

Damn magazine cost me five bucks. Now I had to look at it.

I was sliding my card through the time clock when I realized what I should have said to Tom that would've saved me some money.

"Already got it. Thanks, though."

Next time I'll tell him I have a subscription. That'll shut him up.

The moon was full. It stalked me across the treetops, following along, keeping me company. It stopped when I did. Waited as I hid the scooter under the brush off the road. Hung behind as I eased through the woods. Looked over my shoulder.

Together, we watched Glen's house.

There was a light on in what I had come to refer to as the bedroom. The curtains glowed. I focused my new binoculars. I could see a dim shadow standing, then moving. I wondered if I could attach a camera to these? Take better pictures. Closer pictures.

Then the patio light came on, crawling out into the yard, illuminating the back of Glen's house. The door opened and Glen came out carrying a tripod. He sat down on the picnic table bench closest to the woods. Away from the house. I heard three clicks. Watched as his tripod legs descended, growing longer. He set it on the cement, spread the legs open wide. Then he got up and went back into the house.

I couldn't see what he was carrying when he came back out. He held it close to his body, wrapped in a towel. I realized what it was when he began to attach it to the tripod.

A telescope.

I felt a shiver of excitement course through me. This was weird. Here I was watching Glen through optical magnification. And he was doing the same. It had to be more than a coincidence, the parallels that ran through our lives. Would we converge somewhere over the horizon as parallel lines seem to do?

What was he watching?

*Me?*

No way. It was too dark. He didn't know I was here, but I hunkered down quietly, using my arboreal surroundings to my advantage. Holding the binoculars at my chest. Using my eyes. I had an okay view. Some branches, but nothing too obstructing.

Did I gasp when he turned the telescope and it pointed directly at me? But he wasn't looking in it. He had just set it randomly in this direction. He stood for a moment and stretched, a loud cross between a sigh and a yawn. Then he sat back down and put his eye to the telescope.

I froze. How would I explain this if he spotted me?

But the telescope rose up. And held. He played with the focus knob.

My traveling companion. He was spying on the moon. Observing the celestial orb as I was him. I had learned another unknown fact about Glen. He enjoyed astronomy, and I enjoyed watching his enjoyment. Sharing another moment. It was far removed from *spying*, what we were doing together. It was an expansion of our consciousness, giving us more touchstones—connections—for our creative endeavors. More wells from which to draw the water of our ideas.

The moon kept its eyes on both of us. Did it wonder what we were doing, or were there more interesting things going on elsewhere? Maybe it wasn't looking at us at all. It didn't know Glen was studying it, just as Glen didn't know I was studying him.

We both felt its pull in our blood and I was reminded of the roots of the word *lunatic.*

# CHAPTER THIRTY-FIVE

I was at the mall after work, still in uniform, walking through the New Non-Fiction aisle of the superstore on my way to Fiction to see what new stuff was out. Maybe get an idea for a story or a novel. Stop by the Reference section and check out the books about writing. Possibly treat myself to something nice between some covers.

"Ezra?"

It was Glen. *Be cool, Ezra.*

"Oh. Hey, Jason."

"What are you doing here?"

Here was a prose master. Someone who could turn a phrase and in a few words give you the total picture. An image of size and scope or script, a small detail that would add life and depth to a scene. And here I was in a bookstore, looking at books. And he asked what I'm doing. Was he having a brain fart or what?

"Trying to decide between the Jaguar or the Benz."

He frowned and then turned it into an embarrassed smile.

"Oh, yeah. Stupid of me. Kinda obvious, isn't it?"

I returned his smile. Maybe I could learn something. "What are you looking for?"

"Just browsing," he said. "Hoping something will leap out at me."

We were on the same page. Again.

"Me, too."

He reached out to the new poetry books across the aisle from non-fiction and plucked a slim volume from the shelf. Showed it to me.

"Ever read her?"

"No."

He handed me the book. "Can't go wrong."

*Adrift.* A book of poems by Margaret Reade.

I scanned the back cover blurbs. "Sounds interesting." Bad word choice and I must not have said it too enthusiastically.

"Sorry. Just a suggestion."

"No. Really. It does sound interesting."

I knew I was going to buy it just on Glen's recommendation. Maybe not with him standing there, and maybe not this night, but I made a note of the title. The author. Maybe poetry was one of the secrets to his prose.

He checked his watch.

"Look, I'm sorry. I'd love to stay and grab a coffee, but I'm running late."

"Next time," I said. "I've got to get home, anyway. Morning comes too early."

"Yeah. See ya."

He took another copy of *Adrift* from the shelf and got in a short line at the checkout. I put mine back on the shelf and looked at Glen.

He was looking at me.

I waved as I rounded a row of shelves heading for the exit. I cut it too close. Almost knocked down some woman with a walker who was looking at calendars.


It was good that Glen had seen me in the bookstore. It would have been hard to explain if he had seen me in the parking lot, removing my scooter from the trunk for a quick trip to the woods behind his house.

But he wasn't going home. He had an appointment. Unless

he was lying to me. So the scooter stayed in the trunk and I went into follow-that-car mode. I was getting excited, feeling the adrenaline pump. This was different. This was new.

I watched Glen leave the store, a small bag swinging from his hand. He got into his car and left the lot. I knew the first turn he could make was at least a mile down the road so I gave him a ten-second head start.

He didn't take the first turn, kept driving straight ahead. I stayed back several car lengths, enjoying the game. This would be easy until he entered town and hit all the lights on the main thoroughfare. If he thought he was being followed—but why would he be?—this was where he'd catch me, but I could always turn off and head home.

I didn't think he knew my car. Just to be safe, I slowed down. Hung back. He went through a yellow on the last light in town and turned right.

There was a No Right on Red sign. I stopped at the red light and watched his taillights disappearing. I didn't want to lose him. There was no oncoming traffic. No cop cars in sight. I signaled, made the turn, and I was back on the chase, my foot automatically pushing the gas. Picking up speed. No car had come between us. Those had to be his lights up ahead. You did it, Ezra. It's okay. Ease up now. Drop back a bit. Let him lead.

Lights began appearing from a series of buildings. The hospital.

I knew where he was going.


It was too early to take up my place behind the drive-in. They didn't close until ten. What if she didn't let him in? They didn't appear to be on the best of terms. I had to continue my pursuit and get a hiding spot as close as I could to where he ended his journey.

His signal was flashing. He was turning.

He stopped and opened his door. What was he doing? What

was I doing? I couldn't drive by. He'd see me. There was no reason I should be in this area at this time.

I threw my signal on in the opposite direction. Turned into the long driveway of an older house outside the new subdivision.

I almost ran over a teenaged kid who was sweeping the asphalt. He squinted at me.

"Who is it?" he asked.

"I'm sorry to bother you. I'm lost."

"Where do you want to go?"

"I can't remember the name. It's an ice cream place. Near the lake."

"Curt's Creamery?"

"That's it. Am I far from it?"

"No. Take a left out of the drive. At the first light make a right. Follow that road around the lake. You can't miss it."

"Thank you."

"Welcome. Better hurry, though. They're probably gettin' ready to close."

I waved to the teen as I backed out of the driveway. I nosed out onto the highway and looked right. Glen's car was gone. Screw the directions. I turned right. Let the kid think I'd made a mistake.

I killed the lights before I turned onto Dr. Anderson's street. I lifted my foot from the gas and let the car carry itself, rolling into a spot a few houses down. The front porch light burned. Glen's car was in the driveway.

I wanted to get out. Go around to the side of the house. Maybe I could see or hear something, but the houses were too close together. All I needed was some nosey neighbor calling the cops or yelling at me, getting Glen to the door in time to see me jump into my car and peel out.

\* \* \*

```
"You following me?" The Author asked.
  "No."
  "What? You're stalking my friend then?"
  "No."
  "Or are you stalking me?"
  I couldn't speak.
  "Do we need to have a talk with the police?"
```

I eased my foot down and turned the wheel. The car moved slowly off the curb, away from the house.

I had another cup of peanut butter and chocolate ice cream. A red-haired boy with some pale skin peeking out from behind a cascade of freckles was dragging a trashcan.

"We're closin' up, sir."

"Okay if I finish my cup?"

"Curt doesn't want anyone stayin' after we leave."

I stood up. Headed for my car.

"Sorry, mister."

I thought about saying, "Tell Curt he's an asshole," but didn't want to be remembered as that guy. I dropped my cup at the kid's feet. Crunched over the gravel. Got into my car and drove away. I was not in a good mood.

I was about a mile down the road, waiting on a side street, the binoculars on the seat beside me. About a quarter before eleven I pulled out and went back to Curt's. Did a slow drive by. Redhead was gone.

I took my spot in the back and waited to get out until the spotlights on the picnic tables went off. Then I opened the trunk and took out my tarp. I closed the trunk enough to extinguish the light, but not enough so it closed completely, just in case I needed to make a fast exit. It's funny how your mind goes into escape mode once it's been trained that way.

I lay down on the tarp, hidden by the picnic table, and raised my binoculars.



If I was reading the body language correctly, there was tension on the back deck. Dr. Anderson was not relaxing in the chaise lounge as she had done the other night. She was sitting across from Glen, a round metal table between them, an unopened umbrella sprouting from its middle.

I wished for my camera, but even the longer lens would only render this as two people. A splash of light surrounded by darkness. Even blown up it would be difficult to tell what it was. Too grainy. I could call it *Two People In A Dark Storm*, the grain like ebony raindrops.

Glen was leaning forward, talking. I strained to hear him, but the sound of a hushed voice doesn't travel over water as well as a louder one does. And, while he looked intense, he was in control, not angry. Almost...pleading? Was he apologizing?

Now Dr. Anderson was leaning in, lifting something off the table. A book I hadn't noticed. She began to read. Glen relaxed, leaned back in his chair. His legs straight out, arms dangling at his side. She was reading to him. I couldn't tell for sure, but it looked like she was reading to him. He was letting her voice and the words wash over him. It had to be the book he'd bought earlier in the bookstore—the book he'd showed me.

*Can't go wrong.*

But there was more to it. This was something between them. An act of intimacy. A ritual. At this moment these two people were bonded, as close as any two people could be.

Dr. Anderson closed the book. Set it on the table and stood up. Glen watched her walk to the door. Go inside.

*GO AFTER HER!* I wanted to scream it across the lake. *"GO AFTER HER!"*

But he didn't. Not right away.

He sat on the deck another half hour, just staring into the night. Then he got up and went inside. The deck lights went out.

I was up and scrambling, the binoculars swinging around my neck. I gathered the tarp into an armload. Hurried it back into the trunk of the car.

I had to get out of here and beat Glen back to his house.

After what I had just seen, he had to be inspired. He would write until sunup, and I was going to stay right there with him. Studying. Absorbing. Learning.

But he never came home. I stayed until the sky started to glow. Until the woods turned pre-dawn blue. Then I went home.

Had he stayed at her house? Slept with her? There was an intimacy. It was palpable, even across the lake. But she had gone into the house at least thirty minutes before him. And it was late. She was probably already asleep when he went in and closed the door. Shut off the light. Had he awakened her? Or had he lain down softly on the bed beside her so as not to interrupt her sleep, but to continue to maintain the closeness.

Or did he sleep on the sofa? In a second bedroom?

Maybe he didn't sleep at all. Maybe he was so inspired he sat at her dining room table and wrote through the night.

And I had missed it.

Like I've said, one of the best things about being a postal carrier is that if you finish your route before your shift is over, the time is yours. You just have to be back at the shop at the scheduled end of your shift to card out. And I was.

I had hurried through the day, including my stop at Glen's, finishing in just under four hours. A personal best.

And the three-hour nap at my apartment? Paid for by your tax dollars. Thanks.

I went over to the bookstore after clocking out and found the book Glen had shown me the night before. *Adrift* by Margaret Reade. I took it to an overstuffed chair and sat down.

There are a couple of things I always do whenever I open a book. One is to check out the dedication, so when I write my novel I'll have an idea of how to go about dedicating it, and to whom. The early books in an author's career are usually earmarked for parents, children, old friends, husbands and wives. If the writer turns out a long list of novels, the dedication is usually someone who's been listed earlier on the acknowledgements page.

And that's the second thing I studied. The acknowledgements page. It often lists the more important people in the writing process. Those who have read the manuscript in varying stages. The agent. The editor. The publisher. A writing group. People who have helped shape or contributed ideas to the finished work. A writing magazine suggested studying this page when you wanted to find an agent for your book. You pick an author whose style and content are similar to yours, find that author's agent (usually listed on the acknowledgements page), and send them a query letter about your own novel. You tell the agent how much you enjoy their client's work, and explain that since your work is reminiscent (yet totally original) of that author, perhaps they would like to read your book, and, if they like it, represent you.

But the dedication stopped me cold.

*To the Good Doctor.*

Another title from Glen's book of short stories. Was Margaret Reade a fan of Glen's? Her name meant nothing to me. I didn't recall it from any thank you in Glen's novels. I'd have to check when I got home just to be sure.

I turned to the inside back cover, where the author's photo usually rode atop a short bio.

*Margaret Reade caught her publisher's attention with two self-published chapbooks. She prefers to stay out of the public's eye, saying she would rather observe than be observed. She feels recognition may hinder her ability to render the truth of her poetry, much of which lies in "the telling detail" that numerous critics, other writers, and her readers find so stunning. Miss Reade enjoys a simple existence in the Pacific Northwest, where she is carefully observing Life in preparation for her next book of poems.*

There was no author photo. But that bio came across as a bit pretentious.

I flipped to the front of the book and looked through the acknowledgements. Something unusual caught my eye: a bunch of initials. As if Margaret didn't want to reveal her sources. Her influences. Maybe she thought someone would link them to her if she used the entire name. Compromise her anonymity.

But below the dedication was the link—the connection—between Margaret and Glen.

*And to Al Field, whose open mind sees outside the box, a special thanks to you.*

They shared the same agent. They had to know each other. And they both valued their privacy so there would be no mail with giveaway postmarks or return addresses.

If they talked at all, it would be by telephone or email.

I returned to the acknowledgements and ran down the list of initials. They were alphabetical, and they were both there. GD. And, right behind it, separated by a coma, JF.

I got up from the chair and went back to the poetry section.

Margaret Reade had written only one other book of poetry. I pulled it from the shelf without opening it. Took both books to the cashier.

Making the connection between Glen and Margaret had me jazzed. I stopped by the liquor store and bought a bottle of champagne to celebrate. Hit the supermarket next. Tossed the ingredients for what people in Maine call American Chop Suey into my cart. In the Midwest it's known as Johnny Marzetti— closer to Italian than Asian. Macaroni, ground beef, green peppers, onions. All held together by tomato sauce. In Maine they sprinkle grated Parmesan cheese over it. I prefer to bake it with the cheese inside. Mozzarella. Let it bind everything together. And I add fresh sweet peas.

It's filling. It's fattening. And it's delicious.

I left the casserole dish soaking in the sink. Emptied two trays of ice into a bucket, and rotated in the half bottle of champagne I had left. Carried it and a flute into the "living room" and set it down on the coffee table next to Margaret Reade's two slim volumes of poetry. I filled the glass, sat down, and picked up *Adrift*, her first book, the one Glen had recommended. The page with the poem titles had nothing that referred to *The Good Doctor*.

I started reading from the beginning. The poems were good. Almost photographic in their rendering, but what Margaret chose to enlighten was something that would not be easily noticed in a photograph. A small detail behind the main subject. A scar on a thumb. A small plant struggling for survival in the shadow of a giant tree. The crack in a mirror running across the reflection of a lover's chest. They were simple. Easy to understand. Yet revealingly intimate.

The other volume, the first book, was *At Anchor* and I had purchased a first edition. Two years old. It must not have sold through the initial printing. How many books were in a poetry print run? What are the criteria for a best-selling poetry book? I would guess not as many copies as even a mid-list fiction writer might sell. Did Glen and Margaret discuss their sales? Or lack thereof? Did they accept it, or rage against the stupidity of book buyers? Were they jealous of lesser authors who sold more books?

Some of the same initials were listed. Again, GD. Only now AF. Before JF. I had never seen a dedication such as this. It wasn't to a person, it was...

*To Solitude,*
*The giver of many gifts.*

A real pick-me-up, right? But it turned out that almost every poem was positive. Ripe with the fruit of love. Stunning depictions of the wilderness used as a backdrop for an affair played out across the pages in a not-so-modern Garden of Eden. I noticed a great similarity between Maine and the Pacific Northwest. Not many people know Maine as mountainous. Certainly not as majestic as the Cascades, but the western side of Maine ripples with a continuation of New Hampshire's White Mountains, the Oxford Hills, and the Mahoosuc Range, which contains some of the roughest going to be found on the Appalachian Trail.

And it was in the first book where I found the poem that gave life to the next book's dedication. The last poem in the book. Almost an introduction to the next book.

*The Good Doctor.*

*Hands heal by touch alone*
*Soft, searching*

*Finding Pain.*
*Warm breath cools the space*
*Open, giving*
*Easing pain.*

*The good doctor stops.*
*House calls may cost too much*
*When love becomes*
*A beggar's crutch.*

*Tissue scars.*
*Sense memory remains.*
*In and out*
*Of picture frames.*
*He walks the woods*
*To ease his grief*
*Each coral step*
*A cutting reef*

*She*
*Encased in silver*
*Just out of*
*Reach.*

*A backwards glance.*
*A simple nod.*
*A key is turned.*
*Where is God?*

It's a punch to the gut. The end of Eden. There is nothing more, and I wanted more. Even though it was all over the symbolic map. Maybe not even any good. I'm not that much up on poetry, but it read like a scream.

And then the lyrical door shut. Like the poet didn't trust herself. Her anger might be too much. So she let it mature, not into an all-consuming rage, an obsession, but into a mellow throb. A feeling she could unearth and look upon as an artifact.

And that's what was missing in the second book. I didn't notice it at first because the poems were good. And if you only read the second book, it would be fine. You'd put it down, satisfied. The poet did a good job. Words made pictures. You'd put the book back on the shelf, let the poems drift away because they didn't have the immediacy of the first book. The personal dive into the experience. The juice. We were swimming in the author's senses. In the second book, we were at arm's length. The rough stones had been cut into finely faceted gems. Too perfect. The first book was rough stones. Grunts and snorts and laughs and screams.

I read both books again, making notes, memorizing phrases that touched me. I was studying the poems with more intensity than I had for the postal exam. I was taking a class in Margaret Reade, maybe an introductory course: a prerequisite to Glen Dower 201.

Jason Firth and I could discuss this. He would see I had the instincts of a writer.

Just like him.

# CHAPTER THIRTY-SIX

I was eating my lunch in the usual spot, off to the side of the road, before my ascent to Glen's place. I was perusing my notes on Margaret Reade. Phrases were bubbling in my brain. There's a whole other section of gray matter that clicks on when you want to learn. It's amazing. My mind had become a sponge. It was all about my attitude. I finally understood what my father had been trying to teach me.

*"It's time for a little attitude readjustment, Ezra."*

But his methods—which often involved "non-verbal" communication—did little to encourage my participation. It's hard to study if you can't sit down.

I set my notebook in the back of the mail cart with my empty lunch bag and soda bottle. Picked up Glen's mail. Nothing much of interest today. A couple of catalogs. Some get-rich-quick newsletter addressed to "Occupant." No bills. If he was outside we could have our discussion about Margaret Reade and her poetry. Maybe I could even knock on the door. He was the one who said I should read her. I could thank him. Draw him into conversation. Maybe even see the inside of the house when he invites me in to continue the conversation.

I was halfway up the hill when an engine turned over. If an engine could sound angry, this one did.

"Damn."

He was going somewhere. I stepped off to the side of the

road, ready to wave. I was hoping he'd stop so we could talk a bit, but it wasn't Glen. It was Dr. Anderson in her silver sports car. And the phrases popped and connected.

The Good Doctor. *Encased in silver.*

I stood there. I'm sure my mouth was wide open at the idea that had just entered my head. I lifted a hand to wave. Held it there, immobile. Dr. Anderson sped by, paying me no attention. I could've been a tree stump. I don't think she even saw me, her eyes straight ahead, her foot heavy on the gas. The road rising up in a swirl of dust and gravel in her wake.

*House calls may cost too much.*


It may have been slow to come to me, but when it did it struck me like a lightning bolt. I should have made the leap before. Back when I first compared Margaret Reade and Glen Dower. The same agent. The stylistic similarities. Their separate desire for solitude.

The lightning bolt—right in the pre-frontal cortex.

It was not separate, but the same.

Margaret Reade was a pen name for Glen Dower.

*And to Al Field, whose open mind sees outside the box.*

Who also doesn't stereotype. Who doesn't slot Glen into some preconceived genre classification. I needed to get my reasonable mind around this. If it was true. I wanted to doubt it, but my every instinct was keyed up, screaming. *Yes, it's true! And you're the only one who knows!* The only one peeling off the scab of Glen's hurt. Prodding the scar by reading his life in the poems he wrote as Margaret Reade.

And he wanted me to do it. He was the one who mentioned the book to me. Hell, he literally put it in my hands.

What do I do now?

Nothing. The situation had to stay the same. He was Jason Firth. I'd never heard of Glen Dower. As far as I was concerned Margaret Reade was a poet who lived in the Pacific Northwest.

Jason had recommended her, not Glen. We could still have our discussion. By detailing my insights into Margaret Reade, Glen would see how well I knew him. We would become closer because of it.

Or would we? For the first time, I had an inkling that maybe I didn't know this man as well as I thought I did. Glen was Jason. Glen was Margaret. He was a wonderful writer. A talented man. Bursting with too many words and thoughts for one person. How could he keep all those possibilities straight?

I started walking up the road to Glen's house just as his car flew over the hill. I made a quick dive for the side of the road.

"What's the damage, Orlando?" I asked.

He didn't answer. He was watching someone walk through the door.

"Hey, Ezra. Orlando."

"Jason."

Glen looked at me and said, "Let me buy you a nightcap."

He motioned to Orlando. I nodded as Glen sat down.

"I was hoping to find you here," he said. "I wanted to apologize for this afternoon. I saw it from the window. You were almost road kill." He paused and added, "Twice."

"No apology needed."

"Yeah, there is. She was in a hurry, and wasn't paying any attention. And I wasn't much better. It's a good thing you've got quick reflexes. For a postman."

Orlando put a fresh pint in front of me.

"What'll you have, Jason?"

"Better make it a diet soda, Orlando. Thanks."

I sipped my drink while Glen waited. When his soda arrived, he raised his glass and tipped it against mine.

"*Iechyd da.*" (Think "*Ya kee da.*")

"What?"

"A Welsh toast. To your good health."

"Thanks. Cheers."

He seemed in a good mood. This could be the optimal time.

"I read that book of poems. *Adrift*."

He smiled. "Margaret Reade. What'd you think?"

"I liked them. Liked the first book better."

He froze a second, then set his glass down and turned to face me.

"You bought the first book?"

"I liked the poems. Went to see if she had written anything else."

"Why'd you like the first one better?"

"It was rawer. More open. If I were a critic, I'd probably go with the second book only because it's more...accessible. Everything was...more polished."

*Look at me.* I used a gemology analogy without apology. *Ha!*

He nodded and said, "You prefer the subjective over the objective."

"I prefer the real over the made up no matter how well it's crafted." Oh, God. That's great. It's where I wanted to go. The perfect introduction to my own reading habits. I saw the line play out. The bait splash and sink. I gave a gentle tug to make it shake. To tease the fish. *One too many metaphors, I know.* "Guess it's why I read non-fiction."

"Exclusively?"

"Yeah. But I did enjoy those poems. Margaret Reade is a nice change. Thanks for recommending her." I stood. Drained the last of my beer. "And for the drink."

"You're welcome."


I was down the steps when Glen made his own exit from Paulie's.

"Ezra?"

"Yeah?"

"Just wanted you to know I've been thinking I need to read over those poems again after our talk. Your ideas were perceptive.

Thanks."

*Fight it.* Don't let that smile engulf your whole head. It's nothing more than a compliment. Not an admission of guilt. And he'd been very gracious with the compliments.

"Thank you. 'Night, Ezra. You okay walking?"

"I'm good and close, Jason. Thanks. G'night."

I was walking home when I heard his car start. He passed by slowly. Gave a toot of the horn. I waved.

I didn't need to jump for my life this time.


The store had closed hours ago and was supposed to be empty. It wasn't. He didn't expect company. He wasn't paid to deal with company. The job was to get in and get out as quickly as he could without being seen. She was screwing that up.

"Who are you?" the girl asked, her voice quivering.

"No one you know, Sweetheart."

He removed the blade from the clip on his belt.

"You don't need to do that," she begged. "I won't tell anyone. I don't even know who you are."

"I know. And I need to make sure it stays that way."

He made a bit more of a mess than usual, but he figured the flames would take care of that.

# CHAPTER THIRTY-SEVEN

If I timed it right, I could get over to the photo shop, pick up the enlargements of Glen, and get back to clock out of work on time. I could then take the photos to my apartment and squirrel them away where no one would see them.

I could see the small crowd and yellow caution tape a block away. I found a parking spot in the strip mall lot, sat, and stared. It was hard to process what I was looking at.

There had been a fire at the photo store. The front window was gone and I could smell the wet smoke as the firefighters finished up their job. The yellow tape fluttered in the breeze. Ashes lifted and settled like dirty snowflakes carried by the wind.

I got out of the car feeling sick to my stomach. The photos I'd taken of Glen were probably among those windswept ashes. But maybe not. Maybe Sally Ann had gotten them and the enlargements out, holding the prints tightly to her, so the flames couldn't claim them.

The stores on either side of the photo shop were open, their common walls streaked with carbon, thick plastic sheets holding out the wind.

"What happened?"

The pimply kid I'd seen behind the counter some days before was probably tired of answering the question. He just shook his head.

"There was a fire," he said, as if I'd asked him the time of day.

"I can see that. Did everybody get out okay?"

He became more serious.

"No."

"Sally Ann...?"

"You knew her?"

"Yeah. Is she all right?"

His face reddened. "She was so sweet..."

*Was.* He said was.

"She didn't make it?"

"No."


He had to have been mistaken. People don't just...stop being alive. Not up here in Maine. I went back to the post office, swiped out, and drove over to Myrna's No Lobster. Myrna and her husband were sitting at the counter having a piece of pie. The lunch rush was over and supper was still a couple of hours away.

Myrna looked up when I came in. The word sullen came to my mind.

"Hey. Ezra, right?"

"Very good. Thanks for remembering."

"What'll you have, honey?" The question came out as if from habit.

"Pop. Orange."

There was a moment of confusion.

"Sorry. I keep forgetting. Soda."

She got up and slowly walked behind the counter, as if her shoes were too tight and she didn't feel like moving.

"I was at the photo shop," I said.

She stopped. Used an arm to support herself as she leaned over the counter.

"Then you know."

I pretended not to have heard what the guy told me. I'm not sure why I felt the need to lie; I just did. "It's why I came here. To see Sally Ann. See if she's all right."

Myrna's head dropped. Her voice was a sad mumble I didn't understand.

"What?"

"She was such a sweet girl."

The word *was* again. I radiated an anguish I did not truly feel. Could I write about that feeling without actually experiencing it? I knew I'd try.

"No..." I tried. But I wasn't sorry for sweet little Sally Ann. I was angry. "Myrna? Forget the soda. I'm sorry to intrude on your grief."

I turned around and walked out. The lock pick in my pocket felt like so much lead.


It was front page news in the local paper the next day, even though it had happened in the next county over. Small towns are like that. They may not always agree with how the other town conducts business, or be on the best of terms when Friday night pits one high school against the other on the football field, but when grief pays a call, they put their differences aside and close ranks like the best of families. And Sally Ann had family in both counties. Knew a lot of people in each because her two jobs crossed county lines.


A couple of days passed and then came Sally Ann's funeral.

"Shame you have to see so much death so soon, Ezra. Just moving up here and all."

I had turned off the road and was driving Rosa Higgins back to the house. She had been quiet most of the ride to and from Sally Ann's funeral.

"Roy's understandable. He was older and didn't take good care of himself. But Sally Ann...to take someone so young..."

"No guarantees, Rosa. On any of us."

"I guess."

But it had been freakish. According to the paper, some chemicals in the dark room caught fire and exploded. Sally Ann was working late that night; she should have been home in bed. Or studying. If Sally Ann had been closer to the door, she would still be alive today, but she had been in the back. The explosion blew out the wall, sending the heavy storage shelf over on top of her, crushing her skull, the flames devouring— my word, not the papers—her flesh.

I stopped the car. Rosa sat there, staring at nothing.

"Least she died quick." She removed her seatbelt and opened the door. "Feel like some lemonade, Ezra?"

"Not really. Thanks, though."

Keep company with the living. I could tell she didn't want to go back into that big empty house. Not today.

"You want to go over to Myrna's? Get something to eat?"

"I'd like that, Ezra. Thank you." She closed the door, pulled her seatbelt back on, and buckled herself in as I turned the car around. She leaned forward a bit, studying the sky, the trees. Rested her hand on my arm. "Couple of months now and pumpkin season'll be upon us."

I gave her a grin. "You are such a tease, Rosa."

That got a smile. Barely.


Lots of people had the same idea. Myrna's was full, but not loud. A somber tone prevailed, as if everyone were paying their last respects to Sally Ann here, where her life used to lift people's spirits.

Myrna got up from a booth in the back and waved us over to join her.

"Joe's been up all night baking pies. It's how he handles grief. He loved that little girl. We all did."

It wasn't Joe in the booth. It was Glen. *Jason.*

"Hey, Ezra. Rosa."

"Jason."

He slid over so Rosa could sit next to him. I took the seat across from them. He took her hands in his and gave her a kiss on the cheek.

"You all right?" Glen asked.

"She should be here, Jason."

"I know." Glen picked up a fork and carved off a small bite of apple cinnamon pie. Lifted it to Rosa. "Try this. It won't make you forget, but it'll make you feel better."

It was like communion, the way Rosa closed her eyes. Her lips turned up at the taste and tears started flowing.

"Excuse me."

She got up, wiping at her eyes, and walked away.

"She's taking it hard, Jason."

He studied me for a moment.

"She didn't tell you, did she?"

"Tell me what?"

"I think she would have. She likes you. Probably too hard to do without breaking down."

"What?" I leaned forward.

"When Sally Ann was little, her parents split up. Her mom took off for Bangor. No communication other than a birthday gift and a Christmas present each year. Her dad had to work. Rosa had taught Sally Ann's mom how to quilt, and the baby would crawl around their feet as they worked their thread. Rosa would babysit Sally Ann until her daddy came home from work. Did that until Sally Ann was in junior high and could look after herself at home. They had developed quite a bond. Sally Ann would always stop by to see Rosa. Every Saturday."

"Today."

He nodded. Dug the fork into his pie.

"You should get some of this. It's good." He pulled the pie from the tines and spoke while he chewed. "And it's," he choked up here, "free. In memory of Sally Ann."

# CHAPTER THIRTY-EIGHT

The next few days plodded by as if the world were working its way through a viscous haze. I didn't even see Rosa, and that was rare. She usually came out on the porch and waved to me a couple times a week, or was waiting at the mailbox for a bit of conversation. I thought about driving up to the house and knocking to make sure she was all right, but I never did.

"Tomorrow," I told myself, but another day passed and my mail cart kept moving on up the road. No horn-honking on my end and still no wave from the porch. I was worried for her, but I think I was even more afraid of what I'd find if I did knock on her door.

My anger at Sally Ann's death took a few days to cool. Why the hell had she been working late that night? And then my anger turned to guilt for feeling that way. She had been my silent partner. I pictured her zipping her lips. Winking at a secret shared. It wasn't her fault. How could I have turned her death into something about me? Was I that selfish? I wanted those great shots of Glen enlarged, and I knew I might never get such good pictures of him again. Why didn't I—?

I took the camera to the woods a couple times, hoping I could get another decent shot. I don't remember even putting it up to my eye. Oh, Glen was there as always, writing up a storm, the new novel taking over his life. I still had that feeling of excitement about what he was writing. I was anxious to read it, to see what trip he would take me on this time, but the image he presented was the same one I had shot many times before. The top of his head above the raised lid of the laptop. I needed those shots to make up for the ones lost in the fire. But there was nothing new to see. I was beginning to doubt that I had even learned anything from him, other than to write you needed to put your butt onto the seat, your fingers onto the keyboard, and then pour your mind out onto the blank page. And you needed to do it a lot, with great regularity. Not the peripatetic swipes at paper I'd been taking.

I didn't even have a keyboard worthy of a real writer, but there was nothing wrong with pen and paper. It had stood the test of time, and it wasn't subject to power outages or erroneous deletions. Or the poking of the wrong key at the wrong time. Pen and paper was retro, and everyone knows retro is hip.

I knew I should spend some of my savings for a better laptop, though, even if I used it as nothing more than an expensive type-writer. My fingers can find the keys, thanks to a high school personal typing class. I was a bit rusty, but I was sure I could pick it up again. Maybe the expense would give me the impetus I needed to actually put my ass on the chair. And, once I got moving, I'd be typing words faster than I could compose them in my head.

I'd barely even jotted down most of the ideas I'd been coming up with. All I had to show for my time in Maine were some photographs, a couple of verses about a fish, and some character notes on an alien being.

I could have the fish battle the alien and win, thereby saving mankind. Then someone could catch the fish, eat it, and provide a twist for an ending.

I was dancing around the question, and it was time I made a decision. Was I just a postman who liked to read, and, therefore, had a peripheral interest in writing, or was I a writer?

I spent some money on a new laptop.

"This is what I do," Houston told the blonde. "I can't do anything else."

She smiled, her golden hair spilling over the pillow, opened her eyes and looked at him.

"I thought you were a detective, too."

Now it was Houston's turn to smile. As much of a smile as he would ever allow himself. Then he rolled off the woman, reached for his cigarettes, lit one and passed it to the blonde, and lit another for himself.

"That's what I was talking about."

She felt him grow hard. Not where she had hoped for, but inside. A door, which had been open just slightly, had closed a bit. It was dark in there. And cold. A small sliver of light gave hope. But was it enough?

"Oh." She wondered if she should leave. Maybe when he slept. Not now. She had seen him angry.

Houston exhaled a sighing cloud.

"I like the knots," he explained. "The untying. Finding the loose strand and working it until it gives up something else. Then working that something else. Sometimes the knots are easy. Straightforward. But other times they can get pretty complicated. Those are my favorites, even when I'm waist deep in shit and can't find my way out, I keep pulling. Eventually something comes loose. Eventually the rope is straightened out. All the knots are gone."

He had never spoken this many words to her before. She turned onto her side and watched his face, its profile a dark, craggy rock.

"And I'm just another knot?"

"No." He ran a rough hand over her smooth terrain. "You are a pleasure." His face was

partially lit as the cigarette glowed, shadowing the short scar above his lips. "You know
this thing isn't over yet, don't you, Tammy?"

"Are you talking about us?"

He kissed her softly. "Let's see how it plays
out. You may not like what I've got to do."

Tammy reached out, her hand cupping the back
of his head, and drew him into a long, searching kiss. "I'll be here."

He stared at her darkened face, her eyes
just bright enough to see. They were alive with
want. "Even after I've killed your father?"

She was silent. Her eyes closed softly, and,
when they opened, he knew she would stick
around.

"Let me help you."

Then she pulled him with her as she rolled
onto her back and he was atop her once again.
And this time the hardness was right.

I looked back over the words I'd just put to paper. I *was* a writer.

Sure, I had borrowed Glen's character Houston, but I could
come up with one of my own. And, yes, if you'd ever heard him
talk about why he writes, you'll know where I got the knot
idea. But it worked. Glen was Houston, as all writers are a bit
of their character or characters. What else do we have to go on
but our own knowledge and view of the world? And who's to say
that with regular writing hours I couldn't turn the above scene
into a fine mystery full of corruption, sex, and lace panties.

I just had to make the time to write.

Work had been the one constant in my life since Sally Ann's
death. I had plodded and trudged for a week and a half. Now I
hopped and skipped.

And other things were turning around, too.

Rosa was waiting at the mailbox, dressed in tweeds, blending in with the autumn colors. She had a red wagon with her. A big cardboard box in its cargo area.

"Miss me, Ezra?"

"You know I did, Rosa." We both started to tear up. "I'm sorry. I wanted to come up and see if you were okay, but...I was scared."

"Of what you'd find?"

I nodded.

"Well, you would have found a sad old woman, I'll tell you that, but she would have been alive. I took salvation in my art. It was what Sally Ann would have wanted. It was what Roy and Martha would have wanted. It was hard at first, but I came around and so I did it." She nodded toward the wagon. "This is for you."

"Gee, Rosa, I'm a bit big for a wagon." She smiled and wiped a tear. "Besides, I've got this swell mail truck."

"Don't be an ass, Ezra. The wagon stays with me. The box is for you."

I eyed the box. "Looks like the plumpest pumpkin pie I've ever seen."

"That's coming. I just got the ingredients yesterday."

"Lard?"

"Lard."

I stepped out of the mail truck and we hugged. Then I put the box into the back of the truck and hugged her again. Gave her a kiss on the cheek.

"I've missed you, you old crone."

"And I've missed you, you young shit."

I got back into the cart, tooted the horn, and rode off. I watched Rosa waving in the rearview until I couldn't see her anymore.

\* \* \*

I went home for lunch, fixed up a spinach and cheese omelet. Then I opened Rosa's package. It was a quilt. But it wasn't just patches and designs. It was a memorial to Sally Ann. The lower border was green. A woman in black and a man in a gray uniform were standing by a mailbox. Trees and bushes, flowers and vines trailed up the sides, eventually mixing with a bright blue sky dotted with puffy white clouds. Riding one of those clouds was an angel.

It was Sally Ann and she was beautiful.

I couldn't help thinking, as I draped it over my bed, what it would be worth at auction.

# CHAPTER THIRTY-NINE

I finished my lunch without going through Glen's mail. It no longer held any fascination. What difference would it make in my life? Though it always did seem to amaze me how much junk mail he got. Computers just seem to spit out addresses the way a farmer spits chaw, not caring where their mess ends up.

For someone whose work involved being outdoors most of the time, I never obsessed about the weather. There was nothing I could do about it. It is what it is. But this day was as close to perfect as weather could get. Crystal clear azure skies. Not a cloud. Slanting sun. throwing gold in its path, gilding and shadowing the land like an old artist's rendering, the fall leaves adding texture and design. And the temperature: cool and crisp. I hadn't even broken a sweat by the time I got to the straightaway. If ever there was a day for good fortune to smile upon me, this was it.

It was even cooler in the grove of trees lining the roadway up to Glen's house. Shaded. And there at the end of the shadow, like a hero's house in a spotlight, was the sun-worshipped home of my favorite writer and newest friend, Glen Dower.

I went into mail carrier mode. I remembered what the guy I'd bought the gun from had said about going postal and smiled. Eyes down. Watching my steps. As I approached the mailbox, my hand fished into the almost empty mail sack and closed around what remained.

I raised my head, pulled the mailbox lid open, and slipped in the last of my day's load. I stole a look at the house as I turned to go.

Glen was coming out the front door.

"Ezra!"

*Whoa. Didn't see that coming.* "Hey, Jason. Some kinda day, huh?"

"Perfect. I was wondering if I could talk to you for a minute."

"Is there something wrong?" *Was there?*

He smiled and waved off the question. "No, not at all. Everything's grand."

*Everything's grand.* The expression his character Blue had used just before everything went crazy wrong. Did Jason have a complaint? Had he seen me in the woods? Did he realize he's quoting one of his characters? *Now I was thinking crazy wrong.*

He glanced at the mailbag. "I must be your last stop of the day."

"Always. I planned it that way. Easier coming up the hill with an empty bag."

"Smart. Where are my manners?" He was opening the gate. "Come in."

I don't know why, but I turned to look back down the road. But I was the only one there.

"I'm sorry," he said. "I thought you were done for the day. If you've got more to do we can talk here."

He was inviting me in. Me. No one ever got past that front door. Not unless he's known you for a while, but then he had known me for a while: the friendly neighborhood postman.

I passed through the gate. "Nope. All done. Just gotta hand in the bag and go home. What's on your mind?"

"I've got a huge favor to ask." He rubbed his hands together. "What would you say to a cold beer?"

"Hello, good looking?"

He laughed and stuck out his hand. It felt good, firmer than the last few times. Friendlier.

We were walking up the slate squares to the front door. I

was going to go into the house. I was going to sit at a table and have a beer—at least one—with him. Would it be the writing table? Probably not. He had to have some other table where he ate meals. I had never seen him eat at the writing table; he ate his sandwich either standing up or while walking from the kitchen to the computer.

And he wants to ask a favor! I hoped I was capable of helping him. What could it be?

He was turning and walking across the yard.

I stopped. My mind screamed, *Follow him, you idiot!*

He led me around the side of the house to the back patio. He must have been planning this. The old picnic table had a plate of sandwiches under plastic wrap. A cooler sat on the table next to assorted condiments on a red-checked, waxy tablecloth. The ketchup bottle was sweating in the afternoon sun. Just like me.

```
He stood there, sweating like a bottle of cool
ketchup on a hot picnic table, his eyes on my
gun.
```

But the sun wasn't bothering me that much. He opened the cooler. There must have been five or six different brands of beer. He selected one and twisted off the top.

"Help yourself."

"That one looks pretty good to me."

He handed me the open bottle, pulled out its twin, and opened it.

"Great minds think alike."

He held the bottle out. I tapped mine against it.

"Cheers. Have a seat." He busied himself unwrapping sandwiches. "I've got some ham and cheese, chicken, and my favorite..." his hand picked up a sandwich on whole wheat, "...good old peanut butter and jelly."

"PB and J beats all."

He laughed. "I knew I liked you." He handed me the sandwich and took another one out for himself.

"Thanks." I took a bite and nodded my appreciation. "This is nice 'n all, but you didn't have to go to this much trouble." I smiled. "So...who do you want me to kill?"

He laughed. I could feel myself blush red, but I felt real good. I had in some small way paid back a lot of the laughs he had given me. Maybe one day I could tell him that.

"No, no. It's nothing that complicated." He took a slug of his beer. "But I've got to tell you some stuff first, so you know what you're getting into."

I put a concerned look on. "Fair enough."

His gaze was steel. "I'm not Jason Firth. That's an alias."

I tried to keep my face steady. Did I react? I don't think so. Time for another joke.

"You dodgin' bill collectors or an ex-wife?"

He smiled. "None of the above. My real name is Glen Dower."

He was telling me the truth about himself. He trusted me. All my planning was bearing fruit. We *were* going to be friends. He was watching me. I should have a reaction.

"You in the witness protection program?"

He grinned and shook his head. "No. Jason Firth is my *nom de Maine*. The name Glen Dower doesn't mean anything to you?"

"Not really." Doubt in my voice. *Maybe?* I was getting good at this lying. "Should it?"

"It's a little ego thing on my part," he said. "I'm a writer."

"Of...?"

"Books."

"Really?" *I was good at this.* "Anything I might have read?"

"Oh, that's right. You only read non-fiction. I do fiction. Mysteries, sci-fi. Some horror."

"Like vampires and stuff?"

He nodded.

"I've got a niece who reads that stuff," I said. "Maybe she knows you. I'll ask." I looked around. "You must do okay. This is a great place."

"Got lucky with my first couple novels. I couldn't afford to buy this place today."

"I know what you mean. I was kinda lucky with my place."

He didn't respond, he just leaned onto the table. "I've got to go away for a week. On business."

"Oh." It was a postal matter, nothing personal. I tried not to look too disappointed. "So you want me to put a hold on your mail?"

"Yes, but what I'd really like...if it's possible...is for you to stay here and housesit."

"Me?" *Oh, yes. Me!* No sooner had I sworn to obey a Glen-free diet, than the whole Glen refrigerator opens up and bids me entrance. This would be so much more instructive than my sojourn in the woods. The professor was handing me the answer book to a graduate-level exam. I could put the diet off for a week, gorge myself, and then go full bore into my writing, stuffed to the gills with whatever I could learn. Sated. Elated. It had to be fated!

Glen was waiting for an answer. *Be cool, Ezra.*

"Be nice getting out of my place for a spell." I nodded. "Guess I could do that. Sure."

He leaned back, exhaled. "Great. Thanks." Leaned forward again. "Now here's where it gets complicated. If, after what I'm about to tell you, you want to cancel, I'll understand."

"What? The place is haunted?"

That got another laugh. "No, no ghosts I know of. Yet." He paused. I could see him trying to decide how to explain whatever it was he had to say. "Ahhh, there's no easy way to do this. Bear with me. If I seem to ramble, I apologize, but you've got to know before..."

He let the sentence trail off as he took another swallow of his beer then used the back of his hand to wipe his mouth. "I've become what's called a cult writer. You know what that is?"

"Occult's kind of like horror, right?"

He chuckled. "*A cult*, not *occult*. I'm a cult writer. I've got fans like any writer with an audience. It's just that...well, my fans have been known to go a bit overboard."

I had to set my bottle down. My hand had started to shake. I was feeling hot. Like my insides were expanding, about to burst my skin. I had to relax. He was telling me this. He trusted me. He didn't—couldn't—know I'm one of those...fans? *Right?*

I put my hand under the table and gripped my leg. My voice sounded garbled to me. "Like how?"

"For starters, there's this website. About me. I don't know who started it, and I can't stop it, but there's all this chatter about where I might live. Where people think they've seen me."

"Like Elvis sightings?"

"Not that bad. A much lesser scale."

He had visited the website. I could only imagine what the talk would be about if they knew he was there with them.

"And they found this place?"

"Not that I know of. But if they did, I could come home from my trip to a shambles. Things would be gone. Stolen. Personal things. They'd take them for souvenirs. My life would be all over their website. My things on Ebay."

"You're that famous?"

He shrugged it off. "Enough people know me and buy my books that I get by. But if you were here, and anyone found the place, they'd think it was yours. You'd sort of be me for a week. But not Glen Dower. They'd think you were Jason Firth."

I decided to act worried. Concerned. "These people? They're not violent?"

"Not so far, and I really don't think they'll ever find this place. I haven't had contact with them for years. Since I left the city and moved up here."

"Don't they know what you look like? From your books?"

"I don't do author photos anymore. Anyone who would take

the trouble to find me here would..." He managed a smile. "Which is why, if you were here, it would be perfect. They'd see you and know you're not me. They'd disappear."

I pretended to give that some thought. Like I might have anything else I needed to do. "Mmm-hmm," I finally said. "Doesn't sound too hard to me. I think I'm up to it."

"Thanks, but there's a bit more. It may seem strange, and, again, I'll understand if you don't want to do it."

What could possibly be wrong with this deal? No one on the website knows where this place is. I'm the only one, and I have no intention of letting them in on my secret.

"If you stay here, I'd like you to *stay* here. Not go to work. For the entire week. Call in sick or something."

Not go to work? Could I do that? He must have seen the shadow fall across my face.

"I mean, you can go out," he said. "The store, Paulie's, whatever. But I'd like you to be here most of the time. Like I am. I'd just feel more secure, knowing you were here."

"When do you want to do this?"

"Next month."

"I'll ask tomorrow. I can't promise, but I'll do my best."

"That's all a mule can do," he said.

"What?"

"Something I heard someone say once. You can only do your best. That's all a mule can do. That's all any of us can do."

"It would help if I had something I needed to do. Some reason to give them for taking a week off."

"We'll come up with something," he said after taking another sip while staring me straight in the eyes. "But the real reason is obvious, isn't it?" He leaned into me. "After all, Ezra, you and I both know exactly who and what you are."

# CHAPTER FORTY

I took a very nervous, very slow sip of my beer. It seemed to have lost its taste.

"What's that, Glen?" I asked, ready to make a dash for the door.

He smiled. "You're a writer, of course, Ezra. What did you think I meant?"

It was all I could do to keep my beer from coming up the same path it had gone down. My swallow could have been heard down the hill at my last stop.

"Why do you say that?" I asked.

"It's obvious. The questions you ask; the ones you don't. You're a good listener. I smelled writer on you after our first real conversation." He paused then said, "So. How to proceed?" Glen took a bite of his sandwich and chewed. "I know. Let's play a writer's game."

"I really don't write."

"Sure you do. Well, you can. Everyone *can*. But the way you spoke about Margaret Reade's poems? I firmly believe anyone who can think and speak that clearly, can write."

"Yeah, letters and stuff. Not my own stories."

"Ever relate stories in a letter?"

"Sure."

"Long letters, sometimes?"

I nodded.

"Well, you take that story and embellish it. Add characters. Maybe one of those characters has something going on with another character no one knows about. Now you've got a subplot going. Pretty soon it's a short story or something longer. Maybe a..."

Glen's hands were facing me, palms up. His fingers moving, typing invisible word in my direction. Urging me to think. I tried to look confused. It wasn't hard. Put a bit of disbelief into my answer.

"A novel? Me?"

"Bingo! The man gets it in one try. You can play this game, Ezra."

"What's this game called?"

"*What If?*"

*Pay attention here, Ezra,* I told myself. This was a lesson. Lesson Number One in the advanced class. But he didn't know I actually wrote. I couldn't show my hand too soon.

"How do we play it?"

"You just ask yourself 'What if?'"

"What if?"

"Yep. Here's the story so far: I'm leaving on a trip. You're staying at my place. We need your boss to think...?"

I was going to say, "I'm not around?" but we knew that already.

"I'm going on vacation?"

"That's good." But he grimaced. Maybe it wasn't that good.

"But you're new. Have you worked long enough to earn a vacation?"

*Wow. Good thought. Ah...*

"What if," I said, "my niece was getting married?"

"Better. Much better. Keep playing."

"And she lives back in Cincy...and wants her uncle...me...to give her away because her dad passed away years ago?"

"Good!" He touched his nose with his forefinger. His smile made me laugh.

"Hey, this is fun. Is this what you do when you write your books?" *Oh, boy!*

"Kind of. You take one step and see where you are. You take another step. Then there's a wall in your way. You figure out how to get around the wall. Your boss is the wall here."

"And we need to get around her, so she thinks I'm going on vacation, but I'm really going to be here."

"Don't even mention vacation. The family angle is much better. Work it some more."

"I'll tell her I need the week off. It's a three-day drive out..." I saw that grimace again. "What?"

"That doesn't leave you a lot of time to spend with the family. There's always stuff to do leading up to the wedding. Dinners, parties..."

"You're right. I'd need more time." My smile grew.

"What?"

"I could fly! That's only a couple of hours."

"Good thought, Ezra. Now you're editing yourself. Just like a real writer would do."

I took a pen out of my pocket. A *Sorry I Missed You* form from my bag.

"What are the dates?"


I hardly remember walking down the hill. My mind was ablaze. Glen had given me the perfect in to talk about my writing. *What If?* I'd get the story of why I had to go to my niece's wedding done first. And then I'd give him a real story I had written! Tell him I had so much fun with *What If?* that this new story just poured out of me. That would doubly impress him.

I was twenty yards past the mail cart when I remembered I was still at work. I was totally into concocting the story for my boss, bits and pieces coming together, I'd walked right past my method of transportation.

I turned around, climbed aboard, hit the horn for a couple

farewell toots, and raised some dust heading down the hill. I was going to clock out and go home. *And write.*

# CHAPTER FORTY-ONE

That blank page just kept staring back at me. Daring me. Why couldn't I think of something? I tried the fish with a wish, but all I could see was some shark gobbling it up. And I couldn't have Glen read a kid's story. He writes adult fiction. I had to give him something approximate to his level.

Maybe I'd spent too much time on my "vacation" scenario. But I think it's solid. I knew he'd like it. I knew my boss would go for it. Maybe that was enough. *Maybe.*

But if I came up with a story, something I had written, in addition to my niece's wedding idea, he'd be blown away. I'd make a big impression. He'd see I was a real writer.

I never realized how loud the ticking of that clock was.

I should have been in the writing shed. Not in this apartment. No wonder I couldn't write.

No excuses. *You are a writer. You can write anywhere. You wrote stories in Cincinnati, and that apartment was no better or worse than this one. But you weren't putting this pressure on yourself then. You were free to write whatever you wanted. No judgments.*

I couldn't write because Glen was weighing too heavily on my mind. What if he didn't like what I wrote? So don't write. Was it as simple as that?

But I thought of a way around that. I went into the bedroom. Bottom drawer in my old dresser. No clothes there. Just memorabilia. High school track medals. Diplomas. And everything I ever wrote for submission.

I grabbed the old blue cloth three-ring binder and returned to the living room. I started looking over stories. Searching for something Glen might find readable.

I became lost in the words and the worlds I had created many years ago.

The clock didn't bother me at all.

Two days later, I drove the cart to the top of the hill. Walked right by the mailbox. Up to the front door. Rang the bell and knocked.

A quick parting of a curtain in the side window. Then I heard locks being turned. The door opened a few inches. I could see Glen's face. I thrust a single sheet of paper at him.

"Here," I said. "Look at this."

"I don't have my glasses with me. What is it?"

"I got the week! And this is my What If diploma. It's a receipt for airline tickets to Cincinnati. My boss said yes!"

"Thank you, Ezra. But airline tickets? Did you have to actually buy them?"

"Icing on the cake. I made the reservations while at work. Printed out the receipt. Showed it to my boss. It's proof. She hoped I'd have a great time. We did it! We...we...What-Iffed her!"

He looked at me with pride. "*You* did, Ezra. *You* did it. I just planted the seed."

"And that's not all." I reached down to the bottom of the mailbag. Took out Glen's mail, wrapped in a rubber band, and handed it to him. "I wrote a story!"

"You what?" He made a face like somebody had farted. And not just a small one but a big Take-No-Prisoners-Fast-Food-Burrito Blast.

But I plowed on, over the wall in the way. "It's in with your mail. I hope you don't mind. I was so jazzed up with *What If?* I got my excuse for the boss ready and just kept going. I was on fire. It was such a great feeling."

Glen didn't say anything. He was holding his mail in both hands, looking down at it as if it were so much sludge. His face was flushed. His jaw set. He rolled the parcel up in his right hand and slapped it repeatedly against his other palm.

This must be what Orlando was talking about. How Glen had a temper. How it flared quick and hot. As if he were a different person.

"Hey, I'm sorry, Glen. You don't have to read it. I just wanted to show you how much you inspired me..."

*Stop*, I told myself. If you keep going, you'll blow it. Say something out of place. He'll remember you. From the readings. From the tour. You'll lose it all. I couldn't think of anything. The look in his eyes. Like he was looking through me. Or deep into me, trying to read my thoughts. Then...as quickly as he'd flared up...he changed. Smiled. And laughed. And he was the old Glen again.

"No. It's okay, Ezra." He turned and tossed the bundle into the darkness behind him. "It's just a surprise, that's all. And I'm really flattered I could get you so riled up as to write a story."

"It's probably not any good. At least, not as good as what you write..."

"Hey, you don't know. You've never read any of my stuff, so it may very well be every bit as good as anything of mine, right?"

*How do I reply to that?* I didn't.

"I'll read it and let you know."

"You will?"

He nodded his head. "And I'll pay you back for the airline tickets you're never going to use." He took the receipt from my hand, folded it and put it into his shirt pocket. "You really won the *What-If* game, Ezra. I don't think I ever would have thought of that."

# CHAPTER FORTY-TWO

I was sitting in the cart daydreaming about how much Glen would love my story. How he'd call his agent about me. How we were about to become brothers in words. All this in the length of one red light before turning in the mail cart and clocking out.

"Excuse me, sir? Mailman?" A voice behind me.

"Yes, sir?" I turned. "Help you?"

Oh, shit. I know this guy. Not from Maine. But from where?

*Oh shit.* He's lost weight, but he's still got the same buzz cut he had at the gay bar on Glen's last book tour.

"I hope so." He cocked his head sideways and studied me. "Hey! It's you!"

"Um...sorry, sir." I kept my voice from displaying any panic I might have been feeling. "I don't think I know you. I get that a lot, looking like other folks. Especially since I shaved my beard. Must be my Scots-Irish mutt mix."

"From the book tour. Glen Dower's book tour?" He thought a moment. "St. Louis, I think. But it could have been somewhere in Ohio. We had dinner together in some bar." He snapped his fingers. "You gave the bartender a copy of his latest book."

Jesus, it had to be this guy. Why couldn't it have been the stripper? That would have been much better. You need to think, Ezra. Put that writer's mind to work. Just as the guy got a huge smile and pointed at me.

"Ira! That's it. Ira."

The traffic light turned to green. I mentally patted myself on the back for telling that lie so many months ago. I nosed the cart to the curb so cars could get around me. "Nope, sorry. Name's Ezra."

I'd forgotten I'd given them a fake name all those months ago. But, this was my new life. And I needed to get this guy out of it.

"Wow. What are the...? You look identical to this guy I knew...I met on a book tour." He reached into his jacket pocket. "You know Glen Dower?"

"I've read a couple of the books. Nice, but nothing to get all excited about. I'm not all that into vampires and creepy stuff."

"Ira—that's the guy you look like—and I think differently on that score. We believe he's one of the finest authors to come down the pike."

"That's terrific," I said. "Glad you get excited about books." I needed this conversation to end before he began to catch on.

"Oh, yeah. Big time." He took a piece of paper from his pocket. Unfolded it. "Take a look. Seen this guy around here? Maybe on your route?"

It was an old author photo from one of Glen's books. Before he'd shaved off the mustache. Before this same guy and his buddies bothered him so much he had all his photos removed.

*Stone face, Ezra. Poker mode.* I was holding a lousy hand and needed to bluff this guy out of the game.

I took the photo. Studied it. Handed it back.

"Nope. This the writer you like? Dower?"

"Glen Dower, yes." He nodded. "I think he may live in the area."

"Hell, I don't mean to point out the obvious, but whyn't you just do an Internet search for him? Everybody's on the Internet."

"I have." He looked around like someone might be eavesdropping on our conversation. Leaned in toward me. Lowered his voice. "I manage a website about Glen. Sometimes people post things about seeing him..."

"So?"

"He's become a recluse." He grimaced. "Some people"—he spit that part out—"think I was part of the reason he up and disappeared. Maybe so, maybe not. But one of our best people wrote in recently. They were in Maine on vacation and thought they might have seen him in some seaside restaurant."

"Like an Elvis sighting?"

He smiled. "Not quite. Far as we know, Glen is still alive."

I smiled back. "And Elvis isn't?"

"Go ahead and joke." He handed me the photo again. "Take another look. It's been some years. He might be a bit fleshier. A bit grayer. But think on it."

I made a sincere show of studying the photo. If you knew Glen well you might have been able to pick him out of this younger man, but I don't think anyone here in town would be able to name him. Maybe Rosa. But Orlando? No. Possibly Dr. Anderson, but I don't think she would.

I shook my head. "I'm sorry. I don't know anyone around here who looks like this man." I handed the photo back. "Sorry."

"Well, thanks for the look." He folded up the page. Returned it to his pocket. He looked at me again. Hard. "You sure you're not Ira?" he asked, getting a little too close for comfort.

"I think I know who I am, mister." *I knew exactly who I was.* "And why do you think he's here? Why Purgatory? We're a pretty good drive from the ocean. If he was seen at the shore maybe he's holed up in one of those cutesy little seaside places." I shook my head. "Or if he's really a recluse, there's quite a bit of craggy coves with small towns hidden away among the rocks and trees. That might be a place to start. If he's even here at all. Hell, he coulda been on vacation, too."

*Good one, Ezra. That oughta shake him up.*

He considered it. "You might be right. I scoured a map of Maine before I even came up here. Purgatory just seemed to fit in with what I know of his sense of humor. From reading the books. In between the lines. Over and over."

And that's when I knew God or whatever had a sense of humor, too. Because driving up the street toward us was Glen Dower himself. James had his back to him, and I tried to keep myself from staring, possibly making James turn and look. I was just happy the light was green, allowing Glen to breeze on through and be gone. But not before noticing us. I thought he was gonna honk or wave. Maybe call out "Hey, Ezra." But something made him turn his head as he drove by, offering us nothing but a patch of gray hair peeking out from under a ball cap and hanging over the collar of a black jacket. I smiled inwardly. If this were a suspense movie, Glen would have probably gotten the red light. The violins would intensify. James would have noticed the car, but dropped the photo and bent down to pick it up. As he stood, the light would change, and Glen would drive away. *That was good.*

"Can I show you something, Ezra?" the guy asked.

"Free country."

He took out an old canvas bag and set it down on the mail cart. Unzipped it. Rummaged around through the same Maine guidebooks I had bought. Pulled one from the mix. No. Not a guidebook. Glen's book of short stories. He thumbed some pages and then read aloud.

"*'The knitting store was like the general store of old. A place where folks gathered to sit and talk. Share the local gossip. It was a grand place for a winter's eve. Warm and fuzzy, with fingers young and gnarled pushing needles through many-colored skeins of wool. Its front window, when not frosted over, gave a fine view onto the town square, its gazebo blanketed with snow, dampening the memory notes of the small combos that spread their music like fresh air during the rest of the year.'*"

It was from the opening of *The Quilt*. I didn't have to try and place it. It was Rosa who had popped it into my memory, but this guy was smart. Spot on.

"That last sentence was a long 'un, huh?"

"You get the idea, though. I just read it badly, running outta breath like that." He folded the book over his thumb and used it to point down the street Glen had just driven up. "You work here, so you know *The Quilter's Rest* down the block. Just across from the town square. And the gazebo. It's just like from the story."

I followed his direction. Nodded my assent.

"That's some fine detective work, Mister."

"Oh, sorry. That's rude. Here I am..." He put the book under his arm. Offered his hand. "James. James Mendon."

I shook it. "Ezra. *Ezra* Lockert. But this is Maine, James. There's probably a quilting store off every town square in the entire state. Winters are harsh. Lotsa folks stay inside with hobbies. Knitting, sewing..."

"Writing?"

"There's that. We got a lot of writers in this state. Past and present."

"I'm sure he lives up here. Somewhere."

"Well..." I motioned to the road before me. "I gotta be going. Good luck with your search. All I'm telling you is I've never seen anyone like that picture in these parts. But you got a card or something? I'll keep an eye out. Let you know if I do see your Mr. Dower."

"I'd appreciate that."

He returned the book to the backpack. Took out a small leather case from a front-zippered compartment. Took a card from it. "There's phone, my email and temporary address on there. I'm staying in New England for a bit."

I looked at the card. "New Hampshire, huh?"

"Yes. Thought he might've been living there for a while, but that seaside sighting changed my mind a bit."

"Card doesn't say what you do for a living."

He smiled. "I'm retired. School teacher."

"Really? You're wearing your age well. Don't even look close to retirement age."

"I'm young. And lucky. Put in my thirty and didn't let the

door hit me where the good Lord split me." He hoisted the backpack, put his arms through the straps, and jostled it until it was comfortable. "Grandmother died. Left me her farm. Lotta acres. Sold some off for a housing development. Still got fifty more for security. And the house."

"So now you do…your search? For this writer guy."

"That's mostly it. And I will find Glen Dower. I feel it. I just do."

"Well, good luck with that." I turned the key. Started the cart. "I gotta get this rig back to work and clock out."

We shook hands again.

"Good to meet you, Ezra."

"You, too. Tell Ira hey if you talk to him. And congratulate him on his good looks."

He laughed at that. "And you tell him hi from me if you do the same."

"Will do. Good luck with your search."

"Thanks. Think I'll move it on. If you haven't seen him, he's probably not around here."

"Be funny if he was living on the farm next to you in New Hampshire."

He smiled. "Wouldn't it?"

I turned the wheels toward the road. James had taken a couple steps back to the sidewalk. "Hey, James?"

"Yeah?"

"What are you gonna do if you find this Glen Dower?"

He was silent a moment.

"I'm not sure."

"I'd be careful if I were you. Sounds like maybe he doesn't want to be found. Have you considered that? Sometimes people are hiding for a reason. Don't know what they'll do if they're found."

He nodded like it wasn't the first time he'd thought of that. "I know. Maybe just say hi and thank him for all the wonderful books. My biggest wish? Maybe we could be friends. Correspond.

I've written letters to his publisher and agent and asked them to be forwarded. Got a note back saying they had done so. But never anything from Glen."

"That's what I mean, James. Sounds like he doesn't wanna be found."


I had picked up some carryout for dinner, but I couldn't eat. Should I call Glen and tell him about James Mendon? If I stayed at Glen's house and James somehow found it, would he believe it was mine? Would I scare Glen needlessly by even bringing it up?

After all, James had said he was continuing his search elsewhere. Maybe I should call Glen and let him know I had helped him dodge a bullet.

I was reaching for the phone when it rang.

"Hello?"

"Ezra?" It was Glen.

"Yeah?"

"It's Glen."

"Hey. How are you?"

"That guy you were talking to today. When I drove by?"

"Yeah?"

"Who was he?"

"Turns out he's a fan of yours. Loves your books. He's looking for you."

"Why was he talking to you?"

"He had an old picture of you. He showed it to me because I'm the mailman in the area. He figured if anyone would recognize you I would."

"What'd you tell him?"

"I played dumb with him," I said. "Told him I had never seen anyone who looks like that picture around here."

There was silence on the line. The kind that hurts your ears.

"Glen?" I said.

"Yeah, I'm here."

"That picture? I doubt anyone who knows you around here will put it to what you look like now."

"What else did this guy say?"

"He said he'd written to your publisher and agent. They told him they had forwarded his letters, but he never got a reply from you."

"What's his name?"

"James. Can't remember the last name. I've got his card around here somewhere. Think it starts with an M."

"Why'd you take his card?"

I heard some papers ruffling.

"Make him think I'd let him know if anyone looking like his photo popped up in the area." I paused. "You know I'd never do that, don't you?"

"Do I?" There was that tone in his voice. The one that came with the temper.

"Glen, I would never threaten your privacy."

Silence again. Then more papers.

"Mendon?"

"What?"

"His last name? Was it Mendon?"

"I think so," I said, picking the card up. "Yeah. Mendon. How'd you know that?"

"He's the guy who started the website about me. Nosy asshole."

"He said he just wanted to thank you for your books," I tried. "Maybe correspond. Be a friend. He got an email from another fan who said they may have seen you on the coast of Maine. That's why he was in the area."

"How long is he staying?"

"I think he may be hanging around for a bit. Exploring Purgatory."

"Really?"

"Yeah. Funny thing?" And here's where I used what he had taught me. Hopefully it scored some points. "I thought about the *What-If* game. Told him a lot of people vacation on the Maine coast. Hell, you may have been on vacation yourself, if it was even you the person saw."

He laughed. Not a joyous "the joke's on him" sort of laugh, but almost a guilty snicker.

"That's good, Ezra. Maybe you are a writer. I'll have to get right to your story."

"Gee, thanks, Glen."

"Don't mention it." Silence for a moment. "Ezra?"

"Yeah?"

"Let me know if you see him again."

"I will."

"Great. Thanks. See you tomorrow."

The phone being hung up cut me off before I could say good-bye.

*I had delivered Glen's mail and looked up to the house.*

*The front door was open.*

*I remember thinking, "How odd." I opened the small gate, its creaking totally out of proportion to the size of the hinge, and walked up to the front door. Daylight fell over the floor and dissipated quickly into the darkness beyond.*

*I rapped a rhythm on the open door.*

*"Glen? You there? Door's open."*

*Not a sound.*

*"Glen?"*

*Then, something muffled. Sounded like "Ezzz-rahhh..."*

*"Glen? That you?"*

*I took a step into the house. Another. I could make out variations in the darkness. Silhouettes of objects.*

*"Glen? You all right?"*

*The door slammed shut behind me.*

*I was in total darkness. The air seemed to be moving, clinging, wrapping over me. Carrying me. I was falling backward.*

# CHAPTER FORTY-THREE

And that gave me an idea. I got out of bed. It was a little after two in the morning. I had four hours before the cursed alarm would ring, signaling the beginning of another day of labor. I was going to spend that time writing.

Starting with the dream—nightmare?—I had just traveled through. If it made that much of an impression on me, it would surely stir others. My readers.

I must've jumped two feet into the air when the alarm broke the silence. I was totally lost in the world I was creating. A dark, jagged world inside of a dream. A mind. My subconscious must have been storing strange impulses, ideas, for...who knows how long? I had no idea where any of it came from, but it was making sense in some otherworldly way.

It had something to do with my dual roles as student and stalker.

The writer in me separated the two. Made them my characters. Like my life. Me and Glen. Only I set it in another dimension. Turned it into a story of a Master and Acolyte. No names. Just Master and Acolyte. The Acolyte learns much from the Master over time, but desires to be free. To live a life on his own terms.

I had maybe ten pages, but they were the best ten pages I had ever written.

Here was something I could stay with. Could grow with.

But right now I had to get to my...job.

I did my route by rote. (I made a mental note to remember that phrase.) Took my lunch in the normal spot down the hill from Glen's house. Got a mustard drip on my notebook. I wanted to talk to Glen about this new idea, but I couldn't do that. He'd want to know where it came from, and what do I say then?

"It's loosely based on me stalking you even before I moved up here," I said to The Author.

"Sounds good," he said. "Let's see what the cops and my lawyer have to say about it."

Right.

I didn't even go through Glen's mail until I was tossing it into the bag, and the fat cream-colored envelope with the gold embossed return address shouted at me.

*The Field Agency!*

The old feelings came rushing back, and they would not be stilled.

Glen was sitting on the front step reading a paperback novel. He had the book folded back, cover meeting cover. I cringed. There'd be a huge crease in the spine. He had to know that. *Come on, Glen, show some respect for other authors.*

When he saw me approaching the mailbox, he put the book pages down onto the step, and got up.

"Hey, Ezra."

"Hi, Glen."

I handed him the mail, a portion of which from the major

on-line book retailer that continued to sink its sharpened teeth into indie bookstores.

"Couldn't help but notice the book you ordered. More poetry?"

"Nope," he said. "Someone's interested in one of my old novels. I get first crack at the screenplay. And this is a book on how to write one."

"That's great." *The great Glen Dower ordering a book on writing?*

He shuffled through the rest of the mail but didn't find what he must have been looking for. Because it was under the seat of my cart.

"I'm waiting for some papers from my agent. You know, dot the t's, cross the i's."

"I'll keep a look out for them." *Does he know I'm lying? Is my face giving me away?* "Um, Glen...about the story I gave you? Maybe I was intruding..."

He waved that off. "It was unexpected, that's for sure. You ever read a mystery novel called *Blues By The Case*?"

*One of my favorites. What's he getting at?*

"No. Doesn't sound familiar. Why?"

"Something I wrote years ago. It did okay. Maybe you saw the movie version."

I had. Four times. Less than I've read the book.

"No. Doesn't ring a bell. Who was in it?"

"Bunch of unknowns. It may have killed a few careers. Did almost no box office." He gathered his mail into a small pile. "Thought you might have. Your story, *A Six-pack of Sadness*, reminded me of it."

"Really?" *I could have been an actor.* "Is that a good thing?"

He laughed. "I'm not sure. If you've never read my stuff, yes, it's a good thing. If you have, I might have to sue you for plagiarism."

He had a leer on his face that sent my heart rate up about fifty beats a minute. I could feel my mind stammering. Trying to come up with some response. *Plead ignorance, Ezra.*

"Plagiarism?"

"It's copying someone's work and presenting it as your own."

"I know what it means. I just don't follow you."

"Your story is good, Ezra, but it clearly follows the structure of my novel. Similarities in the characters, their motivations. Even the way the lead character speaks. If I were a critic, I'd say the best thing you've done is encapsulate a three-hundred-plus-page novel in twenty pages."

I stayed calm. On the outside. "But I wrote that story, Glen. I did. And I told you; I've never read anything you've written. I'm sorry. I don't know what to say."

"I believe you. Maybe you saw the movie on late-night cable and forgot. A lot of people did. Maybe someone told you about the book. I don't know. But if none of that happened, Ezra, you can really write."

I had no answer for him except, "Thank you."

"So tomorrow I want you to bring everything you've got. Stories, whatever. Okay?"

*Don't tell him about the novel, Ezra. This is everything. What he has now. Tell him.*

"That's it, Glen. *Six-pack of Sadness* is all I've got."

"I can't believe that. Unless you're the most natural born writer I've ever met—that this is all you've got. Nothing else?"

*The most natural born writer he's ever met?* This was my first story and he thought I was a natural. Maybe I could play this somehow. Put some spin on it.

"That's it. Other than some stuff from high school. And some more *What Ifs* I've done in the last couple days."

"Bring it all. High school, whatever, Ezra."

I couldn't find my voice. I was nodding like some bobble-head doll.

"Okay. Yeah. Thank you. Thank you."

I shook his hand like I was pumping water from a well. He

was laughing. I was laughing.

"So? Tomorrow?"

"Definitely. I'll bring it all around. Thank you."

I released his hand, adjusted the mailbag on my shoulder and turned to walk down the hill. Then he yelled out some words I couldn't even have hoped to hear.

"Oh, I almost forgot. While you're here, feel free to work at my writing table."

I called out "Thank you!" for the thousandth time.

All was right with the world.

Sometimes the old ways are the best. A little steam, the glue loosens, the flap folds back. I practiced on a couple of similar envelopes I had bought at the stationery store. It accomplished the task, but I didn't like what it looked like when I resealed the flap. Swollen. Tampered with.

I should just leave it alone and deliver it tomorrow. But I couldn't help feeling I might learn something about deals or agents. Author-agent relationships. It could be invaluable. Something I could discuss with Glen and Al Field when I was about to be published.

I studied the envelope as a burglar would case a house. How do I gain access? I checked the front. The back. The sides were the giveaway, where the paper was glued to form the rectangle. The envelope could be opened there, also, and then the contents could be slid out.

I went back to the other envelopes and tried the steam on the sides. It took longer than the main seal along the flap, but it worked. However, it had the same telltale appearance as when it was resealed. Like it had been tampered with.

I was getting hungry so I let the envelope sit on the table while I put some soup in a pan and made a peanut butter and jelly sandwich. I filled a tall glass with ice and added cold water. I took everything into the living room and turned on the news while I ate.

Let my subconscious deal with the envelope.

And there it was on the news. The answer. Doctors somewhere were separating twin boys joined at the hip with a scalpel.

Who says there's nothing worthwhile on television?


The sporting goods store was open. The thin blade of the filleting knife proved to be perfect. Back home, I slid the enclosed documents out onto the table. There was a cover letter from Al Field. *Dear Glen...blah blah blah...Sincerely...*

The film contract was next. I scanned it quickly. Wow. They were paying Glen $100,000 to adapt his novel *Death Enters Darkly* into a screenplay with a title change to *The Big Breakup*. His title was better, but not as commercial. I got lost in the legalese, so I lifted the stapled pages to put back under the cover letter.

There was another contract. A mere two pages, but it got me more excited than any big deal screenplay could. It was for a new novel with a working title of *The Visitor*.

I knew Glen was writing again. This had to be the book he was working on.

*The Visitor*.

As I perused, I began to understand why it had been so long. His former publisher had dropped him. According to the terms listed by his agent and the new publisher, Old Arts, the deal was for two novels. No advance, but once the novel had recouped its printing and marketing costs, his author's royalty rate went from ten per cent to an equal split with the publisher.

A risky deal that could prove to be astronomical. I felt so glad for Glen. I knew this book would break him wide open. It had to. It just felt right. He had been at it so long, slogging it out, getting noticed, building a fan—and fanatic—base. And Sci-Fi had become big business since his last try many years ago. Aliens from other worlds were hot.

I put the movie contract on top of the book contract, the cover letter over them both. I refolded them along the original creases and slid them back into the envelope.

A little glue on a small paintbrush. A slow swipe along the opened edge. A little pressure. Perfect.

I occupied myself for the rest of the evening by getting my own compositions together. I reread some of the stories to make sure they didn't reflect knowledge of Glen's output. It seemed strange, but I couldn't remember producing them. How had I come up with *this idea*? Where did *that turn of phrase* come from? It was like reading something new from an unknown author. I felt like a grown woman reading her teenage diary. This was a lifetime ago. Anyone would forget. Did Glen? Did other writers? Once their words were set, bound in book form, did they forget them? Did they pick up the book years later and read it for a bit, then look at the dust jacket to make sure their name was on it? And that was entire novel-length books. Mine were just stories. But they held up. They even got better with age.

Like whiskey and wine.

I decided to hold off on handing over the beginnings of the novel for now. I didn't want to tip Glen off to his influential position in my life.

# CHAPTER FORTY-FOUR

I was keen to find Glen on the front step again, reading and waiting for me. He had seemed to place some importance on the letter from his agent. I thought his eagerness might make him anticipate my arrival. I could hand him the envelope, and we would connect with his good fortune. He may not realize it, but I sure would.

No such luck. The house was draped in silence. Literally. All the curtains were pulled. I couldn't tell if he was home or not. Maybe in the back, at the table, writing.

I thought about going to the door and ringing the bell, but if he was working I'd disturb him, and then he'd connect me to his writing in a negative way.

But I had in my possession an excuse. My stories. I had put them all in an expandable folder. I left the rejection letters at home. No sense in calling attention to my previous lies. That would be of no benefit.

I had felt a sense of worthiness wrapping that red string around the button on the folder. I enclosed three short stories I could explain away as stuff I had scribbled over the last couple of days. He'd see how he and his *What-If* method had inspired me.

I put the mail on top of the folder. Everything in the mailbox. I was surprised the folder fit, but there was enough play in the sides I could almost roll it up. I wrote a short note on a postal form.

*Jason,* (on the off chance anyone else read this) *Thanks again. Ezra.*

I wanted to return and see if he was writing. See his reaction when he got the mail. He'd opened his correspondence before at his writing table or in the kitchen. I could see both from my spot. But by the time I got home, got changed, and returned, he probably would have been done with all that. So I decided not to go home.

I made a decision, knowing full well how dangerous it was. The peril added to the attractiveness of my choice. This was not watching to learn. This was watching to share. To enjoy his happiness. I had to see Glen's reaction to his agent's letter.

No, that's not true. I had an idea what his reaction would be. He'd read the contracts, sign them, put them in a return envelope, and have them ready for me tomorrow. That's how he was. Efficient. Something turned up, he addressed it. I knew that much from all I had seen.

What I really wanted to see was his reaction to what I had written. It would help me to be ready for the next time we talked.

I turned the mail cart toward the back road. Toward my entrance to the woods.

I didn't like leaving the cart by the side of the road, but it was necessary. I parked it just off the side of the road. Passenger-side wheels barely on the roadway. Plenty of room for cars to get around, but there was never any real traffic.

I walked into the woods, wearing my postal uniform. Would it stand out from the trees? The bushes? How do I explain it if I got it caught on a branch and ripped it? Could I get it repaired or would I have to buy a new uniform? However bad it was, I'd have to pay for it out of my own pocket. I had already used up the money allotted to me for uniform purchase by the postal service.

What would I say?

"Nature called. I had to go."

So simple they had to buy it.

It turned out it didn't matter. Glen wasn't at his writing table or in the kitchen. But he could be inside somewhere, reading a book or taking a nap. And the trees were shedding their leaves. The bushes turning golden brown. This had to be one of my last trips. Soon there would be no cover to protect me from his keen eyes.

I gave it five minutes. When he hadn't put in an appearance, I went back to my cart.

And there he was. Glen. Sitting in my cart. *Holy shit!*

"Hey, Ezra."

"Hey, Glen." *This is not right. Set your alibi, Ezra.* I put my hand down and checked my zipper. Gave it a tug upwards. "When you gotta go, you gotta go."

He laughed.

"I was gonna give you another minute and call out. See if you were all right."

"What are you doing out here?"

"Walking. I was writing and got to a part that kind of confused me, so I took a walk." He looked around the woods. "It helps work out the problem, consciously or subconsciously."

"You get the problem straightened out?"

"Not all of it, but I think I've got a handle on it."

"Good."

He stepped out of the cart.

"I hope you don't mind, but I looked in your mailbag."

"Long as you didn't steal anything," I joked. "Federal offense."

"Just looking. I thought your stories might be in there. I'm kind of anxious to read them."

That made my day; a writer of Glen's caliber was looking forward to reading my stuff. He thought of me as a fellow writer.

An equal.

"They're in the mailbox with your mail."

"Good. I'll get to them as soon as I can."

"Take your time. I'm honored you'd even do such a thing." Then I remembered. "Oh, that letter you were looking for? From your agent? I think it's in today's mail."

"Great. I hope there's a check in it. I can use it."

I knew there wasn't, but I couldn't tell him that. Is he having money problems? "It's kind of a thick white envelope with some firm's return address. Gold script."

"Sounds like it." He extended his hand. "I better get back to work. See you later."

We shook hands.

"Hop in. I'll give you a ride back to the house."

He waved me off.

"It'll be faster if I cut through the woods." He took a step toward the side of the road. "You know, Ezra, it's a good thing I wasn't in my writing room."

"Why?"

"It looks out over the woods. Imagine if I looked up and saw you standing there taking a leak." He shivered. "It would probably warp my mind. Send me farther around that bend. Some folks think I've already traveled beyond the point of no return."

Now it was my turn to laugh.

"I couldn't see your house, so your delicate artistic sensibilities would have been preserved."

"Spoken like a born writer." He waved. "Take care."

Glen thought I spoke like a born writer. Maybe that was it. I could use my real voice, my speaking voice, and make it my literary voice.

Glen had helped me find the narrator for my novel. *Me.*

I watched him walk into the woods, my gratitude chasing after him, but it stopped short. He was walking through the opening I used when I walked to my spot.

Had I covered my tracks? Would he be able to tell someone

had been standing out there? Was there an impression in the soil? An obvious scar on the smooth skin of Mother Earth?

I wanted to follow, but couldn't move. A voice said, "Go ahead, but wait until he's in the house. Then watch him open the mail. Read your stories." I took a step toward the woods.

It was too dangerous. My clothing was wrong. I had been stupid even coming out here dressed as I was. What if he thought about me peeing in the woods and looked up, smiling with the image. Looked out toward the road beyond the woods, straining to see as far as he could.

And there I was in my uniform. Staring back at him.

I couldn't chance it.

I got in my cart, did a U-turn, and headed back for the post office.

# CHAPTER FORTY-FIVE

Each day I expected to see Glen waiting for me at the mailbox to talk about my stories, but a few days went by without a sign of him. Almost as if he had left early for his business trip without telling me. The feeling depressed me as his house remained dark.

At night, I dressed in black and hugged the tree. I had to watch for him. And I did. For hours. But the blinds had been lowered in the kitchen. He didn't appear in the writing room, the one room that apparently had no curtains. But the next day the mail was gone from the box.

He was in there.


Tuesday I learned the reason for Glen's withdrawal.

I was delivering the local weekly newspaper to the homes along my route. The paper had installed U-shaped metal brackets onto the mailbox posts of their subscribers, a decal with the paper's name on the surface. I would roll up the paper and fit it into the bracket. It would open a bit and lodge itself securely in place, waiting to be picked up.

When I first started delivering the paper, I was a little upset. They were using me to save on the expenses of a paperboy. (Or, more likely, a man or woman with a stationwagon who could do the work of half a dozen paperboys.) I even mentioned it to the editor/publisher/owner of the paper when I saw her on the street. I complained about all the extra weight I had to carry.

"Ezra, we're not some big publishing concern. It's a small weekly paper. I barely make enough to print the thing let alone turn a profit. I can't afford to pay someone to deliver it."

And then she hit me with the zinger we both knew was out there.

"Besides, you don't have to carry the weight. Your cart does."

She had explained that she got a special rate from the post office that cost less than having to pay a delivery person. And she herself had another full-time job. The paper was something to keep the community in touch. A labor of love. Her reporters were not paid. They took their own pictures. If the story was big enough, the wire services would pick it up. She let her reporters keep the extra money, felt it was only fair for all the unpaid work they did.

If there was money left over at the end of the year, they all went out for a big meal. Then started over the next day. From zero.

So I delivered their papers, but still complained. That got me invited to the next dinner.

I even took a little more care with how I delivered them.

I'd roll them up so the paper's name was showing. Place it gently in the hook. When it expanded to fill the space, I'd arrange it with the name facing out to greet the subscriber. I subscribed myself and thought about writing for them, but so far, I hadn't had any ideas small enough for a local weekly.

That Tuesday, I had taken the first paper out of my bag and glanced at the front page as I began to roll it.

It was her picture. Dr. Anderson.

*The Good Doctor, Encased in Silver.*

The black and white picture next to hers told the story better than words. A car smashed and mangled. The headline screamed *Dangerous Road Claims Another Driver.*

I thought there was more to the story than that and flashed back to the half-empty pint glass on the bar next to Glen's vodka.

I rolled the paper and slipped it into the bracket.

I didn't know what to do when I arrived at Glen's. I didn't want to leave the paper out in the hook, its missive of tragedy visible to the world. It was too impersonal.

I wanted to walk up to the house and offer my condolences. Just be there if he needed anything, but I couldn't. I had to be ignorant and pretend I didn't know he even knew who she was. If he wanted me to know, he would tell me. Share this part of his life with me.

I folded the paper and placed it inside the mailbox; I laid the rest of the mail over it like flowers on a casket.

That was too different. Too noticeable. This was just another tragic accident as far as I was concerned. I had to pretend I didn't know the woman. I wasn't supposed to know Glen knew her. If I treated the paper any differently than I usually did, he would know.

It may lead to his asking questions. Ones I didn't want asked now that we were friends. Now that he was reading my stories.

Or would be—when his grieving was over.

I took the paper from under the mail and rolled it up. Set it in the hook like I had with all the others. Maybe with a bit more care. Then I arranged it so all Glen would see would be the paper's name. I closed the mailbox and walked back down the hill.

There was a light on in the writing room. I could see it through the woods even before I got to my watching place. Glen had pushed his laptop to the side. He was reading the paper. He flipped some pages. Folded. Read some more and set the paper down.

His hands covered his face. Was he crying? His heart must have been torn to pieces, but there was nothing I could do or say.

I put the binoculars to my eyes.

His hands went up, his fingers combed through his hair. His eyes were closed. He dropped his face, his hands cupped the back of his head. He seemed to be shaking.

Then he rose and exited the room. The blinds were still down in the kitchen, but the light was on. I saw his shadow move across the room and then it was gone, back to the writing room. Something metal flashed in his right hand. He sat and picked the paper up.

He was cutting the article out of the paper. When the first page was done, he set it aside. Flipped the pages and trimmed the rest of the paper away. His arm swept it off the table onto the floor.

He positioned the two pieces of newspaper together. Looked at them again. Then just sat there, staring out the window. Into the woods. I don't think he was actually looking. It was a blank-eyed stare. A blurring of the world while his mind was churning. I could have popped out from the tree and waved and he wouldn't have noticed me.

He got up and went back into the kitchen, returned quickly, and lifted one piece of newsprint. He placed it against the wall and taped it into place. Then the second.

He set the tape on the table, sat down, and looked up at the article. At the picture of his friend. Did he hear the crush of metal? The breaking of glass? The anguished scream? Would he write about those auditory assaults to the mind?

Then he leaned over and lifted a rusty red folder from the floor to the table.

I gasped. It was the folder holding my stories.

I watched him untie the string from the button and open the flap. He pulled out everything and tossed the folder aside. He flipped through the pages. Each story was stapled so it would be easy to separate them. He selected one and pulled it out.

Then he turned to the photo of his friend and started reading to her. Reading my story to her like she had read his own poems to him. It was a part of his grieving, his healing, and I was a part of it.

The three of us were in the writing room. I couldn't get any closer than that.


I was almost home when I realized which story he had been sharing with his dearly departed loved one. The story that would help heal the grief.

I could see the editor's red pencil. The single word spread across the first page.

*Maudlin.*

But it wasn't maudlin, and I knew Glen would know how good it was. It just had to be read at the right time, under the proper circumstances. And this was that time. Even though he had questioned the origin of the story. Suggested I had somehow copied him.

He knew it would help heal the rift between his broken heart and his lost love.

My story. *A Sixpack of Sadness.*

# CHAPTER FORTY-SIX

There was a note on Glen's mailbox.

*Ezra, come on around to backyard.*

I wasn't sure what to expect, but I carried his mail around the house with me and found him stripped to the waist. Sweaty. Pretty good upper body. For a writer. He had a shovel in his hands.

"Hey, Ezra."

"Jason."

"You can call me Glen if you want," he stage whispered. "When no one's around."

I nodded toward the holes in the backyard.

"What are you doing...Glen?"

*How long had I been waiting to say that name? And to have him casually answer like it was the most natural thing in the world?*

"Making a fire pit."

The shovel bit into the earth. He strained and sent some dirt flying toward the woods and slammed the blade down. Left the handle standing like a post and wiped his hands on his jeans.

"Seems like forever since I've done anything physical." He walked over to the table and picked up an aluminum pitcher. Beads of moisture dripped onto the wood. He poured iced tea into a glass. "Feels good." He looked at me and smiled. "Probably won't tomorrow." Holding the pitcher out, he asked, "Want some? It's unsweetened."

"Sure. Thanks."

I set his mail on the table and picked up a tumbler. He poured. It was cold and good.

He drank his all the way down and poured another.

"Sorry I haven't gotten back to you about your stories."

What could I say to that? Nothing. I used the drink to mask any comments.

"It's been a tough week." He set his glass down and sat on the bench. "You remember that woman I told you about? Didn't want to see me anymore?"

I paused for effect. "Yeah?"

"She died in a car crash."

I let it dawn on me slowly.

"The one in the paper? The...doctor?"

"It hit me harder than I thought it would."

"Oh my god. The paper didn't say, but was it drunk driving?"

"Almost ironic. One of the reasons she didn't want to see me. She said I drank too much. That I...mistreated her."

"I've seen you drink. It wasn't that bad."

"Count yourself lucky then. I stayed away from the booze for three years. I did it on my own. No meetings so I don't have chips to display my achievement, but I wanted to prove it to her, show her how strong I was. I thought I was being smart, asking her to meet me in a bar."

I nodded. "Paulie's?"

He nodded. "The night you and I met. I was nervous so I had one to calm me down. She saw Orlando filling my second one when she came in. Wasn't too happy, but she sat down. Criticized me. Went right into—" He took a breath. "So I had another. Why? Why self-destruct in front of her? Wasn't I worthy of her company? Three years sober and first-date jitters send me around the bend? When I ordered that third one, she saw what direction the evening was headed and left."

He drank the iced tea. Shook the cubes out to the ground

and pulled his arm back. He threw a sixteen-ounce fastball at the back wall and the glass shattered. My whole body shook. His voice choked off the words.

"What makes one person rub another person so raw? Just by their being around?" Glen started to cry. "She wouldn't let me in. I hurt her one time and she wouldn't let me in ever again. Why?"

I knew he wasn't asking me. It was a question addressed to something he had been wrestling with for years. In his life. In his writing. The transitory connections we make. The impermanent imperfect life we lead. Someone goes on. Someone is left behind. No winner or loser. We're all just surviving.

The next night he asked me again, "You're sure you've never read any of my stuff?"

We were at some lobster dive on the coast. How did Glen find these places? We had to drive to the end of a paved road. Then a dirt road until it ended and a short hike through the woods following little handmade signs with arrows pointing the way.

"Positive." The lie was coming easier now. "Don't tell me my other stories are as close to your writing as the one you've already read?"

"No. Not as close, but they have some of the feel—the nuance—of what I wrote years ago. Not close enough for a lawsuit..." He smiled. "...but there are some similarities in setting and characterization."

"So you're telling me they've been done before?"

"I guess so." He cracked a claw and extracted the meat. Dipped it in the drawn butter. "Probably just some more of that Collective Unconscious floating around, huh?"

*Was he putting me on? Did he know I'd read his books?*
"What's that?"

He tilted his head back and dropped the lobster into his mouth. "Goes by another name, too. The 'There's Nothing New

Under The Sun' theory. Everything's just floating around out there. Basically the Greeks covered all the plots and Shakespeare stole from the Greeks. Sooner or later, everybody gets the same idea. The best we can do is come up with new and interesting characters."

*He said* We! "But you liked the stories?"

"They were okay." He had a mug of Moxie. Maine soda pop. He took a swallow. "But what I really liked..."

He paused. I was getting nervous. He just smiled.

"Come on. What?"

"The fish with a wish story. It's...cute. It could be a great children's book."

"You really think so?"

"I do."

I was overjoyed. The one piece of writing that was totally me. From idea to...to what?

"That's great. What do I do now?"

"You finish it."

"But..."

"You. Finish. It." *Teacher to Student.* "It's a good idea. You're off to a great start. Now's when the hard work begins. And you're going to find out it is work. Mind-numbing, brain-breaking labor. But you can do it, Ezra. You can write this book."

Glen thinks I can. He's in my corner. My coach.

"I can do it," I said aloud.

"That's the attitude! Now I want to see pages. Before I leave and after I get back."

Glen raised the Moxie. We clinked glasses.

"To the world's newest writer. Soon to be author."

"What's the difference?" I asked, already knowing the answer to the old joke.

"Writers write," he said. "Authors get published."

"I'll drink to that."

Glen was laughing heartily. I forced a couple guffaws. The

challenge had been cast and I had accepted. Now I had to write.

I spent that evening plotting out my story. Outlining. Thinking of possible walls my fish could run into. A shark? A fisherman's net? I envisioned a scene where the fish looked through the window of a submarine. The sailors eating tins of tuna. Do submarines have windows?

I put it aside and made some notes on my Master/Acolyte novel. It would start out as sort of a *Pymalion/My Fair Lady* thing. The Acolyte would learn from the Master. The acolyte becomes more knowledgeable and then he would conquer the Master and become the Master himself.

I was on my way. The clock said midnight. I was on my way to bed.

Glen had become one with the shovel. Maybe it was helping him work through his grief.

"Hey, Ezra."

"Hi, Glen." I put his mail on the table and admired the earth he had torn up the length of the front fence. "What now?"

"Flowers. I ran some errands this morning, and when I drove up to the place, it was looking a little drab. I thought some color might help. I might even paint the place."

"I'm going to be here a week. Get the paint. I'll have plenty of time to throw a coat or two on the walls."

"Thanks, but no. You, my friend, are going to put your butt on the chair and write. I expect to see a lot of pages when I get back."

*Perfect! He wanted me to stay focused on becoming a writer.*

"If you insist."

"I do. Do any work last night?"

"Actually, I did. Some outlining for the fish story. But the weirdest thing happened. While I was working on the plot, a new idea just bubbled up out of nowhere."

Glen started laughing. "Oh, man. Already? Be careful, Ezra. There are thousands of desk drawers holding thousands of started stories that were cut short by some new idea that sounded better. Keep at the fish story. Don't dilute your energy. Make some notes if you want, but finish the fish story. Ha! Then go on to the next project. Otherwise, you'll have a multitude of beginnings, but no middles or ends."

"This has happened to you?"

He looked at me and shook his head.

*Oh, God. Had I just insulted him?* He's a proven writer with a shelf of books to his credit. And here's this beginner questioning his advice. I'm an idiot. This is what I came up here for. His advice. His teaching.

"Oh, Glen. I'm so sorry. I had no right..."

He waved me off. "It's okay. Yes. I've been there. That's how I know. I started three different books before I realized I had to choose and finish one. Then the next. Then the next. It's an easy lesson to learn, but a hard one to live by. Take it from someone who has been there."

"I will. I will. Thanks."


The phone rang late Friday night.

"So, you all excited, Ezra?"

"Looking forward to it, Glen."

"You haven't said anything to anyone, have you? About staying here?"

"Not a word."

"Good. I was thinking about that Mendon guy. From the other day? He's got me on edge. Have you seen him anymore?"

I hadn't even thought of him since that day. I figured he gave up and left town. He didn't strike me as all that bright.

"Nope. I'm sure he's gone."

"Good. Sorry if I seem paranoid, Ezra, but there's a lot of

strange people out and about in this world."

"I know what you mean. Don't worry. I'll be alone. No one else."

"Thanks. I'm leaving Sunday night, so I'll say my goodbyes now. Feel free to move in anytime Monday. Thanks again, Ezra."

"Um...Glen?"

"Yeah?"

"What about a key?"

"Oh. Right. That would help, wouldn't it? I'll leave it in the mailbox. In the back. Taped to the top."

"Back top of the mailbox. Got it. Have a good trip."

# CHAPTER FORTY-SEVEN

I couldn't sleep. My heart was hurtling around my chest, my body buzzing as if highly caffeinated. My eyes would not close long enough for me to approach anything resembling rest. The night before Christmas when I was a kid. The anticipation all through the house. I tossed and turned, then just lay there, eyes wide open, the darkness talking to me about the future.

My life was about to take a one-hundred-eighty-degree turn. From postman/wannabe writer to writer/postman. Was I ready? I had always played it safe. Been responsible. A good job, a pension. Put in the years and then...what? How many people faced this same dilemma? Security or risk? I had always taken the safe ride. Don't get me wrong. I was not going to leave the post office. Yet. Not until my novel or children's book was complete and selling well. I knew I could do this. I had meditated on it for so long. Now I was finally going to take that leap of faith over the abyss and land on something solid on the other side. The best part was I had finally made a decision to jump. I was facing the unknown.

And I had an attendant guide named Glen Dower to help me travel the unchartered wilderness. To lead me to a well-deserved end.

But I was still afraid. How many others had confronted these two foes and, at the last minute, stepped back into the comfortable realm of the known? That had been me.

But no longer. Tomorrow I was taking that big step into the undetermined future.

# CHAPTER FORTY-EIGHT

I parked my car outside the gate to Glen Dower's house and extricated the key from the mailbox. All the excitement had come back. I was free to follow my original plan. Not only follow it, improve upon it. I was going to be composing at Glen Dower's writing table, with full access to his house. Imagine what things I could learn, the new air I'd be inhaling. It was all mine for a week. I approached the house slowly so I wouldn't surprise the Master if he were still there. My new world—full of undiscovered wonders—was mere steps away.

I stood at the front door and slid the key into the lock. The key Glen had entrusted to me. Maybe I should make a copy? *No, that would be breaking a trust and I would not do that to Glen.* The lock clicked, I opened the door, and stepped inside.

The inner sanctum of Glen Dower. I closed my eyes and inhaled. This was a moment I'd never forget. The word *ecclesiastical* came to mind. This was a holy moment.

The living room was neat. Clean. Spare. An Oriental rug covered most of the floor. An overstuffed couch faced a large flat-screen TV and stereo system. On the coffee table sat a bottle of wine with a red ribbon around it. A note in Glen's handwriting.

*Ezra, thanks again. Hope this helps you pass the time. (But only after writing!)*

Next to the bottle was a stack of DVDs. Some CDs. I recognized the names from his conversations I had been privy to on his tours.

I folded the note and put it in my pocket. If his most ardent fans—those website people—could see me now they would urinate on themselves with jealousy.

"*He gave me a bottle of wine,*" I'd say. "*Let me housesit his place while I wrote.*"

I moved on to the next room. His library filled with books shelved in alphabetical order by author. Another Oriental rug. The only furniture a chair, a side table, and a reading lamp.

I sat down and sunk into the chair. I tried to find a stronger adjective than comfortable. I picked up the novel on the side table, a bookmark little more than halfway through. Did he forget to take this with him or did he have too much work to do before he saw his agent? Maybe I could read this while I was here. Discuss it with him when he returned. The book was by one of his favorite authors. He had mentioned her during public appearances. I read the inscription.

'*Thanks for your inspiration. Looking forward to your next one.*'

He knew the woman. She was a fan of his as he was of her. Glen and I were alike in that respect. He understood the connection between artist and audience.

I closed the book and set it back on the table. Luxuriated in the warmth of his chair.


The kitchen was large, with a freshness to it, as if it were only utilized sparingly. On the Formica-and-chrome table in the corner was an envelope with my name on it.

*Ezra—Not sure what you like as far as food. If you need anything, this should cover it.*

He had left me two hundred dollars. A completely generous—and unnecessary—gesture.

I opened the refrigerator. It was full of food. More sustenance than I could consume in a week. And several different beers. There were canned goods in the cupboards. Soups. Pastas. He was well-stocked for the coming winter or a premature nor'easter.

I folded the note and put it in my pocket next to the other one. I put the money back in the envelope and left it on the table.


I was crossing the threshold to the next room when I realized its significance. I stepped back into the kitchen. The room before me I had seen solely from my observation post in my arboreal place of study.

*The writing room.*

It was smaller than I had imagined. The air sparked with the electricity of creativity. This sacred place was magic. The hidden heart of his unknown life. The part I alone observed.

I stepped into the room. I felt like an intruder. Much like a poet might feel visiting Dylan Thomas's writing shed and finding the door ajar. Hesitant to enter. Of getting too close to the flame.

And I could write here. It would be more than okay. *It would be sanctioned.*

Glen had literally given me the keys to the church.

I was hoping there would be some of his written pages on the old rectangular oak table, but there weren't. His laptop was not present, but his printer, covered in see-through plastic, sat silently unplugged. He had left my folder in the center of the table with a stack of legal pads, a cup of pens and pencils. His kind gesture was encouraging. I could almost hear Glen say, "Go ahead. Create." It stirred in me a desire to sit down and start writing.

I went to the file cabinet and pulled on each drawer. Locked.

I returned to the table and pulled the chair back, feeling a surge of energy at its touch. I sat in the chair—the pew?—and ran my hands over the table's wide expanse of smooth wood. Snatches of Glen's stories ran up my arms and echoed in my mind.

The vampire's fangs were like sharpened fingers. Death rode the night air.

She could make a strong man fall to his knees. But then most men fell for Blue in one way or another.

Come with me, I've got something I want you to see.

---

I looked out the window and espied my hiding spot. It looked closer from this angle. I had been right; it would have been nigh impossible to stand there in the winter. The lack of foliage would have left me totally exposed, even in snow-based camouflage, and the cold Maine winds would have cut into my viewing time considerably. Winter was the time to hibernate. Time to write. And when spring came I would blossom like a fresh flower, my finished novel on some publisher's vine, maybe even climbing the trellis of the best-seller list.

I had one week to lay my foundation.

Maybe I could find the keys to the filing cabinet. *No! Again, a violation of trust.*

The bathroom was nothing short of sparkling. He used organic shampoo, organic soap, organic toothpaste from Maine.

We used the same disposable razor!

A clean towel was on a bar by the shower. Another, still damp, hung limply from the shower curtain rod. I pulled it down and buried my face in it. Inhaled. I could almost smell the words emanating from the cotton. He had used this towel before he left. I draped it over the bar right next to my clean towel.

On the back of the door was a robe. His robe. I tried it on, and it felt so right, even over my clothes. I tied the sash around my waist and wandered into the next room.

I had guessed correctly from my perch in the woods. The big room at the end of the house, after the bathroom, was the bedroom. There were pictures on the dresser. A man and a woman, they were hunkered down, smiling at the camera. A young German shepherd strained at his leash between them. Glen's house was visible in the background. Maybe I'd meet them on their next visit.

I glanced over the other photos. Darla. *The Good Doctor* Darla who had died in a drunken car crash. She had her own frame.

There she appeared again in a photo with Glen. They had their arms around each other's waists. Her head was resting on his shoulder.

This was stuff no one knew. Gold. The website would be in turmoil if I sent this in.

But it would be a betrayal.

Maybe that's why he asked me to housesit. Was this a test? If I spent one week and kept mute about all I've learned, maybe we'd spend more time together.

He had separate drawers for everything. Underwear. Socks. Jeans. T-shirts.

That made me even more confident he was an outliner of his books, not what some people call a "pantser"—a writer who wrote by the seat of their pants.

The bed was freshly made. A folded quilt lay across the foot of the mattress. Was this *the quilt* he had bought at the church bazaar? The one Rosa and Roy's wife had made? What was her name? Were they the ones who took the photographs of Glen and Darla?

A dark green wool blanket covered the light blue sheets. I lay down and closed my eyes. I would be slumbering where he slept. I took five deep breaths.

The pillow was soft. I rolled onto my belly and hugged the pillow like I do at home. For the next week this would be my home. I could hug this pillow as often as I liked.

I slid off the bed and stood up. My feet bumped something halfway protruding from under the bed.

His slippers, fleece-lined leather moccasins.

I sat on the edge of the bed, took off my shoes, and eased my feet into his slippers. They felt fantastic, a perfect fit. I didn't think I'd wear my shoes the whole time I was there. I would—literally—be walking in the Master's shoes.

Now I knew why he hardly ever went out. There was plenty of food. Lots of books. Movies. Music. I planned to stay here the entire time, wearing nothing but his robe and slippers.

I shuffled over to the closet, feeling like a king. I opened the closet.

He was there. Glen. In the closet. Pointing a gun at me.

"I thought you'd never stop snooping around."

# CHAPTER FORTY-NINE

I was handcuffed—steel cuffs, probably police-issued—with my hands behind my back.

*Now that I knew how this felt, I could better write about the sensation. Cold. Tight.*

"Did you truly believe you could just take over my life?" Glen asked. "That I would let that happen?"

"What are you talking about?"

*What was he talking about? How much did he know?*

He pushed me onto the bed and pointed his finger at me: Teacher to Student.

"I've been watching you, Ezra. You're not as invisible—or as clever—as you think."

I looked up at him. He had the whole thing wrong. Unless this was a writing exercise. Of course, it had to be, but he was taking it a little too close to the edge. We were friends. *Right?*

"Please, Glen." I shook my head to the side. "I understand what you're doing, but this hurts." I was on my back with my weight bearing down on my hands, arms twisting back from my shoulders. I turned on my side as he set the gun down on the nightstand and opened a drawer and took out another pair of handcuffs. A longer link of chain ran between the manacles.

"I've been watching you since before you started watching me," he said. "I knew one of you would go too far. I have to say, I'm kind of glad it was you. At least I could stand you."

He clipped the cuffs around one of my ankles. Then the other. He retrieved the gun.

What did he mean by "one of you?" *I wasn't like those others.* Then I remembered that Mendon guy who was trying to do something close to what I had accomplished. Loser.

"Open your mouth." Glen's smile was sickening. He rushed forward and leaned over me. The arm with the gun extended, maybe an inch from my lips. "Open. Your. Mouth."

"Why do you...?" I shut my eyes and twisted my head to the side, as far away as I could get, pushing for more space on the mattress, the wool blanket digging its scratchy surface into my flesh. His free hand cupped my chin, his thumb and fingers digging into my cheeks. He turned me back to face him.

"Open your fucking mouth or I will end you right now."

*That was a line from* Hell in the Hole, *but I didn't think now was the time to say so.*

I opened wide and squeezed my eyes tight. Tears oozed from my eyes and rolled down my cheeks into my mouth. I almost choked on their saltiness. The metal scraped against my teeth as he rammed the gun home. I gagged and he pulled the gun back a bit.

"Open your eyes, Ezra. I need to see your eyes."

This *was* an exercise. He needed to see how someone's eyes changed when a gun was planted in their mouth. *Nice. How else would you know for sure?*

"Open your goddamned eyes," he repeated.

I heard a click. Forced my eyes open wide. Breathing was hard. The gun was a blur, but I could see that the hammer was raised.

Warmth flooded my crotch. *Damn it! I was one of those panic pissers.* Would he write about that for all the world to know?

He pulled the gun out of my mouth and eased the hammer down. He had a disgusted look on his face as he said, "Don't be a fucking sissy."

I stared at the ceiling. At the lone lighting fixture. Still uncertain this was an exercise, I said, "I'll...I'll leave. Go away. You'll never see me again. Never." If this was an exercise, someone would say something like that in this situation.

He looked disappointed in me. "You'll go away, all right. But at my discretion." He leaned forward, grabbed my belt and yanked. "Stand up."

I struggled. With his help, I stood. He waved the gun at the door.

"Walk."

I took a step forward—hands and ankles restrained by metal—and nearly fell. He grabbed my hair and pulled me upright. I screamed, the pain shooting through me. I took a smaller step. Hobbled to the door and into the hallway.

"Left." *Toward the kitchen.*

Smaller steps now. My tears continued streaming. Sweat came from every body part.

"Please, let me go." *That was something else I believed one would say here.*

"You'll go, but I have something to show you first. Move."

The barrel of the gun stabbed my back, but now I had renewed hope. He said he was going to let me go. I sniffled. Mucous filled my throat. I gagged and struggled forward.

"Stop."

He came around in front of me. His eyes searched my face.

"All I wanted was to be left alone. But you guys couldn't give me that. You have no lives of your own so you attempt to attach yourselves to mine. Like parasites."

The words were wooden. His voice flat. As if he were reading something for the first time. He led me into the dark kitchen. Reached in. I heard a light switch click.

"To the door." *The one that led outside, to the deck.*

That same dead tone. No emotion at all. Scripted lines.

*He was writing! This was part of his method and I was invited to participate.*

There wasn't a lot of slack in the cuffs around my ankles. I moved slowly toward the door that opened onto the deck. Off balance. He wrapped his hand around my belt and held me upright. With his other hand he opened the sliding door. and then pushed me. I

I was on the deck as I felt the sole of Glen's shoe shoe push against my spine. I tumbled hard, head first into the wooden railing. As I started to drift off, I hoped there was a method to this madness.

*Or was this madness the method?*

When I came to, Glen was standing over me. From the smell, I could tell I was on the wet ground. No, strike that. I was *in the ground*. The "fire pit" I had found him digging the other day?

He walked away. Then he was back, standing over me with a shovel in his hands.

"Your book." My mind was racing, reaching for the title. I just had it. *Hell in the Hole*—the one where the guy ends a grudge by literally burying the hatchet. Along with the friend whose head he'd just buried it in. "One of my favorites," I half-whispered.

His lips twisted into a sick parody of a grin. "You really need to expand your reading habits, Ezra. Your stories just scream my name."

I believed now that there was a strong chance I was going to die. And I knew how it would happen. He was going to smash my skull with the shovel. Maybe separate my head from my body. My blood would soak into the dull earth of his backyard. I would be with him forever.

My body tensed. I closed my eyes. Waited for the final blow.

"I hope no one else remembers that plot point," Glen said. "I'm recycling it. A little self-plagiarism never hurt any writer. But what am I going to do? Sue myself?"

I heard the familiar sound of the birds in his back woods.

Then softly, almost lovingly, he said, "Open your eyes again."

I went for petulant. Damn, I'd already pissed myself, so why not? "No."

"Open your eyes, Ezra. I do need to see your eyes for this."

I opened my eyes. Saw him standing over me. He was smiling.

"Yes, I am writing a new book. You're helping me. The working title is *The Visitor*."

That's the book I had read about. In the contract.

"I've been using you as the model for the lead character."

I was cried out. I could feel my tears drying on my skin.

"Me?"

Glen nodded. "Sorry about all this." He shook the shovel. Small motes of pale dust sifted slowly in the air. "This might seem a bit extreme, but I wanted your reaction." *Was I right the first time?* "I'm almost finished with the novel, and I thought it might be good to do a little playacting with you. Show you my thought processes. Maybe inspire you in your own writing."

He looked at his watch.

"After all, I have a plane to catch. And you have a book about a wishful fish to write while I'm gone."

I was going to be free. He had done all this for my help. He could have finished the book on his own, but he wanted my input. I was his protagonist. The hero—anti-hero?—of his new book. His breakthrough novel. It had to be. He had been at it for so long.

I would be famous. People would want to know about me. Important people.

Agents. Publishers.

They all would want to sign me. I would be a writer. Glen's story would be my birth.

I was laughing. Crying newly found tears of joy.

"So bear with me, Ezra. I just need to get your reaction so I can finish the story."

"Why me?" I asked.

He rested the shovel on his shoulder and said, "Why you what?"

"Why'd you pick me? To help with the story?"

He grinned like a fisherman with a prized catch. It didn't comfort me.

"I picked whoever got the closest to me, Ezra. Whoever was willing to make the kinds of sacrifices it would take to not only track me down, but to then make the commitment it took to insinuate himself into my life. To become my...friend." He moved the shovel to the other shoulder and said, "It was almost that Mendon guy. He would not have been nearly as much fun. I mean, look at the sacrifices you were willing to make. And I'm not just talking about all the lies you had to tell—quite like a writer, by the way—and moving your life to Maine."

"What are you talking about?"

The grin again. "Come now, Ezra. Sally Anne?"

*Shit. How did he know about...?* "What about Sally Anne?" I tried.

"Good, Ezra. Stick with the big lie. But please. Everyone else around here may buy the story that she was in the wrong place at the wrong time, but you and I know the truth. Don't we?"

I stayed silent. He didn't.

"You needed to get those pictures back from the photo shop so I wouldn't find out about them. Now, do I believe you went there prepared to kill to retrieve them?" He looked at the piss stain on my pants. "No. But do I believe you did what you felt you had to do to keep your...plot moving forward? Absolutely."

"If you think that's true," I said, "why didn't you say anything?"

"Because it was also keeping *my plot* moving forward. Hell, Ezra. You made my story better by keeping yours alive. You added another dimension to my protagonist. I never thought he'd kill for me, but...I owe you for that."

An idea hit me. "What about Darla?" I asked. "*The Good Doctor?*"

"What about her?" The question did not please him, but he wasted no time talking around it. "Do you know how easy it is to fake a drunk-driving accident, Ezra? Especially up here in God's Country. All the winding, unlit roads. The optional speed limits. Almost too easy."

"Why did she have to die?"

"For the simplest of reasons, my friend. She did not like you. She did not trust you. She saw you for who you were." He paused. "Like she saw me. Like I saw you." He took the shovel off his shoulder and rested the business end on the ground. "She didn't want me to see you anymore so one of you had to go." He pulled on his lower lip. "And to be honest, nothing was more important to me than my next book, so the choice was rather easy."

Even lying in the fire pit with my hands cuffed behind me, I couldn't help but feel honored. *Glen Dower had chosen me.*

"And," he said, "in the spirit of full disclosure, I should probably tell you about Roy."

"What about Roy?"

Glen shook his head. "The old fool was thinking of returning to work. Asking for his old route back. Your route, Ezra. *Our route.*"

That was hard to believe and I said so. "His heart. He had a heart attack right after he retired. He was in no shape to—"

"I know, but he thought he was. And if he had returned, and gotten his route back, where would that have left us?"

*What was he saying?*

"So," he said, "when Roy called me over to have a few drinks, we discussed his possible return from retirement. I tried to persuade him not to, but you know Roy." He looked down at me. "Well, you didn't know him all that well, but the man was stubborn. When he set his mind to something, there was no convincing him otherwise."

"So?"

"So," Glen tapped the shovel against the ground twice, "he needed to have a reason not to return to work. The way I figured it, the best reason was his health. So, I kind of guided him into a heart attack."

I had to repeat that out loud to see if it made sense. It didn't.

"We drank a lot that night, Ezra," Glen explained. "I had Roy running back and forth to the kitchen to get me snacks, up and down the stairs to get me a blanket so we could sit outside. I kept bringing up his poor departed wife and how much he must miss her. Challenged him to split wood. By the time I was done with him, his heart had had enough."

"You *gave* him a heart attack?"

Glen shook his head. "Let's just say I helped facilitate a coronary arrest. I'm not sure there's a law against that, but...maybe that's for another book."

He raised up the shovel again and held it like a baseball bat. Even took a few practice swings. He liked the way it felt. He turned his attention back to me.

Glen began to jab the shovel toward my face, more practice. I had to act scared. It wasn't hard. Give him the emotion he needed to write accurately. To finish his novel.

But the movement was wrong. The shovel should be slicing through the air. Or maybe a pile-driving swing like a sledge-hammer. Over the head and smashing down. This was just a...shoveling motion. Arms moving forward from the hips as if he were shoveling dirt.

Should I mention it to him? No, of course not. He's the writer. It's his story. I can't tell him he's making a mistake. But it's a detail I see and he doesn't. A moment of clarity when I realized he didn't know everything.

Or maybe he was afraid he wouldn't be able to control the more powerful swing. That he might actually hurt me. I needed to give him a reaction. Fear mixed with the certainty of impending death. I opened my eyes wider.

His motion stopped halfway through his next jab. That was it. I had given him what he needed. It was over. We would keep each other's secrets. I was going to be free. *And famous.* He would set the shovel down. Help me up. We'd get a beer and laugh about it before he left for the airport. Before I sat down at his writing table to fully develop my fish with a wish story.

He moved the shovel off to the side next to a bag I hadn't noticed before. He dug into the bag and came out with a shovel full of white powder. Now I was confused again. He looked back at me and said, "Thanks for your help, Ezra."

Before the words "You're welcome" could come out of my mouth, he shoveled the white powder onto my face—in slow motion—burning my eyes and mouth.

I screamed.

He let me scream.

I was still screaming when he brought the shovel down.

# THE VISITOR

Arthur couldn't wait for the rain to begin. The stifling heat had made it even more difficult for him to write these days, especially since he'd always eschewed the so-called luxury of air conditioning. He needed the windows open; he needed to smell the outside air, to hear the wind dancing through the leaves of his arboreal property line, to feel the welcome visit of the Maine summer breeze as it snuck through the windows into his home, not quite uninvited. Even the slapping of the oak branches against the side of the old house would at times create a tempo he would attempt to replicate in the rhythm of his prose.

Yes, at any moment the promised remnants of the latest tropical storm would continue its northerly journey, befall his secluded property, and with it—he hoped—would come the words for which he so desperately searched. While others sought shelter and stocked up on toilet paper and groceries designed more for making French Toast than basic survival food, Arthur longed for inches of rain, the fifty-mile-per-hour wind gusts, the possibility of scattered blackouts due to fallen trees and downed electrical wires.

If Arthur Ray, The Author, were going to live and write in seclusion, then bring it on!

Arthur's other source of inspiration had gotten him started, at least. Ever since Arthur had placed the corpse in the meat freezer in his basement, ideas had been flowing: character, dialogue, setting.

But still no plot. At least not one that hadn't been done before. Even by Arthur, not that he was above lifting from his own body of work.

Oh, yes. The murdered deliveryman was...well, late in delivering plot. Just as that thought crossed his mind, he looked at his blank document. Old Ernest had been right: it *was* the cruelest thing, whether a page or a screen. Arthur felt another of those tightening spasms in his throat that he had been experiencing for the past few days.

Had they started the same day he'd placed Ira in the freezer?

He made a mental note to schedule an appointment with his new doctor and have a discussion about those strange contractions that on occasion made breathing just a little difficult. A shame about his previous preferred medical professional; she had been quite the beauty before succumbing to the horrific injuries she suffered from her ill-advised driving decision.

And he had been the one with the drinking problem?

Sitting in front of his laptop, waiting to hear the distant sounds of thunder, Arthur was instead greeted by another sound: someone ringing his doorbell. *Damn.* If it was who he thought it was, he might have to make more room in the meat freezer.

No it wouldn't be him; it was too early for him and—Arthur was certain—that particular entrance would not be through the front door.

He got up from his writing table and felt a wave of light-headedness. Again, he'd been sitting for too long at the table with only the warm bottle of soda for sustenance. After he answered the door, he'd have to make himself a sandwich and a nice glass of lemonade. Maybe go for a walk in the woods later, after the storm had passed. Breathe in some of that Maine air he'd been paying so much for.

The person at the door was the sheriff. *This could be interesting.* He made a point to pay strict attention to what the sheriff had to say. You never knew when someone—especially an officer of the law—would utter something that would make for good fiction.

*Wait. Should I be worried?*

He reached to open the door and the knob seemed to turn itself. In an attempt to appear unperturbed, Arthur said, "Afternoon, Sheriff."

The sheriff tipped his hat. Arthur figured he'd learned that gesture at the Sheriff Academy. "Afternoon, Alan." The sheriff knew Arthur only by his *nom du Maine.* "Figured I'd swing by before the storm came through."

Arthur stepped aside, inviting the sheriff to enter. "Please," he said, "don't tell me this is about my shooting again."

"Oh, no, sir." *Sir? Official.* "You've stopped that, haven't you?"

Arthur felt some pull from the door and let go of the knob. Normally stubborn due to its advanced age, the door shut by itself. *Huh.*

"Absolutely," Arthur lied. The sheriff was referring to his nighttime habit of shooting at raccoons while drunk. (Arthur being drunk, the raccoons pretty much sober.) And he had stopped. Mostly. Since he'd learned that little trick on-line about making silencers in the privacy of your own home, he had enjoyed his nocturnal hobby without having to bother his nearest neighbors, who really would have to strain to hear even unmuffled gunshots.

"Good, good," the sheriff said. "No, I just have a few questions for you regarding a missing-person report."

"Who's missing?" Arthur knew full well that that would be the first question that would come to an innocent person's mouth. And it would come quickly so there was no need to pretend to think on it.

The sheriff removed his hat. "Ira. Ira Keyes."

Arthur did pretend to think on that a bit, but not too long, because of course he knew him. "The delivery guy. He's missing?"

"Kinda what it looks like. Company says he hasn't been to work the past few days. I'm sure there's a reasonable explanation."

"That's usually the case," Arthur said. "So you've come to see if he's hiding out here? Maybe he and I are looking through his packages for hidden treasures? Would that be the purpose of your visit, Sheriff?"

The sheriff laughed. "That's good, Alan. No."

"You're welcome to search the place. Won't even ask for a warrant."

Another laugh. "Just wondering if maybe Ira mighta mentioned something to you is all. The company said you were one of his more frequent destinations."

*And, indeed, his most final,* Arthur thought. "I order a lot of books from the indie shop in town. Can't always make it there, so I have them delivered." Arthur then pretended that a thought has just occurred to him. "Last time I saw Ira, I think he said something about a wedding. Back home in the Midwest? A niece, I think."

"Iowa," the sheriff said. "His cousin. That's what he told his boss. But we checked that out and there wasn't any wedding that the family—I spoke to an aunt—knew about. Cousin, niece, good friend from college's daughter. No one. Seems like he took a week off and just never came back."

"Well, if he lied to his boss I don't see why he'd confide in me. Who filed the missing-person report?"

The sheriff shook his head. "He's not officially a missing person if you wanna get technical. Ira's an adult of sound mind and body far as we know, and he has the right to up and go wherever he wants. Rita called me and said she was a might worried. Said Ira's not the kind of person to do something like that. Pull a Houdini, I mean."

"She..." *Use the present tense, Arthur* "...knows him well, does she?"

"Quilting supplies. Twice-a-week deliveries sometimes."

"Ah, yes. Rita and her quilts. I have one she made me." He left out the part that it was currently wrapped around Ira's body. "It's around here somewhere."

"Turns out he was big on her pies and they had coffee more than a few times. Said he was the kind of man who made his presence known."

Arthur felt that tightening sensation around his throat again, and rubbed just below his chin with his index finger and thumb. "She would know then. More than I."

"So he said nothing out of the ordinary to you? Nothing that might give me an idea where I can reach out? More for Rita's piece of mind than anything else, 'cause like I said, adult man can do whatever he wants."

*Not anymore.*

"Nope. Sorry I can't be of more help, Sheriff." He stroked his neck again.

"Okay, Alan. Thanks." The sheriff made his way to the door and, with his hand grasping the knob, turned around. "You getting that bug that's been going around?"

"I don't think so. Why?"

"You just keep rubbing your neck is all. That's what my wife does when she's got something brewing in her throat."

"Nope." Arthur slapped his chest twice. "Fit as a fiddle."

"And ready for love?"

"Always ready, Sheriff." He thought again about the unfortunate demise of his doctor. "Anything else I can help you with?"

"Nope. But if anything springs to mind..."

"You're my first call."

"Stay dry, Alan."

The sheriff exited and the door shut, again, almost on its own. Arthur waited until he saw the sheriff get in his car before saying aloud, "That you, Ira? Brewing something in my throat?"

When the expected non-response came, Arthur went to the fridge and put together a turkey and Swiss on whole wheat with mayo that he knew would be consumed by the time he returned to his laptop. He also allowed himself a glass of water.

His last bite didn't go down the right pipe, as his mother used to say, and it was all he could do to not choke or spit it out.

Damn, Ira. Let me eat a sandwich, at least.

He took a long, cleansing sip of water, sat back down at his laptop, and stared at the blank screen. Again the word *cruel* came to mind.

The idea came to him much like the small release of gas that travelled up his esophagus and came out as a deep sigh.

*What if*—he loved those two words more than any other pair—a murder victim came back to take revenge on his killer? Since the killer and victim had been close and had shared many ideas, both big and small, this would make sense if you believed enough in the concept that ideas cannot be killed, and believed also that the dead can—and will—find a way back to the land of the living if they're truly motivated.

*Revenge* might be the wrong, easier motive, Arthur thought. Besides being done to death—ha!—it was not as interesting as the other idea that had just risen to the surface of the author's mind.

What if the murder victim came back to collaborate with his killer? To create a work of fiction that could only be written by the two of them?

That would be motivation. A story that just had to be told, even if one of the writers was no longer breathing.

"Thank you, Ira," Arthur said out loud. "I knew you'd come through." He walked over to his laptop, sat down, put his hands in writing position and looked at the screen.

```
I thought it was over.
```

Arthur knew he hadn't written those words; they were not even in his preferred font. Besides, the screen had been blank when he looked at it not more than thirty seconds ago. He was certain of that. *Wasn't I?*

"What was over?" Arthur asked the room.

His question was again met with silence. The next sound Arthur heard came from outside. It was somewhere between a child's sneeze and the bark of a fox. Not having a pet, Arthur was never one to chase away wildlife, unless it was a black bear. Those he could do without.

He turned his attention back to the screen and repeated aloud the words, "I thought it was over."

Not a bad opening line. The reader would be grasped by the mystery of the simple word.

It.

What was *it?*

This thought was again interrupted by the sound from outside. Arthur was certain now it had come from the woods. The same woods in which Ira Keyes had believed he was well concealed for all those weeks.

Don't tell me...

Arthur stood up and went to the side door. He took in a deep breath—the rain was not too far away now—and looked into the woods. He found the place where Ira had always positioned himself and kept his gaze there. It didn't take long to detect motion. Too big for a fox; not big enough for a black bear. *A deer perhaps?*

Too big; not big enough; not a deer. Arthur knew who it was and would have figured it out sooner had he not been convinced that this encounter would not likely happen so soon.

The suspension of disbelief leads to new discoveries.

"Hello," he called out to the woods. "I can see you."

No response. This one probably thinks he is just as invisible as Ira had thought he was—then and now.

"Really," Arthur said. "I can see you and there's no need to hide. I'm not calling the sheriff back. Also, it's about to rain."

There was some rustling in the bushes and then the man took a quick awkward step forward, as if he had stumbled. Arthur almost laughed at the man's outfit: identical to the camouflage suit Ira had always worn.

"It's okay," Arthur said. "I can tell you're not here to hurt me." He stepped out onto the deck. He raised his hands and said, "Look, no gun. But tell me, please. Press or fan?"

Another awkward step forward, this one definitely resembling a stagger. The guy removed his hat before speaking.

"A fan," he said. "I'm...sorry. I wasn't sure and now I feel..."

"You feel caught, my friend," Arthur finished for him. "We've all been there." He pointed to the woods the man had just stepped out of. "Some of us exactly where you're standing at this very moment."

The man looked behind himself and coughed again. He turned his glance back to Arthur and said, "I can just go." He pointed toward the front of the house. "Like I'd never been here."

"But you are here," Arthur said. "What's done cannot be undone, as the man said. Please come in. The least you can do is introduce yourself. And I can offer you a lemonade or iced tea if you're so inclined."

The man seemed surprised by the offer. *Good. Keep him off balance.*

"That's very kind of you," the man said. "Mr. Ray."

That ended any doubt that Arthur Ray, The Author, may have had about the stranger knowing his true identity. "Call me Arthur," Arthur said. "Since we're about to have a drink together we may as well be on a first-name basis. And yours is...?"

"James. Jimmy, actually. Jimmy Munson."

"Please come in, Jimmy." Arthur gestured toward the door as the man took, once more, another unskilled step forward. "Are you okay, Jimmy? There's no need to be nervous. I am inviting you in."

James looked over his shoulder, confused. "It's just that I feel a...I don't know. I guess my back is acting up," he explained. "Feels like I'm being—"

"Probably just muscle spasms," Arthur said. "You've been crouching there for quite some time now. Three days by my count. The body has a way of letting us know when it's had enough."

Embarrassed, Jimmy nodded unconvincingly. "I guess you're right," he said and followed Arthur's outstretched hand into the house.

As he walked past Arthur, Jimmy said, "I can't believe you're inviting me inside. I thought you'd be...having me arrested."

"Nonsense. You've made an honest—albeit misguided—attempt to reach out to me. The least I can do is extend you the courtesy of a little company and liquid refreshment."

"That's very kind of you. Arthur."

"I only ask that you keep the *Arthur* thing between the two of us. Folks around here know me as Alan."

"Absolutely," Jimmy said. "I'd never dream of—"

"Of course you wouldn't. The same as I wouldn't dream of reporting your trespassing on my property to local law enforcement."

Once they were both inside, Arthur pulled the door to

the deck closed. It stuck a little this time; must have been the humidity.

"So, what'll it be?" he asked.

Jimmy looked confused again.

"Lemonade or iced tea? I could mix 'em. Make you an Arnold Palmer if you'd prefer."

Jimmy seemed distracted. "However you take yours is fine," he said, looking around as if he had just stepped into a place of worship. He must have noticed the laptop because he asked, "Is this where you write?"

Arthur took a pitcher of lemonade and one of iced tea out of the fridge and said, "Here, there, and everywhere. The beauty of a laptop. It goes where I go."

Jimmy snuck a look at the screen and mouthed the words that were written there. Again, he made the experience seem pious.

"*I thought it was over,*" he whispered. The words seemed to stick in his throat, causing him to cough.

"Here." Arthur handed Jimmy a glass. "Sounds like you can use a drink."

"Must be allergies," he said, stroking his neck. "I feel a pressure and scratchiness I don't get back home."

"The sheriff told me there's something going around."

"Maybe that's it," Jimmy said before taking a sip.

"So what do you think?"

More confusion crossed Jimmy's face. "About what?"

"My sentence," Arthur said. "I saw you looking. It's a first draft, but you're a fan. What do you think? And be honest."

Jimmy took another sip. "Wow," he said. "You're asking me?"

Arthur smiled. "As I've said, you've made quite an effort to be here, Jimmy. You are obviously a student of my work. Why wouldn't I ask you?" He took a sip of lemonade. "Kind of a writer's dream, some might say. Having a reader in the room while the writer goes about his craft. So, yes. What do you think?"

"It's good," said Jimmy. Then he allowed himself to say aloud, "*I thought it was over*," and nodded. "Yeah. I love it. Is it the opening?"

"I'm not sure yet," Arthur said. "It could be the beginning, the middle or the end. Too early to tell."

Jimmy nodded; he had just been let in on the author's process.

"What's the next line?" he asked. "Do you know?"

"I think I do." Arthur stepped over to the laptop and typed—but it didn't feel like him typing—three more words. He read them to himself and leaned back. "What do you think?"

James stepped over and read the next three words aloud.

```
I was wrong.
```

# ACKNOWLEDGMENTS AND ABOUT THE AUTHOR

Michael Wallace Herron loved listening to, telling, and writing stories. Not one to look behind, Mike left this novel, *Wannabe*, unfinished as he pursued other works of fiction. After he passed away from COVID in May of 2020, his brother Dennis, his life partner Carole Monferdini, and Tim O'Mara decided that *Wannabe* needed to be completed and shared with as many readers as possible. You've just read the fruit of that decision.

A full acknowledgements page for Mike would go on for thousands of words. He touched—and was inspired by—many people's lives as a music promoter, television news photographer, writer, and the kind of guy who showed up for as much live entertainment as possible. Mike loved living in New York City and the city returned that affection.

He would want to mention by name his parents, Richard and Barbara Herron, his twin brothers Tom (wife Carmo) and Tim (wife Beth), and his youngest brother Dennis (wife Keri.) Mike was also a fiercely loyal uncle to his nieces, Lissa and Shanna—"My Girls."

One of Mike's favorite charities was God's Love, We Deliver—www.glwd.org. All proceeds from *Wannabe* will be donated to this wonderful organization.

From those of us who had the privilege of basking in Mike's glow and delighting in his unfiltered sense of humor to those of you who didn't—We are sorry for your loss.

# OTHER PUBLISHED WORKS

M. Wallace Herron's short story "The River Freezes" appears in the short crime fiction anthology *Down to the River*, also published by Down & Out Books.

On the following pages are a few
more great titles from the
Down & Out Books publishing family.

For a complete list of books and to
sign up for our newsletter,
go to DownAndOutBooks.com.

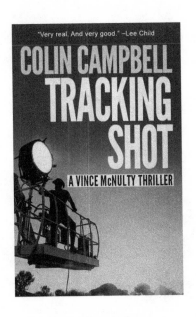

*Tracking Shot*
A Vince McNulty Thriller
Colin Campbell

Down & Out Books
April 2021
978-1-64396-183-5

Several people are killed when a gunman opens fire while Titanic Productions is filming on a courthouse set in Waltham, MA. Did the gunman mistake the set for the real courthouse down the road? Or was it just a message to the real judge?

When the production is shut down, Larry Unger realizes that secondary footage and the cameraman is missing and Vince McNulty must walk a fine line between helping the police and protecting the movie.

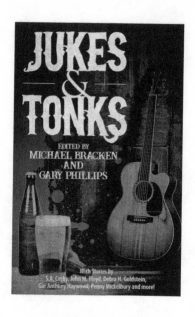

*Jukes & Tonks*
Crime Fiction Inspired by Music
in the Dark and Suspect Choices
Michael Bracken and Gary Phillips, editors

Down & Out Books
April 2021
978-1-64396-184-2

The stories in *Jukes & Tonks* introduce sinners and saints, love begun and love gone wrong, and all manner of unsavory criminal endeavors.

What they have in common is that they plop you down in worlds where the music pulsating from the stage provides the backbeat for tales that are unsparing, heartbreaking, twisty, and a few are as dark as the night.

*Trigger Switch*
Bryon Quertermous

All Due Respect, an imprint of
Down & Out Books
March 2021
978-1-64396-190-3

Dominick Prince has been a magnet for trouble his entire life. A series of poor life choices and their violent consequences have crushed his spirit. Desperate to outrun this burgeoning rage before it fully consumes him, Dominick accepts an offer he doesn't trust from an old high school classmate.

Dutchy Kent says he wants to make one last-ditch effort to prove his acting chops by mounting the New York City debut of a play based on one of Dominick's stories, but the true story involves the real estate empire of a notorious Queens drug dealer and $1.2 million in cash.

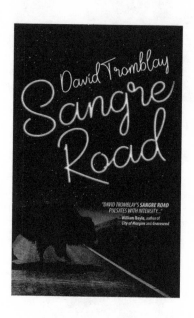

**Sangre Road**
A Moses Kincaid Crime Novel
David Tromblay

Shotgun Honey, an imprint of
Down & Out Books
April 2021
978-1-64396-191-0

Introducing Moses Kincaid, an ornery, brazen, and possibly-punch-drunk bounty hunter who must track down a skip trace into rural Oklahoma; circa summer 1995.

Follow along as he comes up against bikers, prison pecker-woods, zombies, pro midget wrestlers, holes up in no-tell motels and greasy-spoon diners, and gets gifted mouthful after mouthful of heavy-duty pain pills for the bumps and bruises he earns along the way.

CPSIA information can be obtained
at www.ICGtesting.com
Printed in the USA
FSHW010853010521
80873FS